TEA IN CRIMEA

David Kopf

Copyright ©2018 David Kopf

All rights reserved. This book or parts thereof may not be reproduced in any form, stored in any retrieval system, or transmitted in any form by any means — electronic, mechanical, photocopy, recording, or otherwise — without prior written permission of the publisher, except as provided by United States of America copyright law. For permission requests, email office@davidkfiction.com.

ISBN: 978-1-7323802-0-2 (Paperback Edition)

Library of Congress Control Number: 2018906372

Tea in Crimea is a work of fiction. Any references to historic or current events, real people, or real places are used fictitiously. Other names, characters, dialogue places and events are products of the author's imagination and entirely fictional and not intended to depict actual events or people. Any resemblances to actual events or places or persons, living or dead, is entirely coincidental.

Cover illustrations by Tony Millionaire.
Cover design by Wendy Byle, Byle Design & Associates.
Author photography by Nicholas Hope, Classic Capture.

Printed in the United States of America

First edition, first printing 2018

Five Oaks Fiction
Aliso Viejo, California
office@davidkfiction.com
www.davidkfiction.com

For my wife and daughters,
the bright spaces
shining between the words.

Acknowledgements

The input, insights, and hard work of several people helped make *Tea in Crimea* possible, and I offer them my sincere gratitude. While new to the world of books, I have spent the majority of my life writing for and editing periodicals, and know that publishing any work involves a team. Similarly, a book's cover might carry the author's name, but he or she is backed by a crew of creative professionals, and they're due some recognition.

Tea in Crimea began as a serial fiction blog written in real time as the Russian invasion and annexation of Crimea took place. That project wouldn't have been possible without the technical expertise and time investment of Andrea Merideth, who set up the blog and the server that hosted it. Andrea enthusiastically supported this project from day one, and I couldn't be more grateful to her.

Upon finishing the *Tea in Crimea* blog, I realized that, together, the installments constituted enough material for a novel. Several early readers provided critical feedback on those early drafts, including my wife, Robin, who offered her advice as a brilliant woman and fanatical reader; fellow editor and writer Joseph Duffy; and lifelong friend and classics scholar, James Earnest. They all generously donated their valuable time to read, edit, and provide pointed feedback on my early drafts.

After those initial edits, I handed my manuscript off to William Boggess of NY Book Editors, who gave it a full line edit, as well as an in-depth analysis into how *Tea in Crimea* could tell an even more engaging story. William's input drew from years of working on many successful works of fiction, and I'm indebted to him for the lessons he taught me. I respect and value William's process and willingness to work with an author who hails from an entirely different school of editing and writing.

At a time when most book covers resemble movie posters or perfume ads, opting for an illustrated cover could be considered a trifle iconoclastic, but that's precisely why I reached out Tony Millionaire. Tony is a one-of-a-kind illustrator and comic artist who I've admired since the 1990s for always going his own way. Tony's earned some fame, and he's worked on some high-profile projects, and I consider his contribution to this endeavor a great honor.

Similarly, my friend Nicholas Hope of Classic Capture , who has photographed parades of beautiful, well-known people, donated his time and expertise to somehow produce a photogenic version of yours truly for the back cover. It's amazing what talent and experience can accomplish.

Tying these art elements together is Wendy Byle, a graphic designer who I've worked with on several projects as an editor. Wendy's a design professional who knows what I want better than I do, and her cover treatment for *Tea in Crimea* is case in point. Working with Wendy on something other than a magazine was a fun change of pace.

Lastly, a wide variety of friends, family, and well-wishers have egged me on throughout the writing, editing and publishing process. Their support kept me moving through strange, new territory, and I'm grateful for that.

Chapter 1
THIRTY-SIX HOURS LATER

"More tea, Viktor?"

"Absolutely."

Viktor and Sasha sat in the GAZ Tigr's cab, keeping warm with the help of a thermos of hot tea. They started with three containers, but over the course of the last day and a half, they had emptied two. After draining the second, the two Russian soldiers had agreed to stiffen their resolve and resisted opening the third for as long as they could. Their willpower lasted the morning but finally gave out in the face of the damp cold that lingered into the early afternoon.

Viktor stared out the windshield as Sasha fumbled with the well-used container's lid. What the hell were they doing here? Three weeks ago, he and Sasha had been lounging in a restaurant with their wives, savoring a meal of wine and kebabs and laughing until they couldn't breathe. Now, after a steady stream of news reports that the Ukrainian capital of Kyiv had spun out of control, he found himself and his squad freezing in the middle of nowhere in Crimea.

Viktor wasn't sure what was going on in Kyiv, or the rest of Ukraine. He had heard legions of angry ultra-nationalists had deposed President Viktor Yanukovych, who was democratically elected. At least that's what Russian news channels were reporting. Viktor had lived long enough not to believe everything he read online or saw on television. Propaganda was the lifeblood of Russian politics, and that didn't change when the Soviet era gave way to the Federation. Add to that a career in the army, and Viktor's bullshit detector had matured into a well-calibrated instrument.

The only thing he was sure of was that Crimea — at least this part of it — was flat. Flat and boring.

Viktor and his squad had established their checkpoint — which the mission had dubbed Checkpoint Anna — at a crossroads between a paved main road and a dirt farm road. To the southeast, the main road jogged out of sight roughly half a kilometer beyond the intersection. To the northwest, the road continued three-and-a-half kilometers and eventually met up with a radar station that was under guard by two other squads. A sizable forest dominated the east, and to the west lay fields and farms that stretched off to the horizon. The dirt road ran east to west and cut through the forest, where it eventually ran into the town of Dzhankoy, a few kilometers to the east. Trucks took the paved road; tractors took the dirt road. Checkpoint Anna was ordered to block all traffic.

Except there wasn't any traffic to block. The squad could probably take a nap in the woods for the next ten hours without having to worry about a single vehicle passing by their little sandbag fortification.

"Got it!" Sasha exclaimed, having finally won the battle against the troublesome lid on the insulated container of tea. A little of the precious liquid had spilled during Sasha's struggle with the vessel, but the steam rising from inside beckoned like an oasis of warmth. Sasha filled the two stainless cups sitting on the dashboard and handed Viktor one of them before quickly capping the metal bottle.

"Here," Sasha offered the cup to his taller, slimmer counterpart.

"Oh good Lord," Viktor said. "That is exactly what I needed right now. Thanks."

"We should have been stronger," Sasha said. "We should have held out and not opened it. We'll surely freeze after it's empty."

"I know. Just the same, let's enjoy this."

They each took long pulls from their cups, exhaled and stared out the window. The view hadn't changed. The same grey sky, beige fields, black-green pines, brown road — they were parked in the world's shittiest picture postcard.

"The wife will be so jealous," Sasha mused. "She always wanted to see beautiful Crimea. She envies my luxurious lifestyle, seeing the world and all. I can't say that I blame her. We have it pretty damn good relaxing in the Black Sea's vacation capital."

Viktor snickered into his cup, steam from the tea filling his nose as he inhaled.

Outside the truck, Privates Albert, Boris, and Pavel leaned against the sandbag walls of their machine gun position, bored and wishing they were in the Tigr. The military truck might not have been all that warm, but it was better than being out in the open.

Boris reached into a pocket and pulled out a pack of Winstons. He tapped the bottom until a smoke popped up and raised the cigarette to his lips. After producing a quick finger snap of flame from a Zippo knockoff, he puffed and took a drag. The crisp, clean smoke invigorated him as it rushed into his lungs.

"I already can't stand this place," he griped.

Albert and Pavel grunted and nodded in agreement.

Pavel rested his arms on the AK-74M hanging across his chest. "I can't believe we're here. Weren't we just watching Sochi?"

The men grumbled, the memory reminding them that they weren't in their warm homes in front of the television, and reviving the stings of Russia's Olympic hockey frustrations. The loss to Finland, the disallowed goal in the shootout with the Yanks.

"Crimea of all places," Pavel said after a long pause.

"Fucking Crimea," Boris spat.

"And not even the good part," Albert added. "Crimea ought to mean bikinis and well-tanned asses sunbathing on Balaklava Bay. Not some flat, grey stretch of nowhere."

"I joined up to get away from places like this," Pavel said.

"Damn straight," Boris confirmed.

A slight breeze blew across the woods and made the pines tremble a bit.

"Quit jawing and look alive, gentlemen," Sasha said, leaning his heavy frame out of the Tigr's passenger window. "This part of Crimea might be short on your 'bikinis and well-tanned asses,' but you still have a job to do. And that job is manning this checkpoint, so do it."

The three said "Yes, sergeant," standing a little straighter and looking a little sharper.

"Not 'sergeant,' you clods. 'Sasha.' On this mission, I am

just Sasha."

"Yes, Sasha," the three said simultaneously, feeling strange addressing their superior this way.

The uptick in military professionalism did not stop Boris from finishing his cigarette. Who knew how long he'd have to stretch the pack?

*

Sasha and Victor were the "old men" of the squad, in their mid-thirties, while Albert, Boris, and Pavel were in their early twenties. The sergeants had spent a brief part of their childhood living under the Soviets, while the younger members of the squad had only known the Federation.

The three privates were good kids; country boys, unlike Sasha and Victor, who hailed from Samara, one of Russia's largest cities, situated at the confluence of the Volga and the Sama. The two sergeants had met when they first joined up, became fast friends during basic training, and served as best man at each other's weddings. Albert, Boris, and Pavel all hailed from the same rural area outside of Nizhny Novgorod and knew each other before enlisting. For the privates, the army meant a ticket out of a life spent working for shit pay at some corporate farm.

Even when the mission might not be clear.

That certainly was the case with this assignment. Each member of the squad initially understood that their platoon had been called into action for a set of planned exercises outside of Krasnodar. However, multiple platoons, including Viktor's, were instead hustled onto eight Ilyushin IL-76 transport jets bound for Crimea.

While they waited in a hangar before boarding, junior officers drilled them on a series of specific, coordinated missions that each platoon would undertake. Intelligence officers told them that Ukrainian nationalists—some of them fascist extremists—had caused the unrest in Kyiv and had overthrown the democratically elected government. Intelligence also told them that the Russian-speaking majority in Crimea and Eastern Ukraine were under threat from the Ukrainian nationalists. Before these nuts could capture the various military bases—especially critical ones, such as the Russian navy base at Sebastopol—Russian forces would swoop in and take control of the entire Black Sea peninsula.

That part of the mission was crystal clear. Despite the hasty timetable, it sounded like a well-thought-out operation that was part humanitarian and part military in objective—reasonably straightforward stuff.

But then the men were instructed that they were to operate with no Russian insignia, and were under strict orders not to interact with the local populace, and especially the media. If they had to speak in the presence of anyone who was not Russian military, they were to give only their first name. They weren't even allowed to address each other by their surnames. Stranger still, they were all instructed to wear balaclavas to obscure their faces.

No insignia, no talking, covered faces, fascists roaming the Crimean Peninsula—those were the elements of this mission that had really set off Viktor's B.S. detector. If Viktor and his men were fending off Nazis, why were they hiding their identities and national affiliation?

Still, while he felt uneasy about the mission, Viktor noted the plane ride to Crimea was the smoothest he ever had—no turbulence, and a landing that felt about as ordinary as riding an elevator to the ground floor.

Taking control of Belbek airstrip, near Sevastopol, went just as smoothly. Second platoon set up a perimeter and encountered zero resistance. From there, the various platoons disembarked, assembled, packed up their gear, and fanned out across the Crimean Peninsula in GAZ Tigrs—Russia's answer to the Humvee—to accomplish their various missions.

As he watched the planes landing and unloading, Viktor couldn't help thinking that the entire operation resembled an endless stream of gigantic mechanical frogs: They touched down on a concrete lily pad, disgorged 100 or so olive drab eggs, and then leapt off into the night to make way for another jet-fueled amphibian to expel another well-armed spawn.

The only difficulty Viktor's squad had encountered was getting the Tigr to turn over from a cold start. For some reason, the pre-heater was giving them some trouble after sitting in the cold fuselage of a cargo plane. Boris and Sasha—both mechanical marvels as far as Viktor was concerned—identified what turned out to be a loose temperature sensor as the problem, and once they reconnected it, the truck rumbled back to life as the dependable mascot for the Squad.

After that, Squad B was off and running along Crimea's motorways, the dutiful Tigr's Cummins engine resonating throughout the vehicle's cabin as it towed a small trailer filled with sandbags behind them. The trip was a two-hour drive from the airstrip, and the Tigr's heater kept them warm while they flew along the M18 in the middle of the night. The five of them had joked part of the way, keyed up on their travels and the novelty of the situation, but Viktor ultimately ordered the squad to rest up, since they could be manning their checkpoint for some time without relief from another unit.

The Tigr eventually transported the five of them,

officially known as Squad B, to Checkpoint Anna, which was, on first observation, going to be low on ambiance and big on boredom.

*

That was pre-dawn Sunday; thirty-six hours ago. Now it was Monday afternoon.

Viktor and Sasha hadn't heard much chatter on the radio, but what they did hear made it sound like the whole operation was more like an exercise than an actual military mission. There had been zero resistance so far. No casualties. No shooting. There was ... nothing. Per orders, their rifles weren't loaded, with their magazines remaining in their pouches. Viktor felt like he had been sent to go to the market, rather than to do battle with foaming-at-the-mouth fascists.

Since arriving, the members of Squad B had only slept in shifts. They still had plenty of food and water, but Viktor and Sasha sipped their hot tea slowly, trying to make it last.

"You'll have to brew up some more, Sasha."

"Later. Tonight. When we heat up dinner rations."

Viktor nodded and drank the last of his cup. He pondered the now-empty vessel for a moment and then returned his attention to the road.

Albert, Boris, and Pavel kept scanning the road, as well.

"Crimea," Albert said, staring blankly up the road and leaning over the PKP machine gun (aka "the Pecheneg") mounted behind the sandbag wall.

"Crimea," Pavel agreed.

"What a shithole," Boris said. He flicked his cigarette butt down the road.

The wind gusted again. A pair of crows cawed as they flew west over the field. Boris stiffened.

"What the fuck is that?"

Pavel squinted as he looked further up the road, trying to focus on a bit of movement.

"Sergeants, are you looking up the road?"

"'Sasha and Viktor,' Pavel. Not 'sergeant.' 'Sasha and Viktor.'"

"Okay, 'Sasha and Viktor,' are you looking up the road?"

Sasha detected trace elements of sarcasm in Pavel's voice. He too hated this stupid name game. They all did. Abandoning standard military protocol emphasized the weirdness of the situation. Still, Sasha loved that kid's spirit, and it was hard to suppress the smile that Pavel's smart-ass remark had elicited. Sasha squinted up the road, but from his position in the truck, he couldn't see a damn thing.

"Easy, Pavel," Sasha said in the best bored tone of voice he could force and stepped out of the Tigr. He walked a little further to the shoulder of the road and stood behind the small, un-hitched trailer that had previously hauled the sandbags that now formed their checkpoint. Sasha crouched a little bit and peered through his binoculars towards the point where the road took a bend southeast into the woods.

"Viktor, you should come out and take a look at this."

"What is it?"

"Well ... to be honest, I'm not quite sure."

Chapter 2

HER SQUARE

Veronika Melnik sat at her kitchen table and peered out her third-floor window overlooking Independence Square. There was activity down below, despite it being nearly dinnertime. In the weeks after Yanukovych's ouster, the square—the maidan—had started reawakening, including the cafes and restaurants. Her borscht and pampushki seemed like a luxury after the tumult Kyiv had seen during the past few weeks, and accordingly, she relished the meal. A second helping was in order.

Barricades at most of the entry points still blocked access to Independence Square, but the mood had changed down below over the last few days. During the riots, the place almost breathed with violence. The regular police along with the Ministry of Internal Affairs' special Berkut police force, both clad in riot gear, would surge into the square in hopes of exerting absolute control over it, but the Euromaidan activists would then overwhelm the authorities in a flurry of colorful, spirited refusal. The Euromaidan movement would no longer acknowledge, let alone live under an administration that was beholden to Russia instead of Ukraine.

Veronika always thought of Independence Square as her square. That's why she chose the Mira Apartments. She participated in the 1989 student protests and cheered through the 2004 Orange Revolution. And now, once again, Independence Square served as the geographic and spiritual heart and soul of the Euromaidan, the movement that sought alignment with the European Union.

A portmanteau of "Europe" and "Maidan Nezalezhnosti," or Independence Square (where the protests had been forming) the Euromaidan stemmed from an eponymous Twitter hashtag that had mobilized the protests via social media. The movement was born from frustration over President Viktor Yanukovych and Prime Minister Mykola Azarov abandoning their nation's steady movement toward European alignment, which had begun in 2008. Instead, Yanukovych suddenly changed gears and entered private meetings with Russian President Vladimir Putin—who had been waging economic war against Ukraine for nearly a year by then. The pair aimed to strike a deal that would see Ukraine join Russia's Customs Union in exchange for a multi-billion-dollar payout and a break on natural gas prices. The move ran contrary to both parliamentary votes and popular will.

Though Veronika watched the Euromaidan protests through her windows, her little brother Danilo had been down in the square, in the thick of the swirling, chaotic fighting. Naturally, this filled her with worry. When she was young and in the square, Veronika knew when to hold back on the periphery of events and stay out of trouble, but her little brother was braver and more adventurous—to the point of being considerably stupid at times.

The situation hit a fever pitch during January and February when the shooting began, and nothing could have prepared her for knowing Danilo was in the middle of it.

What the hell was he thinking? Danilo wasn't some idealistic school kid. He had graduated university with a Political Science degree, but after a year of interning for a couple parliamentary offices, he changed tacks and went to technical school. He had since been working as an electrician for eight years. Danilo had not yet married, but still ... down there, wearing that motorcycle helmet and gloves, her little brother was one baton—or bullet—away from never seeing his wedding day.

*

The Euromaidan protests had kicked off in full the previous November, but the seeds were planted well before then. In 2008, Ukraine had announced it was working toward a stabilization and association agreement, a process that would eventually bring the nation into the European Union's open marketplace. By March of 2012, the European Union and Ukraine had initiated an Association Agreement. The need for such a relationship had grown acute. Ukraine's economy was in rough shape, its national debt skyrocketed, and the government had explored an International Monetary Fund loan at the same time it was looking at European Union association, a course that, if followed, would eventually see the nation join the EU many years later. By the summer of 2013, the Ukrainian government was making steady progress toward meeting the EU's terms for association and ratifying the internal legislation necessary for the nation to formally sign such an agreement.

In response, Russia launched a trade war in August 2013, blocking all Ukrainian goods, which forced Ukrainian exports and production to plummet. It was clear what Russia wanted: Ukraine taking on a loan from Moscow rather than from the West, and no EU association at all. Ukraine was being pressured to pay fealty to Russia, which was growing increasingly paranoid about the West's influence in the region. Putin didn't want the EU anywhere near his sphere of influence.

Not all Ukrainians saw things the same way. Public opinion of EU association swung based on region. Most in the west of the country—especially in big cities, such as Kyiv—favored EU association. Sentiment in middle of the country was mixed on the issue, and the eastern reaches of the nation—ethnically more Russian than Ukrainian—leaned toward opposing it, but not by a massive margin. Crimea, home to Russia's Black Sea fleet and Russian sunbathers in the summer, opposed association, as well. This was the dilemma of Ukraine as Veronika saw it: some regions of the country identified themselves as Ukrainian more than others.

But even the staunchest supporters of EU association couldn't deny the effectiveness of Russia's trade tactics. As Ukraine's industry dwindled under Russia's blockade, so did President Yanukovych's and the parliament's resolve to support EU association. On November 21, 2013, the government and President Yanukovych announced they would not sign the European Association Agreement.

That night, someone tweeted the hashtag

"#Euromaidan" and two thousand protesters showed up in Independence Square. The movement's momentum exploded. By November 24, a rally on the square attracted nearly two hundred thousand people. On November 30, protestors on the square noticed their smartphones suddenly stopped working. Out of nowhere Berkut special police armed with clubs and stun grenades poured into Independence Square and started cracking heads.

From that point onward, tensions between Yanukovych's government and the Euromaidan, as well as tensions between the protestors and the police rocked back and forth like a seesaw. Sometimes, the chaos and violence would center around the square, and other times it would move to other parts of the city. The rioters would hold the square, and then they would leave the square. There would be periods of calm, and then the calm would be interrupted by intermittent shit storms. During the riots, tear gas canisters, rocks, paving stones, fireworks and sometimes Molotov cocktails seized control of Kyiv's airspace from the resident pigeons while hand-to-hand melee churned below.

The situation escalated to horrifying heights in January, when the first shooting victims started showing up in hospitals and morgues. Many of the fallen Euromaidan supporters had been killed by rounds fired by Kalashnikov assault rifles and Degtyaryov sniper rifles, as well as shots from nine-millimeter handguns and shotguns—all were the types of weapons used by the Berkut.

January saw approximately thirty people shot to death by Yanukovych's forces. An ensuing truce between the protestors and security forces lasted for a little while, but by February 17 fighting had broken out again. On February 18 and 19, another twenty-six were killed, including a journalist who was murdered—shot in the chest—by a group of Titushky who surrounded his car. The Titushky were thugs the Berkut hired from various hooligan gangs. (The irony of cops hiring criminals to do their bidding made Veronika seethe.) Then February 20 happened. That was the big one: Yanukovych's forces gunned down sixty people that day.

The events of those four days in February kept roiling in Veronika's memory like a boiling kettle. She couldn't believe Yanukovych's security forces—she insisted on calling them Yanukovych's forces because she refused to think that those wolves somehow served the citizens of Ukraine—would start shooting at their fellow countrymen. But they had. The Euromaidan supporters were completely outgunned. Only a tiny fraction of the protestors had firearms; most armed themselves with sticks, thrown objects, or foul language.

During those grim days in February, when violence in the Maidan boiled over, Veronika joined her fellow hospital workers and headed for the square. The police were on the offensive and were working in earnest to vanquish the rioters by any means necessary. She and several other nurses and a few physicians from her employer, the Municipal Clinical Hospital, joined about a dozen emergency medical technicians, hopped in a small convoy of ambulances packed with supplies, and rushed to Independence Square after the Berkut and police had launched their first strike of the day against the protestors.

Veronika was horrified at what she saw when they had arrived. When she had left her apartment earlier, the square had looked like how it had for the past several weeks: protestors gathering, and constructing barricades. But upon returning with her fellow hospital staffers, the square appeared as though an angry giant had picked everything up and threw it back down, leaving the square in smoldering, bloody disarray. There was some calm since the continually unfolding chaos had spread to other parts of the city like some giant, migratory beast.

Even in her student protest days, the square hadn't looked like it did that morning. Back when Veronika carried signs and chanted slogans, mainly students comprised the ranks of protesters. However, on that morning everybody—men and women, old and young, from all walks of life—packed into the square, clad in cobbled-together gear to protect them from the riot police. They were rebuilding barricades constructed from tires, oil drums, scrap lumber, dumpsters, picnic tables and whatever else they could find. A few men on bullhorns rallied everyone and shouted out instructions and updates on where the police were heading. The rest were either trying to clean up after the confrontation with the Berkut or tending to wounded friends.

As experienced a nurse as she was, Veronika wasn't prepared for the casualties awaiting them. The police and Berkut, along with Titushky and other pro-Yanukovych thugs, were not stingy when they doled out their beatings. She treated lacerations, abrasions, broken bones, and concussions—and bullet wounds. She and other medical professionals from across the city had set up a combination triage and emergency treatment facility in the lobby and ballroom of the Hotel Kyiv adjacent to the square. As the riots kept spreading throughout the city, the casualties kept coming. She thanked God her little brother Danilo wasn't among them.

*

Veronika still remembered the relief she felt when she

took her first break after fourteen hours of stitching, stapling, bandaging, and dressing. The fighting and general insanity that had been raging outside had finally quieted down. She washed off as much blood as she could, put on a white army helmet and white lab coat hastily spray painted with a red cross on the front and back, and stepped outside to stroll along the square's northeastern border, sipping a coffee in a paper cup. Every drop felt like liquid restoration for her flagging spirit.

"Veronika? Veronika!"

It was Danilo's voice, but it was strangely muffled like he was in a bucket. She saw her little brother rushing toward her wearing a skiing jacket, motorcycle helmet, and his motorcycle gloves. The visor of his helmet had been broken off, but a portion of the clear plastic shield was still attached to one of the hinges, and it stuck in the air like a dog's ear. He looked idiotic. Veronika laughed when she saw him and rushed up for a hug.

"Baby brother! Danilo, I've been so worried about you. What happened?"

Veronika pointed to his battered helmet.

"Ah ... that. A cop in riot gear nearly smashed me on the head with a stick. I dodged, but it tore off the visor. Such a loss. It was a beautiful helmet."

"Never mind the helmet. Are you okay?"

"I'm all right. What about you?"

"I'm fine. Just rattled."

"Well, prepare to be rattled some more. The cops and goons are making moves. We're expecting more trouble. You shouldn't be walking around here drinking coffee. You should go back inside and keep treating people, or better yet, you should get some sleep. You're going to need your rest, big sister."

"How can I possibly sleep knowing you're in this shit? Danilo, they were shooting people here!"

"I know ... I know you're worried. I'm sorry, but we need to show Yanukovych that he can't sell us out to Russia. Anyway, it's not as dangerous as it could be. Some guys are ex-army, and they've been helping us get organized. They showed us tactics for dealing with the police and the thugs. We might not have guns, but we're way better organized than the Titushky now."

"Was that supposed to make me feel better?"

"It was, but I think I'm doing a shitty job of it."

"You are."

"I'm sorry."

"I know. Look, little brother, you have to promise me that if there is any more shooting, you are going to either get the hell out of there or hide like a rabbit if you can't. You have to promise me that."

"I promise."

"And you have to come check in on me occasionally. You can't let me worry that you're lying dead in the middle of some street."

"I will."

"Promise me."

"I promise, Veronika. I promise."

"Now walk with me a little while. I want to stroll with my little brother in the square before I go get some sleep."

*

The following morning Veronika opened her eyes to what sounded like fireworks. There was a "*crack!*" and then another, echoing off buildings in quick, staccato fashion: *Crack! Echo-echo-echo.* Then a long pause. Then, *crack! Echo-echo-echo.*

Still, in her clothes from the night before, Veronika sat up from her bed at her apartment, pivoted her legs over the edge of the mattress, and looked toward the curtained window. Alina Soroka, a fellow nurse and Veronika's friend since high school, was already standing there, staring between the mostly closed curtains. Veronika had invited Alina to stay at her place after a long night tending to the kinds of injuries that invariably result from violent clashes between protestors and riot police.

"It's gunfire," Alina confirmed. "It woke me up a couple minutes ago. The police are shooting. ... At least I think it's the police."

Still groggy, Veronika considered Alina's words for a moment before she processed them.

"Oh God. Danilo."

Veronika sprang up, parted the curtains a little more and looked out. What she saw was horrifying. Small bands of protesters were either running back to the presumed safety of the square or were pinned down in clumps throughout the streets. Nearly all were wearing masks of either balaclavas, scarves, or handkerchiefs, along with helmets of all kinds — motorcycle, construction, army, and even some confiscated police helmets. Many were carrying or hiding behind metal riot shields they had taken from fleeing police. It was eerily quiet. There was no yelling. There were no sounds of fighting. There was almost no noise of any kind, except for an organizer on the square using a bullhorn to shout instructions and the occasional gunshot.

Crack! Echo-echo-echo.

Snipers. Veronika's and Alina's attention turned to a group of six protesters huddled behind their shields, a concrete trash can, and a few trees about a block and a half up Instytuska Street. It was clear a sniper had them pinned down and was not letting up.

Crack! Echo-echo-echo.

"This is horrible!" Alina exclaimed. "They're unarmed! What do we do?"

"We don't do anything," Veronika replied. "There's nothing we can do."

Crack! Echo-echo-echo.

One of the six protesters slumped over. His shocked comrades grabbed at him and tried to pull him closer in to give him better cover from the sniper.

Crack! Echo-echo-echo.

"Oh, God!"

Another one of the six protesters, a man who was partly hiding behind a tree, fell on his side, quickly grabbed his riot shield and laid it on top of himself like a metal blanket. It looked like a bullet had hit him in the leg or hip. He began crawling to better cover, one hand holding the shield and the other pulling him along the pavement. The fallen man waved off his friends who were moving to help him. He was yelling, but of course, Veronika and Alina couldn't hear him from inside their room. They could only see his mouth opening and closing. His frantic movements. His worried, grimacing face.

Veronika ached for him and his friends. He was all alone, but they could do nothing to help him. "Oh God in heaven," she said as she looked on.

Crack! Echo-echo-echo.

A cloud of dust appeared on the pavement next to the crawling man. *Crack! Echo-echo-echo.* Another cloud of dust rose up from nearly the same spot.

Alina called out: "Veronika, look!"

Alina was pointing to another group of protesters taking cover behind the VTB Bank building on the corner. There were five of them — three with shields, one holding a bundled-up canvas stretcher, and one carrying what looked like a can of soda in his hand. They were focusing on the six pinned-down men and seemed to be trying to figure out how to get to them.

Then the one with the soda can did something strange: He opened the top of the can, and instead of drinking it, he hurled it as high as he could into the middle of Instytuska Street. Thick, grey smoke began to pour out of the soda can and clouded the whole block — a smoke grenade.

That's when Veronika noticed the helmet of the man next to the one with the smoke bomb.

"Oh my God, that's Danilo. Danilo is the one holding the stretcher. Do you see him? Oh, my God."

"That's your little brother? Oh, Veronika!"

All Veronika could do was watch. The five rescuers raced diagonally across the block behind the wall of smoke spewing from the canister and went to work as soon as they reached the six pinned-down men. Danilo and the man who threw the smoke bomb pulled the first man who had been hit onto the stretcher and hurried the litter toward the Hotel Kyiv. Two other men dropped their shields and picked up the man who had been shot in the leg and started running as well. The remaining five who could hold shields tried to protect themselves and those who were carrying the wounded.

"It looks like they're okay, Veronika. It looks like they're okay," Alina said, but Veronika was gone, padding down the hallway toward the elevator. Alina quickly followed, closing the door behind her.

Danilo made it unscathed that day, and despite being appalled by her little brother being in the middle of the violence, Veronika was extremely proud of him for helping save those men. That didn't stop her from sobbing and hugging him for what seemed like an hour in the lobby of the Hotel Kyiv before she got back to the rows and rows of wounded.

The Hotel Kyiv and the other aid stations that had quickly sprung up looked and sounded at times nothing short of army field hospitals, filled with blood and screaming. What could she or any of them do to treat rifle rounds to the head? The wounded were sent to a real hospital as quickly as it was possible to get an ambulance to transport them. But many of those shot by snipers had already died long before they were carried to care. She remembered one of the injured activists who had some military experience remarking that the snipers must've received far better training than what the police could provide because their shots were so effective. "Putin's triggermen," he called them.

The square looked nightmarish, filled with tire smoke and screaming. There were spots on the pavement where people slipped in the blood as though it was winter ice.

*

That was thirteen days and eighty-six bodies ago. Now it was March 2, and this morning was much calmer. Veronika continued gazing at Independence Square as she chewed on some pampushki she had dipped in her borscht. Now the Maidan was less a fortress and more a memorial. Friends and family of the fallen had reverentially placed flower arrangements all over the square, and walls and drawings and posters memorializing the events of February 17 through 20 covered the barricades. The Square was changing its mood again.

Someone knocked on her door.

"Just a moment," she announced, and dabbed the corners of her mouth with a napkin.

She swung open the door to see Danilo.

"Hey big sister, mind if I join you?"

"Not at all! I'm glad to see you. Tea?"

"Is that borscht I smell? And garlic? Pampushki?"

"I might be willing to share."

"I might be willing to eat! Did you hear the news?"

"No. I slept in and have been ignoring the TV. What's going on?"

"There are Russian soldiers all over Crimea."

Chapter 3
FIVE MUTE MICE

"What do you mean you're not sure?"

"I mean that I'm not sure. Look, Viktor, get out here and see for yourself."

Viktor hopped out the driver's side door, walked around the front of the Tigr, and crossed the checkpoint to where Sasha was standing. The big man was still looking through his binoculars, muttering.

"Weirdest damn thing …"

Viktor raised his binoculars. Almost as soon as he had peered through them, he lowered the field glasses, blinked a few times, and squinted toward the bend in the road. He looked through the glasses again.

"You're right, Sasha. That is the weirdest damn thing."

Through the binoculars, he could see a strange little

parade of sorts. A man in robes, flanked by another man carrying the Ukrainian flag on one side, and a third man carrying a Ukrainian Orthodox three-bar cross on the other. A group of roughly twenty people followed them. Two men carrying video cameras escorted them, and a few more men either snapping still photographs or taking notes.

The strangely out-of-place procession was making its way up the road, toward Checkpoint Anna, and growing easier to see as it approached. Viktor wondered, *what is it, a religious pilgrimage? A procession of some kind?*

Boris piped up.

"Is that a priest?"

"Looks like it," Viktor responded. "Listen, we are under specific orders: you are not to engage with the civilians — and especially the media — under any circumstances. I want you all to maintain strict discipline on that. Do you understand?"

"Yes ... Viktor," Boris stumbled again on the mission's first name policy.

"Yes, Viktor," Pavel and Albert chimed in.

"Excellent. Keep cool, do not engage, and do not even react. Oh, and keep those balaclavas well over your faces. We do not want your mugs popping up in a newspaper, or on Youtube."

"And if there is any talking to be done, Viktor and I will do it," Sasha added.

The five men of Squad B watched the spectacle continue toward them up the road. When the group got closer, they could hear a man in the crowd reading what sounded like Bible passages, the still camera shutters clacking open and shut, and the crowd of people chanting and sometimes singing. The slogans and hymns grew louder as the civilians drew closer.

"Russia out! Russia out! Russia out!"

"They want us out. Shall we take off?" Pavel joked. Boris and Albert snickered.

"Shut up. I mean it," Viktor snarled. The three privates immediately grew serious and stiffened their postures. Viktor noticed even Sasha moved to pull his balaclava a little higher up on his face.

"No one has a magazine in his weapon, correct?" Viktor asked. "And no one takes a step near that Pecheneg. I don't want anyone doing anything exceptionally idiotic this afternoon."

"No, Viktor," they chorused.

The group of civilians and journalists had nearly reached them.

"Russia out! Russia out! Russia out!" the protestors chanted.

The five held still and silent.

Viktor suddenly thought-up a joke: What did the Russian soldier say to the Ukrainian priest? Nothing. Not one damn thing. He smiled to himself, then got worried the crowd might see his grin before he realized he was wearing a mask. He almost laughed out loud at himself for being so nervous.

The group walked right up to the checkpoint.

"Russia out! Russia out! Russia out!"

While the people chanted, the journalists with cameras scrambled to and fro, trying to get different angles. The man reading the Bible verses maintained a loud but calm tone of voice, which Viktor found oddly soothing. The man carrying the Ukrainian Orthodox cross wore a suit. The man bearing the Ukrainian flag wore a construction helmet painted in the same yellow and blue as his nation's banner.

"Russia out! Russia out! Russia out!"

Viktor's men maintained their composure.

One of the reporters was talking to one of the video cameramen, and pointing near the trailer. The cameraman started heading in the direction of the trailer. Albert began to turn to head them off, but Viktor waved him back.

"He's just getting a shot. No big deal. Keep calm," he advised in an even voice that hopefully only Albert could hear. Albert kept calm.

As the cameraman got into position, the bearded priest walked forward. He wore a gold and crimson chasuble over his white cassock and held a silver-handled brush of sorts in one hand. It was a holy water sprinkler. He walked up to the men and began sprinkling the five members of Squad B as he prayed.

Viktor was praying, too. He hoped to God that his men stayed calm, especially in front of those cameras. Viktor felt holy water splash the part of his face exposed by the balaclava. It felt like rain.

The priest prayed as the crowd continued chanting.

"Russia out! Russia out! Russia out!"

"Why are Russian Soldiers taking over various military and government facilities all over Crimea?"

The voice asking Viktor the question wasn't Ukrainian. It wasn't Russian either. The accent sounded foreign—English.

"Why are you here?"

Viktor looked at the man with the English accent. He looked to be a few years older than Viktor, but not many, and wore a neat mustache and eyeglasses. He was asking Viktor the same question Viktor had been asking himself all day. *Why were they there? Really?*

As Viktor wordlessly pondered the journalist's question, an old lady walked up and began scolding the members of

Squad B.

"Your Putin is making you look like fools! Look at you wearing masks like bandits. Your faces might be hidden, but we know who you are—you're Russians. And you're pretending that you haven't invaded us, but you have. How does it feel to look like fools for your government, eh, Russian soldiers?"

Viktor looked at Sasha and the three privates. They remained stone-faced. *Good.*

The old lady continued her admonishment.

"You know why the priest is blessing you? He's hoping God Almightily grants you enough wisdom to realize the wrong you are doing here and to leave our country. You have no right to be here! Listen to his prayers and do the right thing!"

"She has a point, soldier," said the English journalist in heavily accented, but solid Russian. "About you being Russians, that is. You might not be wearing any insignia, but your equipment is clearly Russian—right down to the Russian military plate on the front of your truck."

It took every ounce of self-discipline Viktor could call upon not to grimace. The license plates were a dead giveaway. They should have removed the plates. But more to the point, why were they hiding? This situation felt increasingly stupid. He gritted his teeth and wished to get back to boredom that had prevailed over Checkpoint Anna earlier. Their duty might have been dull, but at least it had been peaceful.

Just then a new noise was added to the cacophony of chants, prayers, Bible verses and snapping cameras. The sound of an engine rumbled through the woods. A tractor came into view, making its way along the dirt road towards Checkpoint Anna. The tractor pulled a small trailer, and the white, blue, and red tricolor flags of the Russian Federation covered both. Three men and two women rode on the wagon, and the driver was a burly man wearing a wool hunting cap and a scruffy, black beard.

The man brought his rig to a halt and stood up in the driver's seat, removed his cap, extended one arm as though he was making a speech, and began addressing the soldiers in a booming voice that rose above the church group's chanting.

"Russian brothers! It is an honor to have you here in our town! We brought some tea and sandwiches to welcome you!"

The men and women on the trailer hopped off and hustled toward Checkpoint Anna with sandwiches and large foam cups that presumably contained tea.

Sasha stepped toward them and spoke up:

"Please, no. We cannot accept. We are under orders. You must step back from the checkpoint."

The welcoming party paused. The burly man's voice boomed out.

"We understand, my brothers! We appreciate your military service and your dedication to duty! Russia, we are with you!"

"Shut up, you loudmouthed oaf, Dimitry!" shouted the old lady who had been berating the soldiers minutes before. "We don't need your fat ass here! Why don't you go back to your farm so that you can resume drinking?"

The man on the tractor launched in a withering tirade of curse words and insults directed at the woman, calling her "a crusty, old bitch," which in turn set off the protestors and the welcoming party until everyone was screaming at each other. The priest was trying to calm down his group, the tractor driver was doing his best to incite his group, and the journalists were having a field day recording and snapping pictures of the mess.

All except for one journalist, Viktor had noticed. The Englishman hadn't left the spot where he had been standing near Viktor and was surveying the affair with a pensive look on his face. Viktor gathered the man had seen more than one confrontation like this, and he wondered what the newsman was pondering.

Sasha tapped Viktor's elbow and motioned toward the back of the Tigr. The two sergeants walked back and stood near the rear of the vehicle where they could talk more privately while still keeping an eye on the scene.

"These people have to be fucking kidding," Sasha said. "I don't know who I'm more annoyed with, the old lady or our newfound friend on the tractor."

"We have to take control of this situation. If there's a brawl in front of those cameras, we could wind up in deep shit. It's already bad enough with all this shouting and yelling."

"You're right."

They hustled back to their three comrades. Viktor stepped forward and raised his open palms toward the crowd.

"Everyone, you must calm down and move away from the checkpoint."

No one paid him any mind. The yelling and cursing continued, as did the camera shutter clacking. It wouldn't be easy to take control of the situation. Viktor looked at the journalists recording the event and began imagining the dressing down he was going to receive from the Captain if he didn't figure out something fast. *Does sweat show through a balaclava?*

A second tractor pulled up, this time from the western

stretch of the dirt road. It came to a stop, and the old man driving gave his horn a long, loud blast. Everyone shut up and looked at him.

"What is going on here?" he asked. "Who are these soldiers?"

"They are our Russian brothers!" the younger, larger driver of the other tractor yelled.

"They are Russian invaders," the old woman from the crowd shouted back.

"Brothers or invaders, they are blocking the damn road! I need to get to market to buy fertilizer, and I'd like to get back before sundown. Someone clear the way."

The old man sat gazing steel-eyed at Viktor. His face caught Viktor's attention, a mix of Turkic and Russian features. *He must be Crimean Tatar.*

"Well? Is anyone going to move?" the old man chided. "I'd prefer not detouring through Bessonov's field. Come next harvest he'll blame me for his poor haul instead of his agricultural incompetence."

The protestors and partisans began arguing again. The old man looked annoyed. Viktor noticed the Englishman was instructing his cameraman to get a shot of the old man on the tractor. Suddenly, the old man hit the gas and aimed his tractor toward Checkpoint Anna.

Pavel and Boris made moves to ready their weapons. Viktor ordered, "Wait!" and motioned for his men to stand their ground. *What the hell was this old coot doing?*

The tractor lurched up onto the pavement. Right before it hit the sandbags, the old man jerked his steering wheel to the right and slammed on his brakes so that the tractor came to a stop between the church group and the sandbag checkpoint. It now pointed at the nose of the other tractor.

"Get out of the way Dimitry! I need to get to market!"

"Hell no, old man! Why don't you go back to that shithole you call a home and paint your stupid rabbits, eh?"

Viktor noticed most of the crowd looked at each other in puzzlement, trying to understand the strange insult, but the old man didn't seem bothered.

"Move, you drunk oaf!" he demanded.

That set off the yelling and cursing between the various parties all over again. This situation was getting ridiculous. That's when Viktor got an idea. He walked over to the man named Dimitry.

"Look, sir, you seem like a good Russian, and we appreciate your offer of food and your support, but what I really need is your cooperation."

"How's that, brother?"

"I need you to leave. If you pull back, the church group will pull back, and the old man will go on his way, and these reporters will leave. I need to maintain order at this checkpoint. Can you do this for Russia?"

The big, burly man looked a little disappointed, but said, "Absolutely!"

"Thank you, sir. When things calm down, I'll be grateful to enjoy your hospitality."

That seemed to cheer the big man up. He brightened and called to the men and women that had come with him before making a final bellowing announcement to everyone at the intersection:

"We are happy to meet you, Russian brothers, and to have you here! We are sorry that we have to be on our way, but look forward to visiting again!"

This guy was working overtime to tick off his neighbors, Viktor thought.

Dimitry started his tractor and drove between the old man and the crowd, and continued on the dirt road heading west. The old man glared at Dimitry as he passed, then put his tractor in gear and headed the opposite direction, toward the woods and the town of Dzhankoy beyond.

Viktor's maneuver worked. Thanks to the lack of interference from Dimitry, the priest now had the church crowd under control. The priest turned to the Russian soldiers and spoke:

"Bless you, my son. We know you are good. Do God's will and leave us in peace."

The group began singing "Oh Lord, Almighty and Gracious" and turned to head back down the road in the direction they came from. The news media members turned to leave as well, but the Englishman lingered for a moment.

"Good job," he said to Viktor. "That could have gotten out of hand." Viktor couldn't tell if that was a compliment or sarcasm, but the Englishman was down the road before he had a chance to consider the remark.

*

When Squad B was finally alone, and Checkpoint Anna had resumed its usual mind-numbing dullness, the five were able to relax.

"Holy crap," Boris exclaimed after a long exhale. "That was ridiculous."

"Agreed," Albert said. "What the hell?"

"Those people were out of their minds—all of 'em," Pavel decreed. "Did you see that crazy priest's beard? He looked like an avenging angel or a wizard or something!"

Boris lit up a smoke and offered the pack to the other three. Albert took him up on it.

"Can you blame them? This whole country is in turmoil," Viktor explained. "That is why we have to keep a cool head in these situations. Bearing that in mind, you guys did a great job. I know it wasn't easy, but you did an excellent job of keeping your cool—especially with the tractor. I owe you all a round of beers when we get to take a break. Let's keep it up."

"Should we radio back a report?" Sasha asked.

"In a minute, Sasha. But first?"

"What's that?"

"I could do with a cup of tea."

Chapter 4
NEWS TRAVELS

English reporter Stewart Cooper was starting to feel his deadline clamping down on him like a vise. He and Ken Marston—a Canadian freelance cameraman who was Stewart's partner in crime on this ETV job—parted ways with the church protest group at approximately 5 p.m. and rushed to Dzhankoy, where they hoped to find a room with some WiFi. They had no such luck and decided to fill up the rented Geely, pick up some coffees and snacks, and head down the M18 either to Simferopol or further south to Sevastopol in search of some bandwidth to file their piece.

Ken drove while Stewart worked on the laptop, editing Ken's video while adding his voiceover dispatch from the Russian checkpoint. With any luck, they'd have the piece ready to send by the time they could find a hotel. If that didn't work, they could grab some free WiFi at a café and could file that way. Stewart wasn't worried about how they'd file so much as when. He wanted to get this to ETV as quickly as possible, before another media outlet started airing a report from someone else.

In a pinch, they could file lower-resolution video via cellular data, but Ukraine and Crimea only had 3G, so getting video to the ETV producer handling their stuff using that route was a real crapshoot, to say the least, and the poor quality would undoubtedly antagonize their client. Neither he nor Ken had a portable broadband satellite terminal. That sort of expensive equipment wasn't usually necessary in Europe, where the public network infrastructure was modern and typically reliable. Of course, a few bombs or missiles could change all that.

"This is coming together really well," Stewart remarked from the backseat. "This story is practically editing itself."

"That priest in those gold robes was amazing stuff," Ken replied over his shoulder. "He looked like he was from another century."

"Those Russians were tight-lipped, weren't they?"

"Yes. Yes, they were. I guess Putin thinks he can keep this a secret?"

"I have no idea on that. I'm not sure how the Russians are going to spin this. I guess we'll find out when we can get a chance to file and take a moment to find out what's going on."

"So how are you planning to describe those nameless soldiers?"

"I said 'unidentified forces wearing unmarked Russian uniforms and carrying standard-issue Russian weapons.' I also noted that the license plate looked like a Russian military plate. I hope ETV doesn't edit out your shot of that.

It's hard to get all this to fit a short clip. A lot was going on, especially after those tractors arrived. Once production adds in the intro and all that, a ninety -second package doesn't leave us a lot of room. Still, even if it would have been good for the story, I'm glad the situation didn't kick off."

"You can say that again."

Ken re-focused his attention on the road, and Stewart resumed editing. Dzhankoy had been what they had thought would be the final stop on what had been a very long day. They had left Kyiv for Crimea at about 3 a.m., as soon as a local Ukrainian reporter friend had called Stewart to give him a tip about the Russian troops. Now they were heading even further south.

Military vehicle traffic on the roads was heavy, but it was difficult to determine whether the Tigrs and cargo trucks belonged to the Ukrainians or the Russians. If they were Russian, they could have been part of an invasion force, or merely vehicles attached to one of the Russian bases in the Crimea. That ambiguity was par for course in Ukraine. The country was so full of shades of grey that it often defied comprehension at first. At least it appeared that way to Stewart.

Stewart and Ken had driven for nine and a half hours before stopping in Dzhankoy. That's where a market owner had told them about the church group heading to a Russian checkpoint. When they asked the shopkeeper where the checkpoint was, he pointed to the old lady, who was walking by out front. They caught up with the woman, who got excited at hearing Stewart speaking Russian, grabbed his arm, and practically dragged him to where the group was assembling. That march on the Russians was probably one of the biggest things to happen in this town of fewer than forty-thousand people for decades.

At the checkpoint, it was tough to tell what the Russians were thinking or how they were reacting to such a ridiculous three-way confrontation, but he had to give the lead soldier (was he a lieutenant, or a sergeant?) credit for eventually getting control of the situation. Stewart had his fill of violent confrontations after the last few weeks in Kyiv. Footage of riots and snipers were an instant sell to ETV, but reporting violence took its emotional toll. The idea of those sweet country folk coming to blows repulsed Stewart, and he was glad the Russian soldier had figured out a way to cool things down.

Picking up that story was a nice bonus, but now he hoped they were on the way to find the real action — something more significant than a checkpoint next to a field. He was confident they'd find that story in Sevastopol. Stewart had already heard stories and read some social media posts about pro-Russian activists staging protests in the city, and a week ago, armed, pro-Russian militiamen had invaded the Crimean Parliament building. It was rumored they were under the direction of Russian special forces.

"This Geely is okay," Ken said, patting the dashboard. "The Cadillac of Chinese commuter boxes."

"I'm holding out for Jeremy Clarkson's review."

"Hah! I'd like to see Top Gear drift one of these things through hairpins. ... Hey, Simferopol is coming up in about 30 minutes, if my math is right. Think you'll be done by then?"

"I just finished. Let's see if we can't find some WiFi there. I'll get the files prepped."

The little silver car flew down the road. Evening faded into night, and Ken switched on the high beams. There was barely any traffic.

*

They found some WiFi at the Crimean Educational Center in Simferopol, a sort of Internet café set up by Ukraine's Department of Education, and filed their story with no hiccups. Then they grabbed a late meal at a café. As Ken sipped a cup of coffee, Stewart was wrapping up a call with his ETV producer to confirm that everything came through okay.

"That's terrific. Glad to hear it. Yes?" Stewart paused and nodded. "Okay, Ken and I are going to head to Sevastopol now. What's that? Oh! Okay, we'll give it a shot. Thanks for the recommendation. Right. Okay. Bye."

Stewart hung up and turned to Ken.

"William back at ETV tells me we should head to the Best Western once we get to town," he said. "It's our safest bet for a room with minimum hassle."

"Thank the Lord for chain hotels."

"Amen!"

On the way south to the city, they passed a convoy of ten sizeable Russian army trucks—KAMA3s—heading the other direction.

"I have a feeling we'll be seeing more of those," Ken said.

"A lot more," Stewart agreed.

They reached Sevastopol proper within an hour and located the Best Western after twenty minutes of driving in circles trying to get their GPS to acknowledge the new reality of Sevastopol's streets, which were starting to get choked with Russian roadblocks. Luckily, they didn't have to stop at any checkpoints along the way. Maybe it was too early in the operation for everything to be deployed. Ken and Stewart booked a double to save money.

Mercifully, the hotel bar was open, even though it was unpopulated except for the bartender. A drink was in order. Stewart ordered a Johnnie Walker Black, and Ken was happy to see Jim Beam on the shelf. Stewart raised his glass.

"To our first story out of Crimea," he said.

"Indeed, and a strange one, too," Ken replied as the bartender handed him his glass. Here's to more like it."

"To more strange stories — and no bloodshed."

"Amen to that. Any idea how we got into town so easy? Feels like we almost got into town too easily for a city that was in the process of being taken over by an army."

"I'm guessing that the Russians and whoever else is working with them are focusing on getting control of military assets and that sort of thing, and aren't worried about civilian roads," Stewart said.

"Well let's hope they don't start blocking things up. How are we going to get out in the field if they start setting up checkpoints and issuing 'official' media credentials?"

"Tough to say," Stewart said, pondering the situation. "Frankly, I'm more worried how they might try to control the flow of information out of here. They're big on media control. I guess we can't really know, yet."

"Yeah, it's too early to tell, but you have to wonder if Russia is simply protecting their assets, or if this is a full-scale annexation of Crimea," Ken replied. "Or does Putin have his sights set on Eastern Ukraine? All of Ukraine? This whole thing is so fucking weird. That noise coming out of Russia about fascists bugged me."

"Me, too, but you know it's the same old shit these countries use to justify anything they do. Venezuela was calling its opposition 'fascists' and 'Nazis' before it started gunning people down in the streets last week. And Yanukovych said the same thing before the snipers opened up."

Ken looked at his last sip of bourbon before downing it.

"I hate not knowing," he said. "I'll be a whole lot happier when the ground under my feet feels a little more solid."

"Well, there's one thing I'm pretty certain about," Stewart said before finishing his whiskey.

"What's that?"

"We won't leave Crimea as easily as we entered it."

Chapter 5
SETTING A DATE

"I miss you," Danilo said into his iPhone.

"I miss you, too," she replied.

Danilo had met Angelina Voloshin when she was visiting relatives in Kyiv. He was called to her aunt and uncle's home to repair a line that was grounding out and continually popping breakers. He was glad they called because it posed a fire hazard, and it didn't hurt that Angelina had kept him company through the whole job. She was charming and beautiful, with almost-platinum hair and sapphire eyes that dazzled him. Danilo wasted no time in asking her to lunch and a walk in the park. After that, the two saw each other frequently while she was in town.

Danilo followed those initial meetings by meeting her while on a trip to Donetsk to visit some friends. Angelina accompanied Danilo for dinner and a night out clubbing with them, and he spent the evening almost exclusively talking and dancing with her. He worried he had insulted his hosts, especially after subsequently inviting her to most of their activities during his stay, but once he couldn't dream of not including her. Midway through his visit to Donetsk, his luggage resettled in her apartment. He was confident that the two of them would spend their lives together.

Since that trip, the two kept up a steady dialog via text messages and phone calls. Danilo had ridden his motorcycle out to Donetsk a couple times to stay with her. As far as he was concerned, she was beyond marvelous. There was something about her—her smile, the way she entered a room, how she wore her hair—that instantly grabbed his attention by the shirt collar and would not let go. In meeting Angelina, Danilo had discovered a piece of himself that he never knew had been missing.

When the Ukrainian-unity demonstration was set for March 13 in Donetsk, he had slated another ride out to Angelina's. The two strongly felt that they should support the event.

"Come to Donetsk," she had said to him.

"I want to," he replied.

"So why not next Thursday? There's going to be a big rally in support of national unity. You can man the ramparts."

Danilo laughed. "Okay, let's make it a date," he said.

"Good. I'll see you next Thursday."

"Absolutely. I can't wait."

"Neither can I."

After hanging up, Danilo stepped out of his van to take care of his next customer. It turned out to be an older couple with a faulty light switch and wall sconce. He made short work of the job and his clients were incredibly grateful, the man shaking his hand and the lady hugging him.

It was jobs like that one that made Danilo confident in his decision to be an electrician instead of working in government. Directly helping people with something they couldn't do for themselves, on a person-to-person level, paid substantial emotional dividends for him. Working as a parliamentary aide or as a campaign staffer wasn't anywhere near as satisfying.

He thought it would have been. After graduating with his political science degree, Danilo had worked a few internships in the offices of various members of parliament. He'd come home after a long day researching some piece of legislation, take a hot shower, grab some dinner, and sit quietly to ponder his budding career. Those nights, his life would stretch out in front of him like a long reel of movie film, as if he could track his potential future, scene-by-scene, moment-by-moment.

It didn't take long for him to decide that the movie sucked. He envisioned the tests on his ethics: A deal here. A compromise there. Initially, they would seem like simple, almost innocent compromises. He could imagine himself rationalizing that he had to break eggs to make omelets. But then he'd see the bargaining quickly mutate into deeper, more profound acts of moral deconstruction until he was finally some worthless Treasury leech, sneaking expensive meals in the dark corners of Kyiv's fine restaurants while he pondered ways to hide his money.

He saw how older politicians told themselves that after years of personal sacrifice they deserved it, that the Rada somehow owed them. He'd own a nice home and a decent car, but nothing too flashy so that he wouldn't tip anyone off to his shady practices. Perhaps he'd have a wife. Perhaps he'd have a mistress. He'd take Black Sea cruises with her in summer using the excuse that he was going to a policy meeting. And all the while he'd twist himself into a pretzel to justify to himself for betraying his conscience.

Danilo was certain that ousted President Yanukovych must have hashed through similar rationalizations before he finally fled the presidential mansion a few nights ago, leading a long convoy of vans packed with foreign currency, works of art, and other valuables belonging to the public. As if siccing snipers on the Euromaidan wasn't enough, Yanukovych fled to Moscow, and he was pictured sitting at Putin's right hand within 48 hours of his escape — a public demonstration of his national betrayal.

Danilo didn't encounter Yanukovych while interning, but it was that level of systemic corruption permeating the Rada and nearly every government agency in Ukraine that led Danilo to ditch a political career in favor of becoming a tradesman. That cancerous dishonesty pushed Danilo to join the Euromaidan, as well. Danilo felt certain that he was achieving more political change chanting a slogan or marching in the streets than he would have ever accomplished sitting at a laminated, particle board desk in some parliamentary office.

Now when he got home from a long day and got a moment to think about his day, Danilo knew that while he might not be sure what his future held, he knew it would not involve continually feeling that he had betrayed his conscience.

*

The rest of the day went relatively smoothly, with agreeable clients and easy-to-assess problems with straightforward solutions. After some early evening bookwork, he headed home, showered, ate a simple meal, and then went into his apartment building's parking garage to do a little maintenance on his motorcycle to clear his head.

He bought the Kawasaki Versys two years ago, and it had served as a faithful steed ever since. After adding luggage panniers and a top box, he rode his bike all over Ukraine and Crimea, and even did a couple of foreign moto-tours, once around Poland, and another through Romania, Bulgaria, and Greece. Riding the motorcycle, and especially touring on it, made him feel free in a way he couldn't find anywhere else. Many people ride motorcycles to escape, but Danilo rode to feel connected. The bike made him a citizen of planet earth. On the motorcycle, he felt linked to the machine, to the road, and to the world.

He enjoyed working on his motorcycle just as much as riding it. On a functional level, when he wrenched on his motorcycle, he knew it was being properly maintained and would perform reliably and safely. He didn't have to trust that some neophyte technician at the dealer would do the job right. Besides, working on his motorcycle gave Danilo some solitude and a chance to sit and think quietly.

The job for this evening was tightening up the chain. Danilo noticed some rough shifts on the last ride, and a quick check confirmed that his chain had stretched a bit. He donned his shop gloves, put the bike on a pit stand, removed the cotter pin from his hub nut and loosened it until he could make the necessary changes with the adjuster bolts on the swing arm. Each turn of the adjuster bolt moved the rear wheel a bit farther out, helping to tighten the chain. Using the measuring marks on the swing arm and the rear hub, Danilo confirmed that the hub had been pushed back the same amount on each side. He measured the chain tension again to ensure he had done the job correctly, tightened the hub to the correct specification, and inserted a new cotter pin.

Some people might see the process as a chore, but to Danilo, it was a cross between church and a museum. Ever turn of a wrench, every moment taken to ensure everything was clean and well lubricated, every pause to double-check his work filled him with immense satisfaction and calm.

When Danilo wrapped up his work and put away his tools, he went upstairs to clean up for the night. Then he phoned Angelina.

*

Angelina was equally drawn to Danilo. He was a set of compelling contradictions: attractive, but awkward. He was bright, but not conniving. He initially came across as self-assured but was so humble that he almost seemed down on himself. Ultimately, Danilo was genuine. Angelina was a pretty girl and was used to guys hitting on her. Danilo expressed obvious interest in her, but it wasn't a ploy to get inside her pants. His attention was genuine. He wanted to know her and observably grew more fascinated by her as he learned more. That kind of genuine, enthusiastic interest and honest attention was the sincerest compliment anyone had ever paid her.

For Danilo, Angelina imparted a feeling of confidence and sense of optimism in him that he didn't always possess, qualities that both of them enjoyed immensely. When he was with her, it was as though he had been injected with an experimental new drug that made him feel like he could take on the world—the whole solar system. Angelina, in turn, found that confidence infectious and impossible to resist. Her attraction made Danilo feel even brighter. It was as though the pair resonated in harmony with one another. They enjoyed a kind of ideal emotional symbiosis, even on the telephone, which she now answered from bed after his caller ID popped up on the screen.

"Hi," she greeted him after picking up the phone from her nightstand. "Mmm ... It's late."

"Sorry," he said. "Didn't mean to wake you."

"S'okay. What's up?"

"Nothing. I just miss you is all."

"Miss you, too."

"I'm looking forward to next Thursday."

"So am I."

"Good. ... Okay, I better let you go. Just wanted to check in."

"Okay. Good night."

"Good night. See you next week."

She hung up and returned her phone to the nightstand. Sleep came quickly. She dreamed of Danilo riding to Donetsk, to her.

Chapter 6
THE SQUIRREL AND THE SAMOVAR

The "X" scrawled on the front gate of Iskandar Nabiyev's property was ugly both in intent and execution; two sets of marks scratched back-and-forth into the paint. They looked as though the vandal who made them had used something dull, such as a key or a screwdriver, to leave the mark.

The old man guessed as to what the marks meant, but he wasn't positive until he phoned up an old friend living in Dzhankoy proper, who told him that "X"s had been made all over homes in town and on farms in the countryside. The marks had only been scrawled on the homes of Tatars. People in town had seen men reputed to be pro-Russian militants carrying lists and going from house to house during the night, skipping homes owned by ethnic Russians and Ukrainians, but stopping at Tatar households and scratching their marks.

Iskandar went inside and gathered his cleaning supplies. While he couldn't clean off the mark—the scratches were permanent—he cleaned the whole gate. When he was satisfied he had thoroughly washed it, he went into his backyard shed and returned with sandpaper, paint and a brush. Taking his time, the old man lightly sanded the front of the gate, and then painted it in a new coat of the same deep-red it was before.

When he finished, he put the lid on the can, stepped back to the middle of the road, and reviewed his work. The sun was coming out.

"Looks good," he said to no one. "It needed a new coat of paint anyway."

His father had said the same thing in 1944. Similar marks had been made—with white paint that time—on the door to his family's home, and he remembered how his father set about covering the offending blots with a beautiful shade of light blue.

That blue paint wasn't to hide the mark or to escape notice. Everyone knew his family was Tatar. Hell, the entire town where he grew up was at least a quarter Tatar. His father's paint job was to refuse to acknowledge the threat, to act as if it didn't merit recognition.

The problem was that the threat wasn't idle. During the Nazi occupation of Crimea, some Tatars had joined a German regiment, and some Tatar leaders collaborated with the Germans. The hope was that they might finally get out from under the Soviet oppressors that had starved them during the Holodomor, but all it accomplish was to give the Soviet Union a readymade excuse for saying all Tatars were Nazi collaborators.

Stalin's brush was broad. The marks went up on the

houses, and on May 18, 1944, Russian soldiers and Cossack mercenaries rounded up every single Tatar on the Crimean Peninsula in one day. That event was referred to as the Sürgünlik—exile. Iskandar always marveled how efficient both the Nazis and Soviets were when it came to carrying out atrocities and persecution. The Tatars were put on trains bound for faraway places, and the Russians and Cossacks took the Tatar homes, farms, and businesses and pretended as if their owners had never existed at all.

But the Tatars did exist—though many didn't survive. Nearly fifty percent of all the Tatars rounded up by the Russians died from disease, malnutrition, or being worked to death in Stalin's gulags. After the war, the Tatars wound up "existing" (living wasn't the right word for it) in faraway places across the Union, such as Uzbek.

The Sürgün killed Iskandar's little sister, Zilya. She was too young, a toddler, and took ill during the perilous rail journey. The old man remembered the night Zilya died, with his family and two others cooped up in that awful rail car. He recalled what his mother said to him: "She has so little strength to fight with, Iskandar. Pray for her."

Iskandar still prayed for Zilya to this day.

It wasn't until 1967 that Leonid Brezhnev and the rest of the Soviets formally dropped the collaboration charges against the Tatars and officially permitted them to return to Crimea. While the law allowed them to return, the Soviets did nothing to help the Tatars resettle. They never returned the Tatars' property that was stolen. They never paid any reparations. They never recognized the injustice of so many dead. They never acknowledged the loss of Iskandar's little sister.

"The Russians were so generous that they welcomed us back to lives that no longer existed," Iskandar often said when the subject of the Sürgünlik came up.

But many Tatars returned to Crimea and rebuilt. They were still rebuilding to this morning, when these phantoms came around, marking Tatar houses again. Iskandar wasn't certain of their identities but he was sure of one thing: He refused to acknowledge threats from bullies, whether they were loudmouths such as Dimitry Lebel, or Russian soldiers like the ones blocking the road.

*

Satisfied with the gate's new paint job, Iskandar went back inside his home to finish his porridge and one of the oranges he bought as a treat at the market in town. The fruit was marvelous — like eating a piece of the sun.

Once he finished his breakfast, he went back outside to collect his supplies and clean up. Iskandar took special care to clean the brush gently and thoroughly. He loved his brushes, whether they were for painting the house, or for painting pictures.

"If you clean them right, and shape them afterward, they will last for years and years," he told Azat, one of his granddaughters, years back. "They are like friends; you must treat them well if you want them to stick around."

That was back when his wife Aysilu was still alive. He still missed her. Their children and grandchildren visited him often, especially on holidays, and his son and daughter frequently brought him to their homes for visits, as well. But he was an old man living on his own more often than not, and he wished his wife was still there. He'd talk to her spirit, but it wasn't the same. Besides, ghosts can't cook.

Once the brushes were clean, Iskandar decided to start a new painting. He liked painting rabbits most of all, but this morning he would depict a squirrel in a tree. The old man enjoyed watching the squirrels on his property. They were simultaneously industrious and adventurous. While their efforts to get into Iskandar's bird feeders frustrated him, he did admire how hard they'd work to get to the seeds. The fuzzy creatures were natural-born puzzle solvers. They seemed to have fun while earning their living, and Iskandar saw that as a characteristic worthy of some admiration.

Iskandar pinned the four corners of a sheet of watercolor paper to a flat, wooden board, wetted a thick brush, and painted with clean, clear water in various spots. Then he dabbed the bristles in tan and made a puddle of it on a white, plastic palette. The old man cleaned the brush in clear water and added some grey to the tan. He added a little more water to that, wicked the grey-tan mixture into his brush, and then added it to the water on his paper.

The result was a kind of magic that still amazed Iskandar and he knew it would continue to thrill him until he either went blind or died: As his paint-infused brush met the wet paper, the grey-tan mixture left the brush and spread across the page like blood flowing into capillaries, creating the branches of a tree where the little squirrel would eventually be perched.

That was the unique nature of watercolor: the artist only has so much control over the paint and is forced to yield to the mercurial combination of paint and the water. Watercolors were a partnership between painter and paint. Predictability and precision did not factor into this universe. It was the closest art got to nature.

While the first strokes of the tree branches dried, Iskandar worked on the leaves and other portions of the painting. There were times in the process when he needed to let everything dry, so he would get up for a while to tend to a chore or something else before returning to the painting. Watercolors required patience, judgment, and flexibility.

Iskandar worked in translucent layers of paint strokes made one on top of the other. The color reflected off the pigment and through each of the layers to give the painting a quality of dimension and light that he could not generate from other types of paint. When he did his best work, he believed his paintings almost glowed.

"Hey, old man!"

The voice came from out front.

"Hey, old man! I see you've been painting this morning! What, no rabbits?"

It was Dimitry Lebel. Iskandar got up and peered through one of his front windows, which was partially obscured by a small tree. He didn't want to give Dimitry the satisfaction of knowing he had heard his taunt.

"I wonder why you painted your front gate, Nabiyev. Was the paint faded? Was it chipping? Did someone vandalize your gate, old man?"

The large man was pacing back and forth in the road in between the moments he bellowed toward Iskandar's small farmhouse.

"You know, there are fascists in Kyiv, old man!" Dimitry strained the Russian pronunciation of the Capital. "Maybe you'd like to join them—all of you Tatars! You're all Nazis, aren't you? Eh? You can join your friends in Kyiv!"

Satisfied that Dimitry was on a bender and would limit his aggression to yelling, Iskandar went to his kitchen and pulled his trusty samovar from the cupboard. He took the large metal device out on the back stoop, filled it with water, and added some wood kindling to start the fire. Iskandar was so fixated on his effort that he paid no attention to Dimitry's caterwauling out in the road. He went back inside to prepare the kettle. Soon, the samovar was boiling, and he took the venerable device back inside to brew some tea.

Tea prepared without a samovar is not tea. The wood smoke involved in boiling the water gave the drink a unique flavor that was only possible with using the old copper contraption that he and Aysilu had received as a wedding gift. A close friend of his mother's had given it to them. That woman's children had all died in the Sürgünlik, and she had no other relative to whom she could give the samovar, which had been in her family for generations. Iskandar and Aysilu invited the old woman over for tea often before she passed away.

That was the central benefit of a samovar: it encouraged tea to be shared. So much water was boiled that you could not reasonably make tea only for yourself. With a samovar, drinking tea was breaking bread.

Iskandar opened the samovar's spigot and poured hot water into the tea-filled kettle and let the leaves steep. Once the drink was ready, he poured two small cups and placed the kettle on top of the samovar so that it would keep warm. He stepped out front and walked toward the gate.

"Ah! So you're home old man! Did you decide to stop hiding like a rabbit?"

Again with the rabbits. Iskandar ignored the stupid remark. He extended one of the cups toward the big man on the other side of his newly painted gate.

"Dimitry, you must be tired from all this carrying on. How about a nice cup of tea?"

"Go to hell, Nabiyev!"

Iskandar took a long drink from his cup.

"I brewed up a good batch. Look, why don't you have a cup and sober up."

"I would drink piss before I'd drink your tea."

Iskandar finished his cup.

"That is a good cup. Dimitry, you're obviously tired. You must have been out late marking 'X's on everyone's gate. Drink it. It'll perk you up."

"Fuck you, old man. Your days in Crimea are numbered."

And with that, the big man climbed on to his tractor, started the engine, and began driving down the road.

"You're not the first person to say that to me," Iskandar said to the steadily diminishing figure of Dimitry Lebel, and drank the second cup of tea while it was still warm.

Iskandar went back inside his home to finish his painting. He quite liked the little squirrel he had painted. In fact, he decided it was one of his best. He admired his work as he drank another cup.

Chapter 7
TRUTH AND BEAUTY

Peace of a sort had arrived in Kyiv, and after months of the trial and tumult that had crescendoed in chaos, Veronika thought the city finally felt normal. Too bad the weather was shitty. Instead of cliché sunlight breaking through the gloom, the sky remained overcast, and the weather continued to be cold. Then again, this was March on the Dnieper — what did she expect, beach blankets and bathing suits?

It was Thursday. The Russians had been in Crimea since the previous Friday. Six days of occupation. In a move that made Veronika and Danilo laugh, the Russian parliament gave Putin the approval to send troops into Ukraine the day after Russian special forces had already invaded Crimea. Putin was maintaining the masked troops Russia sent to

Crimea the day prior were not Russians soldiers, but rather random, patriotic civilians who must have purchased their identical uniforms, weapons, and vehicles from army surplus stores.

After Russia's parliament gave its blessing, things moved fast: Russian troops spread all over Crimea taking various bases and government buildings. What the Russians didn't secure, various pro-Russia self-defense militias did. They even began setting up roadblocks and checkpoints to control movements. But what was really frightening Veronika was Russia's insistence that there was an anti-Russian threat Eastern Ukraine. Those facts made Kyiv's current calm feel tenuous.

"The Russian TV news is saying that Ukraine is oppressing ethnic Russians," Danilo said as he walked with Veronika down Kreschatyk Street. They were making their way to the National Museum of Art. It was a mission to renew their sense of normalcy.

"That's pretty funny. Apparently, they don't realize how many Russians in Ukraine hate Yanukovych as much as we do."

"It doesn't matter to Russia. Facts are beside the point. What they need is justification for their invasion, and if some nuts from Svoboda showed up to a Euromaidan rally, that's all the footage Russia TV needs to say that the entirety of Ukraine is a bunch of Nazis."

Svoboda was Ukraine's far-right, nationalist party, and in the same way that the Soviets had branded all Tatars as Nazi-collaborators in 1944, Russia's state-controlled media now used the presence of Svoboda members at Euromaidan rallies to paint the Euromaidan as an extreme right-wing movement. The Russians had weaponized misinformation. Putin might have dropped 30,000 troops in the country and propped up pro-Russian militias to capture Crimea — all while barely firing a shot — but it was waging an even more effective war via television news and social media. The goal was to not only frustrate Ukrainians' access to reliable information but confuse how the international media reported events in Ukraine, which in turn delayed or minimized the West's response. Soldiers controlled the land, and propaganda controlled reality.

"I have to say, little brother, you should be more than an electrician," Veronika observed. "Why don't you put that Political Science degree to better use?"

"I like being an electrician," Danilo replied. "Besides, Political Science doesn't pay the bills. This city can only employ so many politicians and government employees, but it has a shit-ton of bad wiring and not enough people who know how to fix it. I wager I'll retire before most of our Parliament members."

"Not if Russia gets its way."

Veronika and her brother turned right and zigzagged east through various streets until they finally made it to the museum. Upon arriving, they decided to eat their picnic lunch in the tree-shrouded lawn that formed a triangle-shaped park in front of the museum. It was a beautiful spot, and as far as Veronika was concerned, the sun felt like it was shining, regardless of the clouds.

The museum was between special exhibits, so after paging through a brochure, Veronika and Danilo decided they would start with the museum's gallery of Twentieth and Twenty-first Century art produced by Ukrainian artists. The gallery showcased works from all over the country. Putin could pretend that Ukraine was split down the middle, half-Russian, and half-Ukrainian, but the museum proved otherwise. Here, art by and for all the people of

Ukraine—Ukrainians, Russians, Tatars, Jews, Belarussians, Romanians, Bulgarians—resided under a single roof.

After finishing their meal, they jogged up the museum's steps and headed to the gallery. Soon, they were awash in a sea of different colors, techniques, and artistic schools. The exhibit was as mixed and varied as one could imagine; explosions of life neatly contained in canvas and surrounded in frames.

From Veronika's perspective, each painting had its own identity. Walking from one painting to the next, taking time to consider them, felt like walking down a street and visiting with each neighbor.

She and Danilo stood before a portrait of a woman. Its artist had wielded a unique style that fell somewhere between post-impressionism and cubism. The painting glowed with intense color and stark lines. After taking it in, Veronika turned her gaze toward her brother and spoke.

"Do you know this artist?"

"I can't say that I do."

"I do. It's by Nathan Altman. He was a Ukrainian Jew from Vinnytsia, born back when the Russians controlled Ukraine. I wonder what our friend Putin would make of him."

"I don't know if Putin would care about him unless he could serve a purpose. If Altman were high enough profile, Putin would probably claim we were oppressing him and that Russia would have to invade Ukraine to save him."

"Tell me, Danilo, what's more true: what people read on the Internet or see on television, or what hangs in this museum?"

Danilo chewed on that point as they toured through other galleries at the museum. Veronika's words echoed in his consciousness the way small sounds are magnified in a museum. Small words become longer statements. Small ideas take on much more significant meaning.

They chatted about the different works they saw and how they fit into the bits of art history that they knew. Afterward, they began walking back down the front steps of the museum, when Verokina turned to her brother.

"Let's get a cup of coffee and then I'd like to take you somewhere else," she said. "We can take the bus."

"Sure, you have me for the rest of the afternoon," Danilo answered with a smile. "I'm yours. Where do you want to go?"

"I'll explain when we get there. It's not far."

The two found a spot for take-out coffee and hopped on the number twenty-four bus heading southeast along the Pechersk Hills, which followed the course of the Dnieper. They sipped at their coffees as the bus eventually carried them down Lavrska Street and stopped near the Church of the Savior at Berestove. The original construction of the church dated back to 1115 when Kyiv was already a grand city with multiple churches and cathedrals, and Moscow had yet to become a wooden fort.

"Are we going to the church?" Danilo asked.

"Not exactly," Veronika said, motioning for her brother to cross the street. "Follow me."

They wandered onto one of the footpaths that crisscrossed the park that encompassed the Perchersk Hills. The area was one of Kyiv's many jewels, and Danilo was happy to have the afternoon to tour around with his big sister. He rarely took any breaks when it came to his business, and he felt like he was on vacation.

As they walked, Danilo noticed they were heading to a spot northeast of the church, but trees obscured their ultimate destination until they got farther down the path.

Then the branches parted, and their location became obvious.

Danilo stopped and stared.

"The genocide memorial," he said. "I've never been here."

"I know," Veronika said. "I've only come once, a few years ago."

The architecture of the monument, officially known as The Memorial in Commemoration of Famines' Victims in Ukraine, exuded emotion. It was an almost too-simple and tucked away reminder of a rarely acknowledged genocide.

*

In 1932 and 1933, Stalin collectivized all farms across the Soviet Union, including Ukraine, bringing them under either state or cooperative ownership. This caused farm output to plummet, and massive famine ensued. But instead of easing up, Stalin pushed forward with his plans. The more Stalin tightened his grip by seizing farms and liquidating private property, the more Ukrainian nationalism took root. Any nationalism that sprouted up provided the Kremlin an easy excuse to forbid Ukrainian farmers from eating any of their yield: Ukraine was full of counter-revolutionaries. Instead, the Soviets forced the farmers to ship Ukraine's agricultural output to Russia, forbade peasants from leaving rural areas in search of food, blockaded any aid to assist the starving, and seized citizens' private food stores at gunpoint. The Soviets starved the country to the point where emaciated corpses lay where they fell in the streets. People stole, murdered and prostituted themselves for food. People ate one another.

Ukraine called Stalin's terror-starvation the Holodomor — hunger extermination. A decade before Hitler started work on the Final Solution and his death camps, Stalin had purposely starved at least five million Ukrainians to death. During and after the mass murder, the Soviet Union denied the Holodomor's existence, describing the famine as a natural disaster and nothing more.

But the Kremlin couldn't bury the bodies deep enough. The memory of the Holodomor wouldn't fade. After the fall of the Soviet Union and historians began to dig, the evidence of the Soviet Union's orchestration of the Holodomor grew glaringly apparent. In 2003, twenty-five nations, including Russia, assembled at the United Nations to sign a joint statement acknowledging the Holodomor. Some countries went further and classified the Holodomor as a crime against humanity, while others—at least ten nations—officially declared it an act of genocide against Ukrainians.

*

Entering the memorial, Danilo and Veronika passed between two winged figures called the Angels of Sorrow, which represented guardians of the dead, and entered a tree-lined, cobblestone path that was framed by twenty-four millstones. The millstones represented the twenty-four thousand people that perished every day at the height of the Holodomor. In the center of the area, a millstone lay on its side on a raised dais and atop it stood the statue of a small, emaciated little girl clutching a bundle of wheat to her chest. Lying at her feet were offerings of fruit and flowers that visitors had left.

The plaque told them that the sculpture was called "Bitter Memory of Childhood," and noted that the Soviets' penalty for picking up any wheat left on a field after harvest was ten years in prison or death.

The two of them stood and stared at the statue for a long time.

"Execution for trying not to starve to death," Danilo finally said. "I can't even imagine that. How does a person do that to another human being? To a kid?"

"The same way they always have," Veronika replied. "They wrap it up in something it's not to make it easy for the functionaries to carry out the dirty work. To Stalin, these weren't families with children starving to death; they were counter-revolutionaries."

"Let's keep walking," Danilo suggested.

Beyond the ring of millstones stood the Candle of Memory, a white, ninety-foot-tall octagonal tower topped with a golden sculpture of a flame. Glass crosses of varying sizes were set into the tower's walls, and a ring of four twenty-foot-tall crosses surrounded its base. Large brass storks soared upward throughout the crosses. The tower overlooked the river from atop a steep slope.

"The crosses are departed souls, and the storks are the rebirth of Ukraine," Veronika read from another plaque as the two walked a slow circle around the tower.

"I can't believe I've never come here," Danilo said. "I've seen the candle light up the hillside at night whenever I drove past, but for some reason, I've never actually visited."

"Probably for the same reasons most Parisians never visit the Eiffel Tower or New Yorkers never go to the Statue of Liberty," his big sister replied. "Besides, it's not like a memorial to a genocide is someplace you want to go every day."

They walked down a graded walkway to the Hall of Memory, which was set into the hillside directly below Candle of Memory. As they toured the different displays, they noticed an older woman with a walker. She must have been at least ninety years old. The old lady lit a candle at a small shrine and appeared to pray for a moment, her eyes closed, and her lips made the shapes of words whispered beneath her slightly bowed head. Then she rang a bell three times, paused a moment and then walked on, pushing her walker in front of her.

"Three bells for three souls," Danilo guessed in a whisper.

Veronika nodded.

"I wonder how many times that bell has rung," she said.

After touring the Hall of Memory, they walked through Blackboard Alley where large blackboards bore the names of more than fourteen thousand towns and villages that were starved during the Holodomor. The entirety of Ukraine suffered during Stalin's forced famine, and that was a fact that would never fade, as sure as a name inscribed in stone.

They finally stopped strolling when they reached the top of a long series of stone steps that intersected with their path. The stairs led down to another path that ran along a wooded area below.

"The view is spectacular," Danilo said, inhaling a deep breath. "I'm glad we came here. It's beautiful."

"It's a beautiful monument to an ugly event," his sister said. "Why don't we walk down to that path? We can walk through the park for a bit and eventually cross back up to the street to catch the bus."

Veronika's suggestion was a good one. The two enjoyed a lovely walk despite the cold weather and the fading, late-afternoon light.

"So what made you decide to take me here?" Danilo asked as they walked under the boughs. "It didn't seem like you planned it this morning."

"I didn't," Veronika replied after a long pause. "We were talking about truth and art in the museum, and something kind of struck me."

"What was that?"

"That the biggest monument to truth in all of Ukraine is this memorial. No newspaper, or website or television news channel could tell more truth than that little girl, or that giant candle, or those engraved stones."

"Or that woman ringing that bell."

Veronika stopped and looked at her brother.

"Especially her," she said. "Truth is particularly important now because I have a feeling that over the next several months—maybe years—we are going be fighting lies upon lies."

Chapter 8
MEN IN CAMOUFLAGE

The first punch sent Stewart back to May of 1988. The swing came from his blind side and he didn't stand a chance of blocking it. As he went sprawling toward the asphalt, he remembered the match. It was Chelsea vs. Middlesboro, the first leg of that year's second division playoffs. Stewart had attended the game with some friends, and while they weren't die-hard Chelsea fans, they did get caught up in the post-game mayhem. In the rush of the riot, Stewart had become separated from his group and cornered by five members of Frontline, Middlesboro's hooligan firm. He didn't stand a chance, and the Middlesboro supporters had at him like jackals.

When you take a few beatings, you learn not to fear them as much, so Stewart wasn't too afraid of the pro-Russian militiamen who had stopped him and his companions at the checkpoint on the highway outside of Sevastopol. Even if they threw a few punches or got in some kicks, it was familiar territory. Sure, you avoid beatings at all costs, but if they happen, you know how to cover up and cry out to give your assailants a sense of satisfaction. It's about minimizing the damage before they decide to try to teach you a more lasting lesson. Besides, yelling in pain came naturally, because it hurts like hell to get kicked in your kidney.

*

Just like back in 1988, the day had started off well enough. It was March 11, fourteen days after Russian troops had poured into Crimea, and five days before the peninsula-wide referendum on Crimean secession that Russia had just announced.

A source had tipped off Stewart and Ken about a pro-Ukraine demonstration that organizers had planned to meet near the parliament building in Sevastopol. The two got there bright and early to get footage of the protest and interviews with organizers and participants. The group was an odd mix of students, regular people from various walks of life, mothers with strollers, old folks, and some random Euromaidan supporters that had traveled from Kyiv. Overwhelmingly, it seemed like a harmless gathering. They were there to wave flags, hold placards, shout slogans and sing songs.

However, they were located across the street from the parliament building, which had sported a Russian flag since it had been taken over by pro-Russian groups. Standing out front were pro-Russian militiamen wearing military-style boots and fatigues, and carrying riot shields painted in the color of the Russian flag. When the pro-Ukraine protestors began singing their national anthem, the militiamen started shouting, "Ross-iya! Ross-iya! Ross-iya!"

The militiamen's voices boomed from the buildings. It was a decidedly different noise from the pro-Ukrainian crowd, aggressive and menacing.

In addition to the militiamen, there were some men dressed in the tall fur caps unique to Cossacks, who were walking up and down the sidewalks of the street that divided the pro-Ukraine group and the men guarding the parliament.

"Cossacks," Ken said. "I'm looking at bona fide Cossacks. I'm not gonna lie — these guys look scary as hell."

"That's what they're hoping for," Stewart replied. "We have to interview one."

"Ugh ... Let's go."

Ken and Stewart approached a Cossack that was pacing in front of the Ukrainian demonstration, watching the crowd. Ken got in position and Stewart opened with a question.

"Excuse me, sir, why are you here at this demonstration?"

"Me? I am here to help support the police and ensure law and order," the Cossack replied. "These fascists are dangerous."

"These people are fascists?" Stewart asked, pointing at the peaceful crowd.

"Yes, many of them. Most of them, I reckon," the man affirmed.

"But this looks like a bunch of students and mothers pushing prams. I don't see any neo-Nazis here."

"These are nationalists and Nazi agitators sent to Sevastopol to oppress Russians and cause an uprising. I'm here to make sure they don't do that."

Stewart was about to ask another question when a man stood between Ken and the Cossack, blocking his shot. The man had close-cropped hair and was wearing a navy blue coat. Pinned to the coat was the trademark orange-and-black striped ribbon of St. George that pro-Russians in Ukraine used to identify themselves to one another. He reminded Stewart of every football hooligan he had ever seen in his youth — louder, bigger, scarier than regular folk.

"Who are you with this camera? What are you doing here?" the man yelled at Ken and Stewart. "Are you Western propagandists here to say Russians are bad people? Get out of here with your lies!"

"We are here asking questions," Stewart calmly replied. "Can you tell me why you're here?"

A couple more men sporting orange-and-black ribbons.

"Let me see your credentials!" The man in the blue coat yelled.

Before Stewart could reply about a dozen of the young, male, pro-Ukrainians that had been at the rally began to insert themselves between Stewart and Ken and the pro-Russian men. Much yelling and gesturing ensued. The Cossack had moved back to speak with three police officers and seemed content to watch the whole thing unfold.

"Some law and order," Stewart remarked, as they stepped back from the scrum.

"What was happening there?" Ken asked, confused. His understanding of both Russian and Ukrainian was virtually non-existent, and he depended on Stewart to do all the talking.

"The Cossack said he was here upholding law and order," Stewart replied.

"Who's that guy kidding? He's here to bust heads."

"Or worse."

Ken started getting video of the two sides arguing, but it quickly fizzled as the pro-Russians backed off. The odds were against them for the moment.

Stewart began interviewing others in the crowd. The only reason he could discern that explained why the pro-Russians were feeling edgy was that the demonstration was happening across from a government building. But ultimately, that excuse felt like bullshit. The pro-Russians were chomping at the bit to kick some ass.

"Fucking ridiculous," he said to Ken.

"What?"

"The militiamen are saying they're convinced that this crowd of students, mothers, and grannies poses an imminent fascist threat and will soon cross the street and besiege them."

"Are you joking?"

"I wish I was. They're spoiling for a fight."

One of the pro-Ukraine demonstration's organizers used a bullhorn to instruct the group that they were going to march to a nearby park to meet up with some other pro-Ukrainian groups and continue their demonstration. The march resembled a nice mid-morning walk, and the atmosphere was somewhat celebratory. Some cars along the way honked their support, while other drivers jeered insults. Many of the demonstrators told Stewart that they had been terrified to voice their support for Ukraine because the pro-Russian groups had been so intimidating and were responding to outspoken supporters of Ukraine with violence. They said the assembly felt liberating, yet somewhat scary.

Many protestors told the reporters that because mostly women had attended this demonstration, that they felt somewhat safe. The Russians were waging a propaganda war, and they couldn't afford footage of pro-Russian thugs beating up old women and young mothers. Based on his interaction with the three men earlier, Stewart wasn't so sure the militiamen had that much restraint.

The demonstration went on in this fashion for a few more hours: they'd occasionally stop, perhaps meet up with another group, trade some stories, yell some slogans, wave some banners and signs, sing some songs, and then walk to another location. One of the groups they met up with was predominantly young men, many of whom were wearing masks. Stewart interviewed one, asking why they were wearing masks.

"We had some trouble with those orange-and-black thugs," the young man replied. "These guys are being shipped in by Russia. We're sure of it."

"What makes you say that?"

"They barely know where they're going. Some of the pro-Russians chased some of us, and it was clear they weren't familiar with the streets."

"Still, there have to be pro-Russian supporters who live here in Crimea."

"Of course there are. And there are Russians who are in favor of staying with Ukraine, too. It's not black and white. But those guys we saw? They aren't from around here. They're trying to stir up shit. Kyiv had them, too. So I'd rather keep my face covered in case they have people taking pictures."

The young men decided to break off from the group that Stewart and Ken had been following, saying they didn't want to attract trouble to a crowd that had women and kids in it. Stewart and Ken wanted to follow them, but they were getting far from their hotel.

"Hey, man, if these guys get into trouble, we'll be on our own," Ken observed. "I want good footage, but we might be taking too big a risk this far from home base."

"You think so?"

"I know so. Look we might be able to run for a while, but this isn't our town. Also, I'm lugging this camera and batteries, so I can't move very fast."

Stewart weighed those factors. Ken was correct. They had to pace themselves.

"You're right. I have to admit we got some good footage—it's not every day you see Cossacks trying to intimidate mothers and their babies."

"Thank God. I thought I was going to have to do more convincing. Let's head home."

The two walked the short distance back to their hotel and spent the rest of the day cutting the footage. Once finished, they had assembled a pretty engaging report and sent it to ETN. A post-filing drink was in order.

In the hotel bar, Stewart saw a familiar face: Bill Lowry, an American reporter.

"Hi there, Bill. Long time, no see," Stewart greeted the American. "This is Ken Marston, my cameraman and a neighbor of yours to the north. Ken, this is Bill Lowry, a scribbler out of New York."

The world of English-language journalists who knew Russian was a relatively small one. Stewart and Bill had met in Kyiv when the Euromaidan protests first began to reach a boil. The three exchanged handshakes and greetings. Bill said that his photographer, who was a Ukrainian named Vasyklo, was up in their room sifting through a ton of shots from the day. The three retired to a table to share drinks and trade stories.

"You two were smart to pass on following those kids,"

Bill remarked. "We caught up with 'em, and my photog and I almost got our asses kicked big time. They ran right into the pro-Russian goon squad, and from there all hell broke loose. There was even a guy with a whip."

"A whip? You're kidding me," Ken said.

"Nope," Bill replied. "There was some crazy fucker with a bullwhip. Like Indiana Jones or something. It was nuts. We got as many shots as we could before we had to bail. I don't even know how we made it back to the hotel, but I pretty much collapsed in the lobby I was so out of breath."

"I wish we had gotten footage of that," Stewart said to Ken's clearly recognizable annoyance.

"No you don't," Bill replied. "This isn't a clash of true believers. There are definitely pro-Russian Crimeans in the bunch, there is no doubt about that, but the guys calling the shots seem way too organized.

"You have to understand," the American continued, "Russia is going to make 100 percent sure Crimea secedes. Frankly, I think it's overkill; if they conducted things fair-and-square, Putin would get Crimea just the same. There are simply too many ethnic Russians here—thanks to Stalin—that the vote is weighted in their favor. But because Putin is so paranoid, Russia is going to stuff the ballot boxes and rig the vote counts to ensure the results."

"So we get Cossacks and provocateurs with whips," Stewart affirmed.

"Pretty much. We're sure to see a good chunk of ballot cooking before this thing is over as well ... Hey, who's for another round?"

Bill told Stewart and Ken that he and Vasyklo planned to drive up to Simferopol, where Russian forces had taken a Ukrainian military hospital. Then they would head back to Sevastopol to check out a Ukrainian army base—still filled with surly Ukrainian soldiers who refused to exit—that was surrounded by Russian troops. That afternoon, a peaceful, pro-Ukrainian demonstration similar to the one Stewart and Ken had followed was supposed to arrive to support the soldiers inside the base. Both would make for great stories, and Bill said he didn't mind sharing since Stewart was doing video and he was doing print.

*

Well before dawn the following morning, they packed up Ken's Geely, and the four of them drove along the small Pivdenna Bay that stabbed like a finger into the southern half of the city. They would round that bay and work their way north to the main motorway to Simferopol. Before they got to the highway, however, they had to take a small connecting road.

They pulled onto that highway in the early morning calm, just as the sun was beginning to rise. Soon, they rolled up to a makeshift checkpoint constructed of oil drums and plywood boards. The men manning the crossing wore camouflage, but their mismatched uniforms and assortment of weapons indicated they were not Russian soldiers. Also, while they were wearing balaclavas, none of them were wearing helmets. One militiaman stood further up the road from the others and motioned with a flashlight for Ken to pull to the side of the road. He complied. The militiaman motioned for Ken to get out.

"I'll do the talking," Stewart said and got out.

"My driver does not speak much Russian," Stewart continued. "May I speak for us?"

"You don't sound Russian. Who are you?" The militiaman replied.

"We are press. Two reporters and two photographers."

"Reporters? Hah! Western spies!"

"Truly, we are journalists. We can show credentials."

"Albert! Vadim! Get over here!"

Two more militiamen, one armed with an older AK-47, came jogging up from the checkpoint.

"All of you! Out of the car!" the man with the flashlight barked.

Stewart motioned for them to exit the car. Ken left the keys in the ignition and the door open as the other three got out.

The man demanded to see their documents and credentials as the other two men acted as heavies. There was no reason their story wouldn't have checked out, but the man wasn't satisfied. Stewart could tell something was wrong. He noticed that Ken had been holding a small digital camera during the process, and guessed Ken was getting video.

"So you are here as propagandists for the West, eh?" the man with the flashlight accused. "You think you are going to help America impose its 'democracy' on us? Your democracy is a sham! You want us to become indebted to the EU and the IMF and become your slaves!"

Stewart didn't like the way this was going—and from the looks on their faces, neither did his companions. As the first militiaman continued his tirade, others from the checkpoint ran up. Soon there were ten men around the four reporters. As the first man yelled, militiamen here and there would yell something as well, or give one of the journalists a shove.

"You think everyone in the world wants to be faggots? You want us to become your faggots? Crimea is not Europe! Crimea is Russia!"

Suddenly, Stewart got clocked on the side of the head. It was enough to send him off balance and to the ground. Ken got socked in the gut and then got a roundhouse kick to the back and went down. Stewart was crawling on the ground trying to head toward Ken while getting kicked in the side and the legs. Bill and Vasyklo were a couple of feet back from the initial attack. Vasyklo got into a boxer's stance. Bill kicked a militiaman's ankle to knock him off balance and pushed him aside to dash to the car, which was less than ten feet away.

"Get in the fuckin' car, God damn it!" Bill yelled as he flung himself in the driver's seat.

Stewart scrambled to Ken as Vasyklo moved backward, drawing some of the militiamen away from the pair on the ground.

"Run!" Vasyklo urged. Stewart could see in dim, spotty light that the man's face had twisted into the same terrified mask they were all wearing.

Stewart grabbed a boot and yanked, sending a militiaman falling backward. Ken was already getting up, and the two helped each other to their feet. They ran to the car and began clambering in as Vasyklo circled the back of the car and dove into the backseat.

Bill put the Geely into reverse and looked behind them as he floored it. Meanwhile, Stewart looked forward from the passenger seat and what he saw sent electric shocks of adrenalin throughout his body: the two men with rifles were trying to line up a shot as their fellow militiamen were running toward the Geely. The only thing that was preventing the car and its four passengers from being riddled with bullets were those rushing militiamen who were accidentally obstructing their comrades' line of fire.

Bill slammed on the brakes, jerked the steering wheel, threw the car into a one-eighty, jammed the transmission into drive, and stomped on the gas. The Geely took off as best as the little car could.

"I knew pulling stupid shit in the high school parking lot would pay off," Bill joked.

"Fucking go!" Stewart screamed.

"Get down!" Ken yelled from the back seat, crouching down but holding his small digital camera toward the rear window. Vasyklo was crouching, too while snapping off shots with his digital SLR in similar fashion. That's when they heard the first shots going off.

Krack! Krack-krack! Krack!

The shots were going wide of the now furiously swerving Geely, which was quickly getting out of range. The militiamen were demonstrating their complete lack of marksmanship. Even so, Bill leaned toward the wheel to stay low, keeping the evasive maneuvers going until they got past a bend in the road.

"Tell me you two got good footage at least," Stewart asked.

"Yes," Vasyklo said. "There's no way I didn't get something."

"I know I got good video of the stop," Ken followed. "The recording of the beating is probably crappy. The escape by car is probably decent, but I have no idea about the gunfire."

"Check and see," Stewart replied.

"I already am."

"What the hell are we going to do?" Bill asked nobody in particular.

"Head to back to the hotel to edit this footage?" Stewart suggested.

"I guess so," the American replied. "I worry that those guys are already on the radio or on the phone to the Russians."

"I suspect those guys were on their own," Vasyklo said. "They are like a lot of these small pro-Russian militia groups that are springing up: They are just trying to knock heads and intimidate people, but they don't have any official ties with the Russian military—at least not until Russian agents can start building a network. I doubt they even have a radio."

That insight put Stewart at ease—at least at as much ease as he could feel given their morning. The four of them agreed to head back to the hotel room, as their reports of the morning's events would be far more newsworthy than the protest at the base. To err on the side of caution, Bill took a different route back to the hotel.

It turned out Ken had gotten some compelling video, and Vasyklo had taken some equally engaging shots. That said, neither of them documented anyone firing a weapon; Ken did manage to get the sound of the guns on his video, however. After a significant amount of careful editing, both stories from the two pairs of journalists were bound to wind up generating considerable traffic for their respective news services before the day was out.

"I never want to go through anything like that again," Bill said. "Excitement is one thing, but ... screw that."

"At least we will get a couple of solid reports out of it," Ken said. "That's an upside."

"We'll be momentarily famous," Vasyklo joked.

"That's true. The high price of fame!" Bill jokingly exclaimed. "Seriously though, I got so caught up in being terrified that I forgot we did some pretty good work. Hey, I'll buy you guys a round of drinks at the hotel bar to celebrate."

"Actually, could we wait until tomorrow for the drinks?" Stewart asked.

"Why's that?" Bill asked.

"Because we are going to be in considerable pain by morning, and I don't need to add a hangover to that."

Chapter 9
THREE KINGS

Dimitry's footsteps fell sloppily on the wet roadway that led to his home. It was night, and he had passed the final streetlight roughly fifteen minutes back. He guessed the remaining walk would take thirty minutes, and trudged along.

He tried to remember where the hell he had left the car he had borrowed from his friend Sergei. Dimitry searched his spotty memory. He recalled driving with Sergei in the vehicle. He, Sergei and Andrei had been sharing a bottle in the stands of a soccer pitch near the railyard in town.

"This town is dead," Sergei had said passing the bottle to Andrei. "There's no decent place to drink or see girls."

Sergei was tall and angular. There was nothing soft about him. Andrei wasn't as tall as Sergei or Dimitry but looked stout enough to pull a boxcar behind him if required. For now, he just pulled on the bottle.

"I'll second that," Andrei said. "Things were a lot more fun when we were younger. Remember that girl Lucya from school?"

"Who doesn't?" Sergei recalled, his eyes lighting up. "I'd wager that champion cocksucker was everybody's first lay."

"Not too bad looking, either," Andrei mused.

"Yep, she had a way ..." Sergei trailed off. "Man, those were great days. ... The greatest."

Dimitry sat looking at his two compatriots in disgust.

"Listen to you two — it's pathetic," he sneered.

"What the hell do you mean by that?" Sergei asked in shock.

"Recalling all your past glories like your cocks are old and shriveled," Dimitry scolded. "This town should be ours. We should be kings!"

Sergei and Andrei looked at Dimitry. The bottle hung from Andrei's hand as they waited for him to continue.

"The Russian army is here now," Dimitry said. "This is our moment. We can change this town and make it ours. All those fucking Ukrainians and Tatars? They can finally learn that Crimea is Russian and that we are in charge.

"And all you want to talk about is Lucya," he continued. "Who cares about that slut? She's probably just a herpes-ridden truckstop whore by now."

Some spark of an idea was firing Dimitry's synapses despite the alcohol, giving him mental momentum that he refused to brake.

"No, if we play our cards right, we won't be musing about the Lucyas of yesteryear," the big man ranted. "If we use this opportunity, we can move up in the world. We can finally have a little power, command a little respect. The kind of respect that people respond to—that women respond to. We can be in charge."

"What are you talking about?" Sergei asked.

"Shut the fuck up and drink, Dimitry," Andrei said.

"Dumbshits," Dimitry scolded. "Let me ask you something: who is in charge right now?"

Sergei and Andrei looked at Dimitry blankly.

"Who is in charge?"

Still no reply.

"Nobody, that's who," Dimitry said.

"Aren't the Russians in charge now?" Andrei asked.

"Look, sure the Russians are here with guns and trucks and everything else," Dimitry explained. "But they're not in charge yet. They just want to kick everyone out who has anything to do with Kyiv, and then they will have to set up their people. They can't do that yet.

Dimitry paused, but his friends didn't seem to understand him any better. "That means we have an opportunity, my friends," he said. "We need to build something. Our own power, our own force. Then, when Russia puts its plans into motion, we will be more likely to be part of that plan."

"And how do you think we can do that?" Sergei asked, taking the vodka from Andrei's weak grasp and drawing a long slug from the bottle.

"We form a militia," Dimitry said.

Sergei nearly did a spit-take. Once he recomposed himself and wiped the vodka off his chin, he looked at Dimitry squarely, and scoffed, "Are you fucking serious? And get ourselves killed?"

"What, are you too much of a pussy to not fight for Russia's right to this land?" Dimitry shot back. "Crimea belongs to Russia and always has. It is our duty to restore it to the motherland. Now that the army is here, we can make sure that happens — and the Russians will be grateful for it."

"Watch your words, big man. I'm no coward," Sergei warned.

"I don't know …" Andrei said. "A militia?"

"A militia," Dimitry confirmed. "The Dzhankoy Self Defense Force. This is our opportunity to make this town ours. Look, aren't you sick of seeing these Muslims all over town? Well now's our chance to send to all those muzzies and dirty Tatar bastards back to Uzbekistan. You've said it yourself a million times, Andrei — we should have never let them back into the country. We can finally fix that."

"I would fucking love to see them go," Andrei agreed. "They act like we owe them something. Fuck those traitors. Let them starve in some frozen shithole."

"I fucking hate 'em, too," Sergei grumbled. "Let's give them the boot."

"So are you with me? Do you want to make this town ours? Do you want to finally have what you deserve?"

Sergei and Andrei both vigorously nodded.

"Fuck yeah," Sergei agreed. "We're with you."

Dimitry clasped his two friend's shoulders. "I knew I could count on you. We're going to change things. This is our day," he said.

The three quickly drained the bottle in celebration of their pact. The idea of the Dzhankoy Self Defense Force had lit a fire in them, and they wanted more.

"Let's get another bottle," Sergei said.

"Yeah, we need to toast the militia," Andrei agreed.

"No, that's not enough," Dimitry said. "We need to do things big. Let's go to Simferopol. Let's drink and fuck all night."

"Yes! Outstanding!" Sergei said. "But … where do we get the money for that?"

"Bottles cost more at a club than at the market," Andrei chimed in.

"Relax boys," Dimitry said, reaching into his coat pocket and pulling out a wad of bills.

"Where the hell did you get that?" Sergei asked.

"Let's just say that more people need to keep their sheds locked up at night," Dimitry replied, grinning.

They all laughed as Dimitry returned the wad of cash to his coat.

"Let's go," he said, standing up and stepping down the stands with Andrei and Sergei following behind. The Dzhankoy Self Defense Force was on the move.

*

They left the pitch and climbed into Sergei's old Subaru; it was clear the car had taken a beating in its life. They stopped to fill the tank and grab another bottle and some smokes for the road. The drive down the M17 was fast and filled with chanted bravado between belts from the bottle.

When they arrived in Simferopol, Dimitry tried to dredge his memory for his old favorite spots. When he was younger, he'd come down with friends every so often to live it up in town, but that had been years ago before he married Yana.

Like a lost dog finding his home, Dimitry's memory eventually led him to the location of some hot spots he recalled, but the names had changed. Regardless, it was clear Crimea's capital still offered some action.

"Hey, look over there," Sergei said.

"Girls!" Andrei exclaimed. "Now we are getting somewhere."

The three men peered out of the Subaru at a short line of people filing into the Galaxy Disco. It was a mix of young men and women who had opted to ignore the recent military incursion in favor of strobe lights and house music.

"There are some minxes over there," Sergei observed.

"Tonight is ours, gentlemen," Dimitry said, putting the car in park. "Let's go."

"Hell yeah," Andrei chimed in.

The three crossed the street and got in line. After ogling one young woman, Sergei looked back and grinned at Andrei.

"I think we're going to have a great night," he said.

Some more people got in line behind them. Dimitry lit a cigarette and offered one to each of his comrades. Before they were halfway through their smokes, the trio reached the head of the line.

"You have to be kidding me," the larger of two doormen said.

"What?" Dimitry asked incredulously.

"This is the Galaxy Disco, not a tractor auction," the doorman replied.

"What do you mean?" Dimitry said.

"Let us in, tight-ass," Sergei demanded.

"Tight ass?" The doorman sneered. "Better than broke-ass. You guys look like you couldn't put together enough money to buy a single round."

"Oh yeah?" Dimitry said, pulling the bundle of bills from his pocket. "What do you call this?"

"I call it a golden opportunity to replace your shitty wardrobe," the doorman said.

A few people behind them started laughing.

"Shut up," Andrei yelled back at the crowd.

"Take off!" Someone from the back said.

Two more doormen arrived, dressed in black suits and black turtlenecks with earpieces. It made for an intimidating display.

"Look, guys," one of the newly arrived doormen said. "I realize you want to have a good time, but you're not going to do that here.

"You see those people behind you?" the doorman continued, pointing to the young people lined up behind the newly established militia. "They're our clientele, and they don't want to party with guys that look like their uncles from down on the farm. It's time for you to leave."

"Fuck you," Dimitry sneered.

"I said it's time for you to leave," the lead doorman repeated, stepping closer to Dimitry and squaring up. The three other bouncers moved forward, too, closing ranks around them. "Go," the doorman commanded. "This is your last warning before you wind up in an ambulance."

Dimitry turned to Andrei and Sergei, "C'mon boys. Fuck this dump. It's for faggots, anyway."

The three walked across the street to Sergei's car as the mocking calls and laughter from the line in front of the club echoed up and down the road. The Dzhankoy Self Defense Force's first mission had met with humiliation. This wasn't a good start for Dimitry.

"That place is a haven for the kind of elitist liberal scum who need to be stamped out," Dimitry said, sitting in the passenger seat. A slight mist was collecting on the windshield, making the neon lights from the disco refract across their faces in flickering pink and bright blue smears. "Start the car. I know where we're going."

"Where?" Sergei asked.

"You'll see. And you'll thank me," Dimitry said with a grin coming across his face. "Come on. Forget those assholes. Let's celebrate."

Dimitry gave Sergei directions, and the Subaru came to a stop outside a smaller establishment that featured equally garish signage. A marquee in the shape of a giant hung over the entrance, and the doors below were painted to look like red marble. Next to the door, a sign said "Kings." A pink neon woman in stockings and a garter blinked and flashed at the door.

"Now this is more like it," enthused Andrei.

"I told you you'd thank me," Dimitry reminded his friends.

"Let's go!" Sergei exclaimed, already halfway out the door.

The interior of Kings offered Dzhankoy's recently assembled Self Defense Force precisely what they had sought: booze and women. The night followed predictably: the drinks started flowing as the girls gyrated suggestively, which caused more drinks to flow. Someone asked for the club's "crazy menu" of special dances; eventually, the three ended up with topless girls grinding in their laps. Finally, Dimitry spent the rest of his money at the cheap hotel down the street, buying himself and his friends a little extra.

The memories of what happened at King's and afterward came to Dimitry in vague flashes and snippets of recollection: A breast here. A leg there. Sergei's laughing face. Andrei being pulled from the stage. The cheap hotel room. His hands on a brunette's hips and thighs. Getting dressed after handing over the last of his wad. He and Andrei loading a passed-out Sergei into the back seat of the Subaru. Careening through the streets of Simferopol with Andrei at the wheel. Throwing a brick at the Galaxy Disco's door and breaking a small window. The long trek home up the M17 with Andrei occasionally rolling down the windows with the vain hope that the blasts of cold air would help him sober up.

*

And then, somehow, Dimitry found himself trudging up the road to his house. He could only guess at what happened to the car and his friends. Perhaps Andrei drove to his house first, then Dimitry took Sergei and the Subura to Sergei's house, and then decided to walk home? For all he knew, his friends and the car could all be sitting in the middle of the soccer pitch where they had started their adventure.

What Dimitry was sure of was that the next half-hour promised a damp, boring walk that he didn't want to make.

In addition to the streetlights reaching their end, the houses thinned out at this point on the road. Suburbia had given way to the farms on the outskirts of town, and Dimitry had seven small farms to pass before getting to his property. He counted them down, seven, six, five … until he came to the corner of his property.

Technically it was his wife Yana's property, but Dimitry was the man of the house. Two-by-fours propped up a sagging fence that separated the yard next to his, and overgrown grass marked the border between the yard and the road. He'd have to stagger the full length of the property before getting to his front gate. Once he did, he quietly opened and closed the gate, walked to his front door, and did his best to silently unlock the entrance. It must've been five-thirty in the morning, and he didn't want to incur the wrath of Yana.

Success! Dimitry thought as he silently closed and re-locked the door behind him, and went to the couch to lay down. He took off his shoes and covered himself with a throw Yana usually kept draped across the back of the sofa and tried to will himself to sleep.

"Oh, there you are."

It was Yana. Dimitry kept his eyes shut.

Yana had been a stunning blonde when they met in their early twenties. Dimitry was instantly drawn to her good looks and athletic body back then. They had been king and queen of their social circle, which consisted mainly of friends from their respective secondary schools. Dimitry had worked his way up to a warehouse foreman, and Yana had a job at the market. Their life together was perfect at first, and the bond between them was so intense that it felt like the will of heaven.

Eventually, Yana and Dimitry married, and when Yana's father passed away, he willed his small farm to her mother, who decided to give it to Yana so that she and Dimitry could run the farm and start a family.

But the family never came. Dimitry wasn't sure why they had failed to conceive. Yana accused him of producing too little sperm because he drank too much alcohol. He never managed to turn from the party-hearty days of their early twenties to a more responsible, adult outlook. Meanwhile, Yana had made that change and had spent more than a decade badgering Dimitry to catch up with her.

He knew she had hoped that having children might change things, and her frustration over the fact that Dimitry wasn't man enough to carry out the task in multiple ways had brought her to the point of exasperation. Yana had loved Dimitry once, and she could love him again, but her biological clock was ticking, and she was giving up hope.

"You must think I'm stupid," she said. "I heard you come through the gate and the front door. You could have raised the dead."

Dimitry kept his eyes closed. He remembered when he first saw Yana. She had stunned him into stammering stupidity. When they finally became an item, he reveled in their near-constant love-making. He felt like more of a man with her than he had ever felt before. Now they rarely slept in the same bed, and she never seemed interested in him. He didn't care if either one of them was a little heavier or older looking; he just wanted her back. He suspected Yana no longer loved him. He had no idea how their relationship had fallen apart, but it had.

"Quit pretending you're sleeping—we both know it's bullshit," she commanded.

He didn't have to open his eyes to know Yana would be standing there with her hands on her hips, waiting for her husband to open his eyes. He kept them shut, but he could feel her refusing to budge. Finally, Dimitry's will gave out. He opened his eyes, and looked at her, blinking.

"Where have you been?" she demanded.

"Out," he replied.

"Out where?"

"Out with the boys."

"Who?"

"Sergei and Andrei."

"Oh, those two success stories? And what did you three kings accomplish while you were out?" Yana used her sarcastic emphasis to leave the word "out" hanging in the air like a hand grenade with the pin pulled.

"We started planning something," the big man said.

"Planning?" Yana replied incredulously. "Planning what? How to buy more booze?"

"No. Something important. Something that could change our position in this town."

Yana leaned back in mock surprise.

"Something important?" she mocked. "You're going to change your position in this town? Dimitry, are you that stupid? You have a home. You have a farm. You have a wife. And you could have a family if you got your act together. But you're too lazy for that, aren't you? You're too desperate to stay twenty-five-years-old forever to realize that you've let a perfectly good farm go to seed. You're too blind to see you've left a beautiful home fall into disrepair."

Dimitry lay on the couch in shock.

"You're lazy," she charged. "And stupid. If you truly wanted to change your position in this town, you'd realize you have everything you need to accomplish that right here in this home; on this farm. You'd put the bottle down and get on that tractor. You'd start trimming back the grass, till the soil, and start fertilizing so you can plant once spring comes around. You'd fix that fence. You'd get that pickup truck running again. You'd start being a man. Instead, you're laying on the couch, drunk and childish."

Dimitry sat up.

"What did you say?" he asked.

"You heard what I said," Yana scolded. "You sound like a child, talking about your 'important' plans."

"They are important," he said, standing up. "The Russian army is here. Crimea is going back to Russia, and when it does, we are going to rise to the top. This is our golden opportunity to make a difference in this place, to gain a little power and prestige."

Yana couldn't contain her laughter.

"Are you serious?" she chuckled as she said. "You sound ridiculous. How are you getting this 'power and prestige?'"

"A militia," he said. "The Dzhankoy Self Defense Force—and I'm leading it."

Yana burst into hysterical laughter.

Dimitry shot across the room from his spot on the couch with a quickness one wouldn't expect from such a large, out-of-shape, and extremely hung-over man. He swept both of his surprised and frightened wife's forearms together under his left armpit and held them tight, and he pinned her up against the wall, his free hand clasping her two cheeks. Yana's eyes welled with tears, and her nostrils flared as he squeezed her face.

"Listen to me, you bitch," Dimitry hissed to his wife. "I've had enough of your shit. I'm still the man of this house."

"The hell you are," she charged back, her voice spitty and distorted by his grasp. "No man behaves like you're acting. Go ahead and beat me, you man-child. You prove my point."

Dimitry released his grip on Yana's face and pointed right between her eyes.

"No, I'll do better than that," he said. "I'll prove you wrong. You laugh at me all you want, but soon I'll have my pick of any farm I want. I'll own a bigger and better plot than this one, and I'll be running things in this town. Will you be calling me a child then?"

"I'll call you delusional," Yana replied, yanking her arms free and batting his index finger out of her face. "You really believe you're going to be somebody? A big shot?"

"I know I will," he said. "The Russians are going to need local leaders, and I'll be one."

Yana sighed. She slipped out from between Dimitry and the wall, walked to the middle of the family room, and turned to address him again.

"You're cracked," she said, pausing to choke back a tear. "… And you smell like booze, hairspray, and cheap perfume."

I was too drunk to shower, Dimitry realized. *Why didn't I think to clean up?*

"Look," Yana continued, her voice wavering, "it's clear you have no idea what you're doing. But you know what? I don't care. I'm tired of this. It's one thing to be mad, it's one thing to be frustrated, because those things mean I care. Now, I'm just tired. I'm exhausted of trying to get you to grasp the idea that you could have a decent life if you'd only work for it."

Dimitry seethed, wishing Yana would go back to scolding him.

"But I guess you see this Russian invasion as Christmas and Putin as your Father Frost," she said. "Life doesn't work that way. But maybe you need to find that out for yourself."

"What do you mean?" Dimitry asked.

"I mean that I want you to leave," she explained. Yana had regained her composure, and some strength returned to her voice. "Go get your bigger farm. Go become a big shot. Go prove me wrong. But realize one thing: You don't get me. Not anymore."

Dimitry just stood there.

"Pack some bags," she instructed. "Stay with one of your fellow militia members. Hatch some big plans, because you need to move on."

And that was that. Yana owned the farm, and Dimitry did not. The rest was just memories. Within an hour, Dimitry had packed his bags and was standing outside the front door. He had made arrangements to stay with Sergei, who had said he would pick up Dimitry in his Subaru, once he could find it. Dimitry walked back down the road he had walked up earlier that morning, this time with two suitcases to his name.

Chapter 10
SIGNS AND WONDERS

Viktor and Sasha stared at the sign for a considerable length of time. The strange billboard definitely made an impression.

The members of Squad B had temporarily swapped their duty of manning Checkpoint Anna with Squad D, and now they were patrolling the streets of Dzhankoy, a town almost as dull as the dusty crossroads. Measuring ten square miles, the town had a population of roughly forty-thousand people, and its only claim to fame was that a major highway and a few rail lines passed through it.

The squad was to patrol the area surrounding the rail station and rail yard in conjunction with two other squads, and then spend some time walking among the shops to demonstrate military control over the area. That second part of the mission irritated Viktor because the members of Squad B were still under instructions to not indicate in any way that they were Russian soldiers. He was sick of being a ghost in olive drab.

Patrolling around "downtown" Dzhankoy amounted to going for a walk and being interrupted by either soldier-obsessed little boys, or pro-Russian Crimeans congratulating them and asking for selfies. That's where Viktor began to get a sense of the propaganda that must have accompanied the invasion. They sounded like programmed robots.

"We are so happy to have fellow Russians here," A middle age man had told him. "You will make sure those fascists in Kyiv don't screw us. Did you know they want to outlaw the Russian language? What happens after that? Thank you so much for protecting us and ensuring the referendum. Long live Russia!"

All Viktor—or any of the squad members—could do in response to those kinds of accolades was nod their acknowledgment. They weren't in a position to share opinions or explain who they were or what their presences signified. Nods seemed to be the best way to handle things. And if someone wanted to stop the soldiers for a picture, the best reply seemed to be "quickly, please" and to get it over with.

When patrolling the shopping area, Viktor and Sasha decided to let Albert, Boris, and Pavel walk around on their own, perhaps flirt with some girls, and have what little fun the situation offered. The younger guys deserved a break, which gave Viktor and Sasha an opportunity to walk and chat where civilians weren't in earshot.

But for now, they were speechless staring at the bizarre sign they found in the middle of town. It was a public service announcement for Crimea's referendum, which was five days away. The billboard was simple: Bold, red letters stated across the top, "March 16: We Choose." A box on the right showed the shape of the Crimean peninsula colored with the Russian tricolor. A box on the left showed the same shape of Crimea, but this was colored bright red and emblazoned with a giant, black swastika stretched across the middle.

"That's some choice," Viktor said.

"Nazis or Russia," Sasha replied. "I wouldn't have a tough time picking."

"Yeah, if that's the choice, then it's an easy one, but give me a break. … Look, we've both been around the block. Do you honestly think fascists have taken over Ukraine?"

"I'm sure there are nationalists in the Euromaidan. And I've been told there's a picture on the Internet of some guys wearing swastikas at a nationalist rally, but …"

"But you haven't seen it with your own eyes."

"And even if I had seen it, and I could prove it was from a rally, I'm not so sure how much that would prove," Sasha argued. "I mean, there's a guy in my hometown with swastika tattoos. So some jerk shows up to a rally or 10 of them show up. So what? There are lots of racists and thugs in the world. I think that Nazi thing is just an easy way to make our case."

"I don't even know what our case is at this point," Viktor said. "What's our case for being here, honestly?"

"I think we're here because Crimea is historically Russian. It should be part of Russia."

"Yeah, but we took over a Ukrainian airbase to get here. And all over Crimea, we're surrounding Ukrainian bases with Ukrainian soldiers inside them. I don't think we can say Crimea is only Russian. The people in that church group were Ukrainians. The old man on the tractor must have been Tatar."

"Okay, so let's say that Crimea is mostly Russian ethnically, and pretty much historically, too. Sevastopol's as much a part of Russia as Moscow is."

"Even if that's true, what do you think the plan is? Have the secession referendum and then merge Crimea into Russia?"

"Pretty much."

Viktor pondered what Sasha had to say as they kept walking. The words made sense, but something still troubled him. As they continued walking, a small figure of a woman approached them from the opposite direction pulling a wheeled, wire shopping basket behind her. As she came into focus Viktor realized it was the old lady from the church group that had protested Checkpoint Anna several days ago.

"Uh-oh, get ready for another scolding."

But when she passed, the old lady kept her eyes toward the ground, not saying a word.

"Where's my scolding?" Sasha asked after she was out of earshot.

"I have no idea. That was the same granny that yelled at us, right?"

"Definitely."

A few blocks further, Viktor and Sasha came upon Albert, Boris, and Pavel with two young women who were taking pictures with them. It was clear the women had gotten dressed up for the occasion. It was also clear their men were turning back into flattered farm boys from the attention. The two sergeants decided to take in the show.

"These clowns have no idea how much trouble they're in," Sasha observed.

Viktor laughed. "Too right. The hunters are actually the prey. It takes me back to watch them."

"It does. ... I wonder how the wives are doing."

"What, you want to spend your weekends fixing the house? You're in beautiful Crimea, the jewel of the Black Sea! Just look at that rail yard; that motorway; that gas station. This kind of scenery is a rare prize, my friend. You joined the army to see the world and lead a life of adventure, didn't you? And you want to go home to your wife?"

"You're right. How could I be such a moron?"

The two held back until the younger soldiers' fan club batted their eyelashes a few more times before saying their goodbyes. This was every officer's and NCO's favorite perk: laying into the privates.

"Just what in the hell do you think you're doing?" Sasha admonished.

"Nothing, sergea—er, I mean, Sasha," Pavel said.

"It didn't look like nothing to me, Pavel. You're not supposed to be interacting with the locals."

"We tried not to," Pavel replied. "But it's hard to figure out how to get them to leave us alone."

"It didn't look to me like you wanted to be left alone. Looking for a little rest and recreation with the locals? Maybe some fraternizing? What if one of those girls turned out to be someone's wife? Or daughter? Where would that put us?"

Flustered, Pavel opened his mouth and closed it a couple of times trying to search for a response. He looked like a guppy gulping water. Viktor and Sasha tried to keep stern looks on their faces while they basked in the moment.

"We weren't trying to do that, Sasha," Boris interjected. "They just asked us for pictures, and we mostly nodded and smiled."

"You sure you didn't give away who you were? Did you confirm you were Russian soldiers? Did you tell them about our unit? Did you tell them about our mission? Answer me, big shot."

Now Boris was making an equally stupid-looking fish impression. Albert was about to speak when Viktor cut him off.

"Relax, fellas. I understand this was innocent, but everyone inside and outside of Crimea wants confirmation of who we are. You must be on your toes at all times. A little flirting could start a rumor mill that winds up on the Internet and compromises the mission."

"Yes, Viktor."

"Good. Remember what the Captain said: This mission is going to be fought mostly with words and pictures, not bullets, so let's not give the enemy any ammunition. Now, let's head back to the rail station. We're set to patrol there for two more hours."

Along the way, Squad B encountered a group of four men, presumably farmers, wearing orange-and-black ribbons. Viktor recognized one of them as the man who had driven the pro-Russian welcoming party up to Checkpoint Anna and began goading the church group into the fracas. The old woman had called him Dimitry if Viktor recalled correctly. The man was huge, taller and broader than Sasha.

"Russian brothers!" Dimitry called, stepping wide into the sidewalk to block the soldiers and extending both hands into the air in a welcoming gesture.

"Not a word," Viktor instructed the men in a hushed voice.

"Russian brothers, it is excellent to see you! We hope you are enjoying our town—soon to be part of Russia again!"

The Russian soldiers nodded. The man named Dimitry peered into Viktor's eyes and studied the part of his face not obscured by his mask.

"Say, you're the soldiers from the checkpoint by the dirt road crossing by Bessonov's field aren't you? Well, don't worry about all those Ukrainian fascists. We've made sure none of that filth will interfere with the referendum. Five days away! We can hardly wait to vote, eh fellas?"

The other men cheered their agreement and began chanting "Ross-iya! Ross-iya! Ross-iya!"

"Thank you," Viktor said. "We need to patrol the train station, so we'll need to get down the road."

"No problem! Thank you for being here, comrades!" Dmitry replied, leading off another round of chanting.

As Squad B continued walking, the choruses of "Ross-iya!" receded into the background and Pavel spoke up.

"Those guys are a big help," the young soldier remarked.

"How's that?" Sasha asked.

"Well, I'm glad we have help making sure no fascists spoil the referendum. I mean, look what they did in Kyiv. Those people have ruined Ukraine."

"Mmmm," Viktor replied in the most non-committal manner he could muster.

"All those nationalists in Ukraine are linking up with the Europeans and the Americans. How morally bankrupt can you get? They're going to wind up slaves to Western bankers. They should have aligned with the Federation. Instead, they listened to a bunch of neo-fascists."

"So these neo-fascists, Pavel, who are they?" Boris butted in to ask.

"All those people who overthrew Yanukovych."

"And what about here? Who are the fascists? Was the

priest a fascist? How about the old lady?"

As Pavel pondered his response, Squad B had arrived at the railway station. Viktor and Sasha deployed the three privates to their specific patrol rounds and then took their positions.

Near the end of their patrol, Viktor and Sasha had just collected the other three into the Tigr to head back to camp when they heard the unmistakable rumble of an approaching convoy. Soon a slow-moving parade of at least thirty Kama3 transport trucks—a dozen of which were towing 152mm Mista-B howitzers—passed through town, heading north on the E105.

"That's a lot of muscle," Boris remarked after taking a long pull from the cigarette he had lit at the end of their patrol.

"Where is that headed? To Ukraine?" Albert asked.

"I don't want to speculate," Viktor replied. "We do what we're told, men. Right now, we're to return to camp—just as soon as this convoy passes through."

Viktor instructed Boris to warm up the Tigr. When the tail end of the convoy came into sight, the men piled into the vehicle. They pulled away from the train station and headed south, passing by the Dzhankoy's shops. Boris lit another Winston and spoke:

"With all those guns, I'm pretty sure you'll get to fight all the fascists you want, Pavel," he teased.

"At least I'm not afraid of them," Pavel replied, an edge in his voice. "Then again, they seem to be mostly old ladies, so I can understand your concern."

Boris's face grew severe. But before he could say anything, Pavel cuffed him on the shoulder.

"Just kidding, comrade. But seriously, we have an opportunity to help free these people with this referendum—fellow Russians no less. The Americans say they are protecting democracy all the time, but we're actually doing it."

"You think so?" Viktor asked.

"Absolutely! I know so."

The truck passed below the "We Choose" billboard. Viktor motioned toward the swastika-emblazoned Crimea.

"Then how come we have to scare them into voting our way?" he queried.

Squad B's Tigr rolled south along the motorway, before taking a right on the road that cut through the woods and fields near Checkpoint Anna, its lights cutting into the country night. The truck's occupants remained mostly silent during the ride, while Viktor wondered how long they would stay near Dzhankoy, and where they would go when they left. Russia felt farther away than it had before.

Chapter 11
A RIDE AND A RIOT

The countryside slipped past Danilo in a green and brown blur. The afternoon was turning to dusk, and the fields, woods, and towns sliding past took on muted tones caught mid-shift between color and shades of grey. Soon, the world around him transitioned into a landscape of light and darkness. Headlights and taillights only briefly turned into actual vehicles when they drove under the occasional roadside light.

Danilo felt like he and the motorcycle were one entity at moments like this. Crouched low against the Kawasaki's tank so that his helmet was partially behind the flyscreen, the sensation of riding was more akin to flying than anything else. Cars were rolling obstacles around which he easily maneuvered, leaning one way and then the next. The engine vibration and warmth he felt in his knees reassured him. This was the exact spot he was meant to be at this very moment. He felt free.

*

Veronika warned him earlier in the day not to ride to Donetsk.

"You know what's going to happen to you, right?" she said.

"No, what?" Danilo replied, already knowing what she would say next.

"It's going to be just like Kyiv. They're going to truck in thugs from across the border to cause trouble."

"They might."

"They will. You know they will."

"And what if they do?"

"This isn't Kyiv, Danilo. Russia is right across the border from Donetsk, and Donetsk is full of pro-Russians. The referendum is three days away. They want as much bad news about Ukraine as they can broadcast. Plus, Putin and the Russian government are looking for an excuse—any excuse—to invade, so if there is trouble in Donetsk, they will blame it on Ukraine. It'll be the same idiotic claims about fascists and all that."

"Well, we're not going to make any trouble. This is a peaceful demonstration. The citizens of Donetsk deserve to be heard. They should have a right to march for what they believe in."

"Of course they do, but you're just playing into Putin's hands. You know there is going to be trouble regardless of how peaceful you are."

"But if the pro-Russians start beating non-violent protestors, won't that make them look bad?"

"It doesn't matter. If there is one drop of blood spilled in Donetsk—even if it is Ukrainian blood—the Russian news media and politicians will blame it entirely on Ukraine. Danilo, how can I make you understand that they are actively looking for an excuse?"

"So what are we supposed to do? Nothing?"

"I don't know. ... I wish I knew. You have to understand, I'm not only worried about you, little brother. It's true that I don't want you hurt. But at the same time, I'm also worried about the country. Ever since 1990, Ukraine has been a work in progress. We cannot let the Russians march in and take over."

"They certainly want to."

"They do, little brother. Don't doubt that for a second. We're a prize on their wall so that they can claim they are an important world power, and we can't give that bastard Putin an inch. ... Danilo, you must promise me: you will do everything you possibly can to make sure the demonstrators around you never return any violence. That may become impossible, but you need to try anyway. One person can sway a crowd. I have seen it happen, back when I was younger than you."

"I promise."

"And another thing: you have to protect this girl, Angelina, at all times. I don't know if she's ever been in a demonstration before, but we both know how bad things can get if things go pear-shaped."

Angelina had been the one who invited Danilo to Donetsk, and he was going—for her as much as for patriotism, whatever that meant. Before, Danilo had viewed politics from a mostly academic perspective. His opinions regarding Ukraine's direction and Yanukovych were conclusions at which he arrived through historic and political study. He felt that after years of a government that kowtowed to Russia, Ukraine deserved to determine its direction. It had been through far too much.

But ever since Kyiv, his logic had veered into emotion. He felt as strongly about Ukraine's direction as he felt about Angelina. He connected with her on an instinctive level.

*

Riding a motorcycle through the countryside, the whole world is reduced to sound. Sure, you see the road — in fact, you can feel it through the bike — you see the cars and the countryside, but the truly significant sensory input is sound. You hear every element of the engine, and you're constantly listening for audible feedback of its performance to ensure that it is running right. You listen for pinging, rattles, or whining bushing and bearings.

You hear the wind whistling through helmet vents, or via the small gap created when the face shield is slightly notched open. A decent helmet cuts down on wind noise, but invariably a tiny portion of it always remains. All other sounds must pass through that wind noise; like an environmental audio filter that forces you to strain to ensure you aren't missing out on any important sounds.

Finally, you hear your engine loud and clear when you pass other vehicles or objects. The sound of your motorcycle bounces off those objects and back at you: *Whiissh-whiissh-whiissh*. It's a sort of self-referential sonar that lets you know you're still there; still moving.

Those sounds became more frequent on his approach to Donetsk as the traffic thickened, signaling that he was getting closer to his destination. Danilo shifted his weight and swung onto an exit that would take him to Angelina's apartment.

Feeling and hearing the engine whine of a downshift, Danilo corkscrewed alongside a guardrail that wrapped itself around a decreased-radius turn—*whiissh-whiissh-whiissh-whiissh-whiissh-whiissh*—and then exploded out into a straightaway. He could feel the motorcycle's suspension contract and expand as the energy produced by the engine unwound itself into the primary gear, yanked the chain taut and set the rear wheel spinning faster. He was equal parts catapult and rocket.

Soon, Danilo was passing through quiet suburbs and approaching the city of Donetsk proper. He grew closer to Angelina with every turn of the tire. In another fifteen minutes he would finally get out of the saddle and into her arms.

Danilo rolled up to Angelina's apartment building, careful not to rev his bike. He let it wind down, swung out the kickstand, killed the engine and shut off the fuel. He unclipped his two pannier bags and walked toward her building. Angelina was standing in the light of the entrance. The moment he saw her, she padded toward him in her slippers and wrapped her arms around his neck.

"I was getting worried about you," she said quietly. "It's past midnight."

"Sorry, I got on the bike as soon as I could pack up after work. I had to make a few coffee stops along the way, too. It was a long ride. I'm exhausted."

"I'll bet. I have some tea and sandwiches inside. Let's get you fed so that you can go to sleep."

"Please."

It wasn't long before Danilo, having feasted on egg-and-sardine sandwiches, flopped unconscious on Angelina's bed. She unbuckled his belt, removed his jeans, switched off the light, and crawled under the sheets with him.

Danilo woke to the smell of breakfast. Angelina was sitting at the table, reading something on her laptop.

"I made tea and have bread and jam," she said. "I also have leftover sandwiches from last night if you want some."

"That sounds fantastic. ... Sorry, I passed out."

"That's okay. There'll be plenty of time for romance later. Let's get our day started."

They spent most of the day walking around Donetsk's downtown Voroshylovskyi District and toured the Donetsk Art Museum for a bit. Eventually, people began collecting for the demonstration. It was shaping up to be more of an anti-war and anti-Russian occupation rally than a Ukrainian unity event.

The protestors paraded along major thoroughfares, carrying Ukrainian flags down the length of their ranks. They sang patriotic songs and chanted slogans about Russia needing to leave Crimea. Danilo was swept away by the mood of the crowd. It felt like the early protests in Kyiv, where average people came out to voice their feelings.

There were pro-Russian counter-protesters, too. A newspaper poll taken earlier had shown that roughly 30 percent of Donetsk's mostly Russian-speaking population preferred a relationship with the Russian Federation. Those groups marched along the sides of pro-unity group's parade, flying their flags and chanting their slogans, as well.

Though Danilo didn't agree with them, their protest felt honest. Both sides were keeping within their ranks and not confronting one another. The dual marches felt like what free people do when they disagree—they support their respective causes. Danilo put his arm around Angelina's waist as they marched along. She kissed his cheek in return.

"I'm glad I came," he said loud enough for her to hear him above the crowd. "I wouldn't miss this for the world."

"I'm glad you came, too," she yelled back and kissed him quickly on the lips. He kissed her back and felt frozen in a perfect moment. When the moment broke, they scrambled to keep pace with the crowd.

As evening fell, the protestors came to a large square. A larger cordon of police had barred off a corner of the square where a large group of pro-Russian demonstrators stood chanting "Ross-iya! Ross-iya! Ross-iya!"

"I don't like the feeling of this," Danilo said, sensing the mood of the demonstrators around him shifting quickly to nervousness.

"What's the matter?" Angelina asked, sounding worried.

"There." Danilo pointed to a group of busses parked beyond the square.

"I've seen that kind of bus before—at the protests in Kyiv. Russian agents shipped in provocateurs from out of town. Now they're doing it here—I'm sure of it."

The confrontation stymied their group for a moment, and Danilo tried to listen over the din to hear if the organizers would shout out a new course.

Boom! Crack-crack-crack! The bangs were loud, but not loud enough to be gunshots. Danilo looked around and saw the pro-Russians were lobbing fireworks at them. The firecrackers and rockets and other pyrotechnics were going off right above the demonstrators' heads. Angelina looked even more concerned.

"Don't worry; stick with me," Danilo said. "Whatever you do, don't lose me."

Boom! Boom! Crack-crack-a-crack-crack! More fireworks. Danilo looked down the length of the parade. There was smoke, probably from smoke bombs. His nose picked up a familiar odor.

"I smell tear gas—here." Danilo handed Angelina a ziplock baggie containing handkerchiefs they had soaked in vinegar the night before as a precaution.

Angelina wrapped the cloth around her face and moved closer to Danilo.

"We have to get upwind," she yelled through the cloth.

They held hands tight, and headed toward a path that led from the square to a boulevard. Danilo looked over toward the police cordon and saw they were having trouble containing the pro-Russians. The guys looked scary, and all wore orange-and-black-striped ribbons of St. George. He started hearing some of the younger guys in the pro-unity rally yelling taunts at the Russians and cursing at them. It was clear things were going to kick off. Danilo grabbed an organizer's bullhorn.

"Don't fight the Russians!" He urged. "This is all a set-up for the Russian media! They want a reason to invade! Don't fight the Russians! Don't fight the Russians! Chant it with me! Don't fight the Russians!"

About half of the crowd around started chanting "Don't fight the Russians" with Danilo while the other half yelled curses at the bussed-in thugs, but everyone in the group focused their attention on the local police cordon, which resembled a levee during a storm. Within minutes, the police lost control of the situation, Russians began streaming through, and a large number of the younger pro-unity protestors started rushing forward to confront them. Danilo tossed the bullhorn back at its owner. Angelina yanked his arm.

"We have to get the hell out of here—now," she yelled.

"I couldn't agree more," he replied.

They ran toward the opening in the square, but a melee between Ukrainian protestors and a group of the black-and-orange-ribboned hooligans blocked the road. Danilo knew by their tactics that organized leaders had bussed them in to provoke violence — he had seen them before in the streets of Kyiv and on the television news. The same types of guys had stormed and occupied Donetsk's City Administration building earlier in the month, right after the Crimea invasion, but the police eventually removed them.

The group of Russians here at the protest were outnumbered but showed no fear. In fact, they looked organized. They had linked arms and were forming a kind of phalanx. If a unity protestor got too close, they would either punch the person, hit them with a club, or spray them with a can of tear gas or pepper spray. A typical demonstrator doesn't carry a club or pepper spray, so it was clear that these guys had been trained and equipped.

Danilo and Angelina attempted to maneuver around this scene when more Ukrainian unity protestors joined their brethren and rushed the Russians en masse. Danilo used the brawl as an opportunity to grab Angelina's arm and rush her out of the square. From the smell, it was clear the tear gas was following them. They ran past a man heading the other direction with blood streaming down his face.

Finally, they broke free of the square. The two ran for several blocks before they could finally hail a cab.

"That was bedlam," Danilo said during the taxi ride.

"Just wait 'til we turn on the TV," Angelina replied.

Back at Angelina's apartment, they turned on her television. Russian channels dominated Donetsk's airwaves, and Russia's propaganda machine was in full swing, generating "news" about how the riots in Donetsk were the fault of Western-backed, neo-fascist insurgents that had started the riot, and that Ukraine's government had lost control of the situation. The Russian news was saying that it was only a matter of time before the eastern half of the country descended into lawlessness. Russian politicians, including Putin, were intoning that if the situation persisted, then they would have to protect ethnic Russians in eastern Ukraine.

The most troubling thing was that someone had stabbed a man to death. The Russian channels neglected to mention that the victim was a pro-Ukrainian unity protester. The Russian reports simply kept his association vague or unmentioned, which led the audience to draw conclusions in line with their biases. Danilo couldn't decide which shocked him more: the stabbing or the cynical media spin.

"I can't believe this is my city," Angelina said.

"This is temporary," Danilo replied. "These are outside agitators. We had this in Kyiv, too. You have to make your way through it. Don't forget, they get bussed in, and they won't be here forever. You live here."

"Still, I want to get out of town for a bit. We should get on your motorcycle and go."

"Let's do it. Where do you want to go?"

"How about Crimea? We could support the protests in Sevastapol."

Danilo felt simultaneously nervous, and intrigued.

"Crimea? Are you sure?"

"Positive."

Chapter 12
RUN-UP TO A REFERENDUM

The morning at Checkpoint Anna was much like any other: mind-numbing. A low mist permeated the sky and clung to the members of Squad B and the surrounding landscape.

Pavel leaned over the sandbags of their small fortress, looked down the southbound road for as far as he could see, and then panned across the field that stretched to the west. Squad B had been in Crimea for nearly 17 days, and when not patrolling Dzhankoy, they manned their checkpoint, which had checked virtually nothing since their arrival. Pavel could count the number of cars they had stopped on his hands and still have his thumbs left over to twiddle.

"Albert, I'm pretty sure I saw a dirt clod moving about 500 meters out from our two o'clock position. It could be hostile," he advised.

"See if it is fascist," Albert drawled.

Pavel sighed. Albert and Boris had both given him considerable grief for buying into the mission's "grand plan" so readily. Even he had to admit that over the past two weeks, they had yet to see a single fascist or Nazi.

"Well, it does look like it might want to merge with the EU," Pavel replied.

"Empty your magazine until it stops moving," Albert replied.

Pavel smiled but then spoke up after a pause.

"Look, I think this referendum is a good thing," he said. "Kyiv is still in chaos, they had a big riot up in Donetsk, and Crimea is mostly Russian. This land should be part of Russia."

"It's none of my business," Albert said. "If these people vote that way tomorrow, then that's fine — anything that gets me back home. But I do have a question."

"What's that?"

"How come these people never voted to secede and become part of Russia before?"

"Well, they probably didn't want to until the Euromaidan took over in Kyiv."

"And three weeks later things were so radically different that they wanted to join the Russian Federation?"

"Sure, why not?"

"I don't know, Pavel. Seems pretty convenient that the people start wanting this as soon as we barge in here and do it anyway."

"Hey, maybe you two political experts should shit-can the chit-chat for a while and concentrate on your military responsibility of guarding this road," Sasha instructed from the passenger window of the Tigr.

Pavel and Albert shut up. Boris walked back from taking a leak in the woods that bordered the eastern side of the road. He popped a cigarette in his mouth, lit up, and joined his comrades in doing nothing.

*

Sasha leaned back in the Tigr and spoke to Viktor.

"We have to keep these guys from talking politics," he said. "They're joking around now, but I'm worried it's going to cut into our cohesion."

"Agreed." Sunday was the referendum, and Viktor got orders that Squad B was supposed to be guarding a polling station in town. If any trouble crops up, he wanted the guys thinking as a team and not questioning each other.

"Do you think there is going to be any trouble tomorrow?" Sasha asked.

"I doubt it," Viktor observed. "The only troublemakers I've seen were that pissed off old lady and that blow-hard Lebel. I know the Tatars and ethnic Ukrainians are supposed to boycott the vote, anyway."

"My guess is that Tatars and Ukrainians will claim the results aren't democratic."

"As if that will mean anything. Crimea will vote to be part of Russia before the sun sets on Sunday."

"Well hey, listen to us. We sound just like the three hens outside."

"We're a threat to unit cohesion, Sasha. I'm going to have to report us."

"That's okay. Maybe the brass will send us to Sochi as punishment. I could use a vacation."

"Hope the toilets work."

"Let's not get ahead of ourselves."

*

Outside the Tigr, the three privates continued talking but kept their voices low to avoid drawing their sergeants' attention.

"How long is this mission gonna last?" Boris complained, tossing his cigarette butt in the road. "I am fucking done already."

"Agreed," Albert replied, his hands stuffed in his pockets.

"Maybe we'll be home by summer," Pavel said.

"I have a feeling we'll be marching on Kyiv by then," Albert said.

"Fuck that," Boris said. "I do not want to go past Armyansk."

"Or Chongar," Albert replied. Armyansk and Chongar were the two land crossings between Ukraine and Crimea, which was as close to an island as a peninsula could be.

"I don't know guys, a change of scenery would be nice," Pavel said. "Consider this: the Army version of an all-expenses-paid tour."

"I want to talk to my travel agent," Boris said, popping another Winston in his mouth and bringing his lit Zippo up to it.

"Brothers!" called a voice from the east.

"Aw fuck," Boris muttered. He pulled his balaclava up over his face, stubbed out his smoke on a sandbag, and returned it to his pack.

"This guy," Albert said.

"He's the worst," Pavel replied in a low tone.

"I have urgent news," said the voice. The big man they knew as Dimitry Lebel appeared, wearing camouflage gear that wasn't military spec, perhaps hunting gear.

"I must speak with your officers."

Boris paused, exhaled a sigh, and raised his hand for

Dimitry to wait, and then turned to the Pav Tigr and motioned to Viktor and Sasha in the cab.

*

"This guy," Viktor said.

"Our local supporter is really beginning to grate on my nerves," Sasha agreed.

"Looks like he's wearing a uniform of some sort. Strange."

"All these guys are forming militias and volunteer forces from what I'm hearing. He's probably set up a half-dozen checkpoints in town to let everybody know who's in charge."

"Have you smelled that guy's breath? I'm pretty sure vodka's in charge."

"Nice. That doesn't surprise me."

"Well, let's see what Chuck Norris has to say."

They slowly opened their doors, swung their bodies out of the truck, hopped onto the pavement, and walked over to the sandbag barrier in no particular hurry. Dimitry stood on the other side of it. He wore a length of St. George ribbon tied around his right arm.

"I must speak with you in private," Dimitry said to Viktor. "I am here on an urgent security matter."

Viktor sighed and walked Dimitry to the back of the Tigr.

"You're wearing camouflage," he said to the man.

"Some of the men in town and I have formed a self-defense unit. This referendum is too critical not to protect. We must become part of Russia," the big man said with a stark seriousness that contrasted from his earlier visit when he had shown up to the checkpoint on a flag-draped tractor and smelling like fifteen distilleries.

"Ah," Viktor replied. "You had urgent news?"

"Yes, we've uncovered a plot to bomb the polling station."

"What?"

"Yes, Muslim Tatars in the area are planning to bomb the polling station during Sunday's referendum."

Viktor paused for a moment. T72hese were serious allegations.

"We know who at least one of the plotters is," Dimitry added.

"You do?"

"Yes. I can take you to the culprit. I'm hoping you can arrest him and get him to inform on his co-conspirators before they have a chance to make good on their plans."

"Hold on. I want you to go to the other side of the barrier," Viktor said. He turned in the direction of Sasha, who was standing by the three privates. "Sasha, come here for a second."

Sasha walked up.

"What's up, Viktor?"

"Our friend says he knows of a conspiracy on the part of local Tatars to bomb the polling station during the referendum."

"Are you fucking kidding me?"

"That's what I wanted to say, but … Look, I don't know if this is true or not, and I have a feeling it's BS, but I think the best course of action is for me to take one of the guys and go check it out."

"What the hell are you talking about? That's a stupid idea. This guy's an idiot."

"Hear me out. First off, in the unlikely event that this kook is right, then it's our duty to follow up on this."

"Okay, true."

"Second, this guy has a big mouth, but he also has pull

in town. We've already seen he has a few local hard cases behind him. If they're strutting around Dzhankoy flexing their muscle, I'd much rather have them chasing a wild goose than getting in the way during the referendum."

"That's a good point. Make sure to tell this Lebel character he needs to get out of our way on Sunday."

"You're right. I'll do that."

"Good."

"Okay, I'm gonna take Boris and leave you with Albert and Pavel. I'll bring a radio, but let's try not to use it. I'd rather this event not draw the Captain's notice unless there's something to it."

Viktor turned and called to Dimitry: "How far away is this person?"

"Twenty minutes on foot," the man called back.

Viktor turned back to Sasha: "Alright, so let's give this an hour; forty minutes walking, plus twenty minutes dealing with the situation. If you don't hear from me by then, do a radio check."

"Got it."

"Boris, collect your gear," Viktor said to the younger soldier. "You're coming with me."

*

The walk suited Viktor. After sitting in a truck or standing on pavement all day, a hike in the countryside felt invigorating, even if the reason for the stroll was quite probably a ridiculous waste of time. The fields they walked through belonged to a man named Bessonov if he recalled correctly. The old Tatar man had mentioned it during the incident with the church group several days back.

"Not too much further now; about ten minutes," Dimitry advised as he walked ahead, not turning around.

Viktor turned back to Boris, who was trailing behind and put his finger to his masked face to let the private know his orders were still to keep his mouth shut at all costs.

The dirt road eventually jogged west and passed through a small line of trees before hitting another paved road. The three turned right and walked along the row of trees.

"Nearly there," Dimitry said. "I'm glad you are following up on this. I believe this man is neck deep in this plot and should be arrested."

Viktor nodded. Boris remained still.

After walking another five minutes, the barbed wire fence that ran along the western side of the road met up with a stone fence that surrounded a yard in front of a small farmhouse. A low wooden gate, recently painted in a deep red, opened on a stone walkway. Viktor walked up and knocked on the front door.

"Just a moment," a voice called from inside.

The door opened to reveal the Tatar man from the incident several days back. He stood in the doorway, one hand on this the knob, the other holding a cup of tea.

"Yes?" the old man asked. "What do you want?"

Viktor paused for a moment. He was a soldier, not a police officer, and wasn't quite sure how to handle the situation. All he knew was that if this wasn't what Dimitry said it was, he wanted to resolve it quickly and with a minimum of fuss.

"We've had a report that there might be weapons on the property."

"Not weapons—Iskandar has bombs!" Dimitry interjected.

"Ah, Dimitry I see," the old man observed. "You're wearing a uniform. Have you joined the Russian army?"

"Give it up, old man," Dimitry replied. "There's no use acting innocent. We know what you're up to, and we're here to stop you."

"Well, it looks like I have three guests," the old man said, opening the door wider. "Please come in."

The man led them into his small home. Viktor noticed that on the kitchen table sat several paint brushes, a rag, a cup of water, a palette of watercolors, and a bit of watercolor paper tacked to a board. A painting of a highly stylized rabbit sitting on a field of grass was in progress.

"Would you gentlemen like a cup of tea?"

"No thank you, sir. May I call you Iskandar?" Viktor replied. "We'll need to inspect the property."

"As you wish. Please let me know how I can help."

"Why don't you direct this soldier to the back rooms, so that he can perform a search," Viktor said, gesturing to Boris. "I'll search out here."

"Very well," Iskandar said. "Come with me."

Boris followed the old man to the bedrooms and bathroom. Viktor began searching the front room. Dimitry joined in, not hiding his obvious contempt for the old man. While Viktor carefully removed a couch cushion, Dimitry was knocking books off a shelf. Viktor stopped searching for a moment.

"You're sure of this man's involvement?" Viktor asked.

"I'm positive," Dimitry replied.

"Well, I'm not seeing anything in this room. Let's check the kitchen."

Again, while Viktor took pains not to disturb the kitchen, Dimitry rousted the cupboards and shelves, tossing items to the ground. The racket attracted the old man.

"Why is this man vandalizing my home?" Iskandar asked Viktor.

"Because you're guilty and we'll find the evidence," Dimitry said, cutting off Viktor before he could reply.

"Look, we'll conduct the search from here on out. Mr. Lebel, you wait over there," Viktor said, gesturing to the fireplace in the sitting room. "Please."

Dimitry looked frustrated but stomped over to the fireplace and crossed his arms.

Boris walked into the room.

"I couldn't find anything the bedrooms or the bathroom."

"Okay," Viktor replied. "Help me finish searching through this kitchen."

As the two continued their teardown of Iskandar's little galley, the old man sat and looked on dispassionately while sipping a cup of tea. Viktor figured the old guy was pissed off beyond belief, but he was hiding it well. Meanwhile, Dimitry appeared increasingly vexed by the process; a human teapot who was coming to a boil.

"The back," Dimitry said in exasperation. "Let's search out back."

Viktor and Boris exchanged glances.

"Alright," Viktor said. "Let's search the back. Boris, can you try to put some of these things back in order?"

"That's not necessary," Iskandar said. "I'll take care of it."

"Are you sure?" Viktor asked.

The old man nodded and picked a path through the mess of pots and pans Dimitry had made in the kitchen and led them onto the back porch. A samovar sat on the concrete stoop with a teapot full of strong zavarka tea keeping warm atop it.

"Where would you like to search?" Iskandar asked.

"That shack," Dimitry said.

They walked over to a green wooden shed, which sat next to a large rabbit hutch. As Viktor approached, Iskandar said, "Be my guest."

Dimitry smirked.

*

The night before, at roughly 1 a.m., Iskandar had just awoken to use the toilet when he heard the creak of his front gate. He hadn't been sleeping well since Dimitry scrawled an "x" in his gate. From the darkness of his sitting room, Iskandar watched Dimitry pad up the drive to the back of his property. He then watched the large man open the wooden doors of his shed and carry in a cardboard box. He kept quiet and continued monitoring the situation — it was a behavior he learned from the small animals in his fields.

When Iskandar was sure Dimitry had left his property, he went out to inspect the shed. It wasn't a long search before he uncovered the box hidden behind some paint cans and other items. The Russian had packed two crudely made pipe bombs into the box. He wondered if they were even functional.

Shocked, he called the local imam, Talat Mustaffa.

"I'm sorry to call so late, but I have a nasty problem and need advice," Iskandar said.

"That's okay," the cleric groggily replied. "Please, go ahead."

Iskandar related what Dimitry had done, and what he found in the shed.

"I'm glad you called. This situation is obviously quite serious. Those bombs are dangerous in more than one way. I'm going to send my nephew over right away. He was in the army reserves. He'll know what to do."

"I'll make some tea."

Roughly an hour later, the Imam's nephew, Musa, arrived in a Toyota pickup truck. Iskandar handed him a cup of tea, switched on the back porch light, and led him to the shed. The young man looked at the box and its contents without touching it.

"Sir, I'd like you to go inside. If anything bad should happen, please call my uncle before you call anyone else. He is waiting by the phone."

"Yes. By all means. Please be careful."

Iskandar retreated to the kitchen and watched from the window. The young man's efforts seemed to take forever, but eventually, Musa appeared in the doorway of the shed holding the box. He nodded toward Iskandar, who walked out to talk to him.

"I've disabled the bombs," Musa said. "To be honest, calling them bombs is giving them a lot of credit. The fuses were crude to the point of dangerous. Still, if triggered, they would cause a lot of damage."

"What do we do now?" Iskandar asked.

"I've put the fuses and other pieces in this box, which I'll take with me. I mixed the gunpowder that was in the bombs with your potting soil. Don't worry; it's full of nitrogen. It's great for your plants."

"Really?"

"Yep. You'll be amazed at the results. It's not a cheap, but very effective fertilizer. Especially with flowers," Musa half-way joked.

"Well, what else should I do?" Iskandar asked.

"Don't do anything. Carry on as usual. People in town have been watching that trash Dimitry and his bigot friends for the past couple of weeks. This invasion has been their golden opportunity to start doing what they've always wanted to do to: bully us and kick us out of Crimea. I don't know about you, but I don't have any intention of going to Uzbekistan or any other place."

"I feel the same way."

"I know. ... I'm sorry you have to go through this, Mr. Nabiyev. ... Again. It's not right."

"Thank you. What are you going to do about Lebel?"

"Nothing. At least, nothing obvious. We're trying our best to spread the word in the community that he's dangerous and to undermine what he and his goons are doing. But the last thing we want is an outright confrontation. That would play into the Russians' hands. Their propagandists would eat that up and spew it back out to justify an even larger invasion."

"What about the referendum? Should we still boycott?"

"Exactly. If only Russians vote, then the result will obviously be a sham."

"I won't vote then."

"Good. Remember, carry on as normal. Don't let on that we've found anything."

"Yes, I will. Thank you."

After Musa left, Iskandar had a hard time sleeping. He paged through an old photo album of pictures of he and his family and stopped on one of him when he was a young man in the late 1950s. A much younger version of himself was standing next to a horse he had named Wind. Iskandar loved riding that animal. Sitting on her back, flying across the Uzbek land they had been forced to resettle in, Iskandar felt free. He recalled feeling as though he was riding the wind. *That horse was a zephyr!*

Eventually, there came a day that he had to start a life with Aysilu, and even with the dowry, they needed money. He had to sell his precious Wind. The horse went to a good home, but the bittersweet parting left a wound. The old man remembered being a young bridegroom, and his father putting his hand on his shoulder and assuring him that he had done the right thing. "It's what a man would do," his father had said.

Iskandar fell asleep that night with the photo album still in his lap, remembering what it was like to fly across golden hillsides astride an animal that was half fire and half spirit.

*

"I don't see anything," Viktor said, emerging from the shed.

"Let me take a look," Dimitry said, pushing past Iskandar, who forced himself to stand quietly at the doorway. Dimitry feigned searching other areas of the shed, but he focused on a spot under the workbench.

Dimitry pulled the potting soil away to reveal ... nothing. He paused. Iskandar heard him breathe in sharply.

"Nothing," Dimitry said to himself as much as anyone else. He turned around and walked out of the shed. He scanned the yard.

"Let me check the rabbit hutch," he said.

"We can see inside the hutch from here," Viktor said. "There's nothing there. It's been about twenty minutes. We need to head back to the checkpoint, and I'll need to make a report to my Captain. I'll need you to come with us, sir."

"I don't get it," Dimitry said.

"I'm guessing your sources were misinformed," Viktor said. "We need to go."

"May I go inside to start cleaning up?" Iskandar asked.

"Yes. Sir, we're sorry for the mess. If you notice anything suspicious, please report it to the local police, and they'll inform us if it's necessary."

"Yes, I will."

"Okay then. Boris, Mr. Lebel, let's head back."

Iskandar watched the two Russian soldiers and Dimitry leave. They walked along the side to the front gate and turned south down the rural road, back to the dirt road that would take them back to their checkpoint.

Iskandar headed inside to start cleaning up.

*

Viktor, Boris, and Dimitry arrived back at Checkpoint Anna on schedule.

"Welcome back," Sasha said.

"Thanks," Viktor replied. "Boris, return to your post.

"Sir," Viktor said to Dimitry, "Could you please step to the back of the truck with me. I'd like to take down some information for my report.

"Certainly," Dimitry replied. He was looking pale.

After collecting various pieces of information on Dimitry, as well as names and contact information of the men that were part of his self-defense group, Viktor then spoke to Dimitry directly.

"Look, I don't know what's going on, but you put me in a very difficult position by sending me on this wild goose chase. I'm sure you're a good guy, but do not come back to this checkpoint with any wild accusations. I have a job to do, and you got in the way of that today."

Dimitry looked stunned. He was searching for words when Viktor started speaking again.

"And whatever you do, I do not want to hear about you and your men interfering with Sunday's referendum. We are providing security for the polling place, and the only reason I want to see you coming near it is to cast your ballot. Understand?"

"I..." Dimitry trailed off.

"Understand?"

"Yes," Dimitry replied. He had gone from pale to red. "I understand."

The big man turned and marched off down the dirt road through the east. Viktor could almost see a black cartoon cloud over his head.

Sasha walked from around the Tigr.

"Man, that guy was fuming."

"Yes, he was," Viktor said. "It turned out he led us to that old man's farmhouse — you know, the Tatar from when the church group came to protest us?"

"Oh yeah. I remember that guy. The big guy was claiming that old man was some kind of terrorist?"

"Yep, and I got the distinct impression that Lebel was trying to frame the old man, too. He seemed shocked that we didn't find anything."

"Well, you better watch out for that guy, because he was muttering some choice profanities as he headed off. He's definitely pissed."

"He's not half as pissed as the Captain is going to be when I report to him that I took Boris off the post and engaged in this jackassery."

"You're going to tell the Captain? Are you crazy?"

"I have to. If this turns into something bigger, my ass will be in a much bigger sling than it is now. Better to own up to my mistake and take my punishment like a man."

"Yeesh. Let's have some lunch. There's tea ready."

"That sounds spectacular."

As the men of Squad B enjoyed their lunch, the sound of an engine came from the west. It was Iskandar on his tractor. They watched him make his approach on the dirt road through Bessonov's field. Once he got close enough to the checkpoint, the men of Squad B paused their lunches and pulled their balaclavas back over their faces.

Viktor instructed Albert to check the old man. Albert wandered out resting one hand on the rifle slung across his midsection and raised the other in the air, signaling the old man to stop. Iskandar brought his tractor to a halt and killed the engine.

"Where are you headed?" Albert asked.

"I'm heading to town," the old man said.

Albert looked at Viktor for approval. The sergeant nodded.

"Head on through," Albert said, waving the man along.

Iskandar put his venerable machine in gear. It was tough to tell who was older: tractor or owner.

"Thank you," the Tatar shouted over the diesel engine. "I have a busy day. I am heading to the hardware store to buy a lock and hasp for my shed, and then I'm going to the nursery to buy some plants. I have some new potting soil I want to try."

Viktor and Sasha exchanged glances as the old man drove down the dirt path to the east.

"Seems pretty friendly given that we just searched his place," Boris said.

"I'm thinking he's lonely," Viktor said.

"More tea?" Sasha asked.

"No," Viktor replied.

No stranger to sarcasm, Sasha filled Viktor's cup.

Chapter 13
PASSING INTO UNCERTAINTY

The morning promised a cold ride. Frost clung to the roofs of parked cars, and streets that had echoed with the sounds of fireworks, shouting, screaming, and sirens the night before were now blanketed in an otherworldly silence.

"Okay, I think that's everything," Danilo said locking the luggage panniers to the motorcycle. His words turned into ghosts in the cold air. "You ready?"

"I think so," Angelina replied. "It's freezing."

"We don't have to do this, you know."

"Actually, I think we do. The referendum is in two days, and I think we can still somehow lend a hand."

"You know this is going to be dangerous, right?"

"Last night was dangerous, but here we are."

"Here we are."

Angelina walked past the idling motorcycle to Danilo, her insulated riding pants making a swish-swish noise with every step. She kissed his cold, blushed cheek.

"Relax," she said. "I'm here to protect you."

"You're here to get me into trouble, I think."

Angelina laughed. "Come on," she said. "Let's go!"

Danilo and Angelina knew that riding to Crimea to participate in pro-Ukraine demonstrations wasn't going to make a difference when it came to Russia's spurious vote for Crimea to join the Russian Federation. However, any civil disobedience would at least remind the foreign press—and the world—that people other than Russians lived in Crimea. In fact, put together, Ukrainians and Tatars represented more than a third of Crimea's population, and neither group wanted to be part of Putin's "Novorossiya." Factor in the ethnic Russians that wanted to stay with Ukraine as well, and Moscow's "Crimea is Russian" story looked even shakier. That message had to get out, and Ukrainian residents of Crimea who might not want to incur the wrath of their Russian neighbors needed as much support as possible.

But riding into Crimea came with substantial risk. The so-called pro-Russian "self-defense" groups that had set up checkpoints into and throughout Crimea were not exactly restrained when it came to their contempt for Ukrainian activists. Also, Crimean police were not likely to protect them as the authorities were heavily pro-Russian.

In fact, by the time Danilo and Angelina decided to travel into Crimea at least five Ukrainian journalists and activists had gone missing in Crimea. Some reportedly were detained, and others were completely missing—gone without a trace. No Crimean authority would confirm the missing individuals' presence in Crimea. Their cars were gone, and their mobile phones had long since gone dead. Overnight, that had become the sharp end of political activism in Crimea.

Angelina clung to Danilo's waist and pressed up against his back as he tucked down. Despite the helmets, insulated riding gear, scarves, gloves, sweaters, thick socks and boots, the pair shivered in the cold wind. In fact, Danilo had to throttle back just to keep the wind chill down.

The Kawasaki carried them southwest through Ukraine, where they would eventually reach Chongar and officially cross into Crimea. The journey would take between five and six hours not counting stops, and they weren't sure what to expect once they got there.

For now, Angelina leaned into Danilo and turned her head toward the countryside that flicked past, watching brown, tan and green fields under a cloudy, grey-blue blanket slip behind her. Field after field receded into not only past geography, but time, as well. Being with Danilo and riding into the unknown felt like passing through a portal. When she returned to Donetsk, she would be a different person.

"We are meant for each other," Danilo had told her as they lay in bed the night before after the riots.

"We are," she had confirmed.

Now Danilo was part of her life, and she was part of his, and they were both rushing at 120 kph toward Crimea. The overnight transformation of their lives was as visceral to Angelina as the acceleration of the bike.

By the time the M18 had brought them to Melitopol, the noon sun had come out, and they rejoiced in its warmth. After some riding around the town, they found a café and enjoyed a big lunch on an outdoor terrace. Bellies full, they pulled their chairs in the sun for a satisfying post-meal bask. Having arrived well after the lunch rush, they had the place to themselves.

"You know, we could always cut south and ride the coast east to Mariupol and then north to your place, or we could ride north from here to Kyiv," Danilo said as they stretched out in the sun. "You could meet my sister. She's fantastic. You'd love her."

"Are you chickening out on me?" Angelina chided.

"Sort of. I don't know how much good we'll do. The referendum is essentially a done deal and crossing into Crimea is dangerous now. Even when they let you through, they still put you through hell."

Neither of them said it out loud, but they both were thinking of Oleksandra Ryazantseva and Kateryna Butko, who had been released by the Russians after a considerable ordeal. The two young Euromaidan activists had tried to drive into Crimea on March 9 but were stopped by an armed checkpoint at the Crimean border consisting of Berkut officers working with the Russians, Cossacks, and members of a local pro-Russian militia group. Once the men had discovered a Ukrainian flag in the trunk of their car and a tattoo on Ryazantseva's arm dedicated to the "Heavenly Squad," the one hundred victims who had perished in February's sniper attacks, the situation instantly grew dangerous. The women were bound and beaten, and the men threatened to chop off Ryazantseva's tattooed arm. They were thrown into cells and eventually sent to Sevastopol where they were isolated and interrogated by the Russian military. After three days' captivity, they were freed and sent to Ukraine.

And that kind of harsh treatment wasn't reserved for activists. Journalists and even members of the Red Cross were being detained and beaten at borders. Angelina knew she and Danilo were taking a serious risk, and she was aware of Danilo's trepidation, but her cause was clear to her.

"We can't just think of the danger. The entirety of Crimea is going through hell," Angelina said. "And while we can't change the outcome of a fake election, at least we can help change the dialog in the media. Russia's propaganda can't be the only voice."

"I know. You're right. It's just that, in a way, I feel like this is riskier than getting shot at in Independence Square."

Danilo and Angelina collected themselves and got back on the bike. The afternoon ride was much more pleasant than the morning's had been. They were able to ditch their scarves and let their sunlit leather jackets keep them warm.

The Kawasaki smoothly filtered through the light, mid-afternoon traffic. Angelina held still as Danilo leaned their weight this way and that to slip between vehicles. Despite the Russian invasion and political upheaval in Crimea, cars and trucks still traveled to the peninsula. Commerce strained to maintain normality for as long as geopolitics would let it. Danilo wove a path through whatever congestion cropped up, and kept their trajectory arrow-straight when there was none. It was a beautiful feeling to travel this way, Angelina decided.

Later that afternoon, the M18 brought them in the area of Chongar. Chongar was a tiny town that sat on one of three land bridges that connected Crimea with Ukraine. A modern, raised motorway bridge allowed the M18 to pass over a narrow strait of water. An older causeway bridge passed over the water directly to the south of that bridge, perhaps 50 meters away.

Angelina could feel their momentum abruptly slow as Danilo sat a little more upright in the saddle as he braked.

He reached up with his clutch hand and lifted his helmet visor to talk. She raised hers, as well.

"Looks like we're here," he yelled over the wind and engine noise.

Danilo was slowing the bike as the cars and the trucks on the road queued up at a checkpoint that had been established by Ukrainian forces. A small concrete building at the side of the road sat between two rows of sandbag barriers that blocked the flow of traffic. Next to the building sat an eight-wheeled armored personnel carrier. Ukraine's blue and yellow flag flew from both the APC and the building. About two dozen Ukrainian soldiers milled around the building and checkpoint. All of them were armed.

Danilo and Angelina waited in line, revving, then stopping, revving, then stopping. Eventually, they made their way to a Ukrainian soldier at the sandbag barriers who held his hand for them to stop.

"Heading into Crimea?" The soldier asked.

"Yes," Danilo answered.

"Where are you coming from?"

"Donetsk."

"Why are you traveling? Surely you know what's going on in Crimea."

"I do. But my girlfriend's sister in Sevastopol is ill, and we're the only ones that can get down there to care for her," Danilo lied

"Is this true?" the soldier asked, turning to Angelina.

"Yes," Angelina also fibbed, confirming the cover story she and Danilo had cooked up while planning their trip. "She has cancer is and is going through chemotherapy."

"Okay, look, traveling into and around Crimea — let alone right before this crazy vote — is a bad idea. I understand your reasons, and I am going to let you go through this checkpoint, but I have to warn you that you might have some difficulty getting back into Ukraine, okay?"

The two nodded. The soldier continued.

"Down there, you can see the traffic lining up again."

The soldier pointed to a spot about a quarter kilometer away.

"That is the Russian checkpoint. Various people man the crossing, and not all of them are real military men. In fact, a lot of them are pretty nervous and wound up civilians with guns. You've probably already heard that they have been detaining reporters and activists and others. Answer their questions straightforwardly and do not act nervous. Do you understand?"

"Yes," the two chorused.

"Okay. Be safe."

The soldier waved Danilo and Angelina through, and Danilo put the bike into gear and took off. Almost instantly they were in another line of cars and trucks as they approached the Russian checkpoint.

Pro-Russian militia members and Berkut officers had assembled the border crossing out of concrete motorway partitions, sandbags, and old car and truck tires. Armed men in various forms of camouflage, almost all of them masked, stood behind the barriers or paced up and down the road. Camouflaged men walked in and out of several one-story buildings that sat on the north side of the road. A Russian tri-color flag flew over their checkpoint. Several Russian PAV Tigrs and a pair of armored personnel carriers were lined up at the side of the road on the Crimean side of the inspection area. The bridge leading into Crimea extended beyond them.

Again, Danilo and Angelina inched toward the border as the traffic in front of them slowly passed through the checkpoint. One by one the cars and trucks passed through the crossing. The wait would have been monotonous if it wasn't for the butterflies in Angelina's stomach that were pushing her to the point of nausea. The vibration of the idling motorcycle didn't help.

Suddenly, there was yelling at the front of the line. Berkut special police officers—Russia had integrated the Crimean Berkut units into its Internal Affairs Ministry—were shouting and brandishing their weapons at a small white car at the head of the line. They yanked the doors open and pulled three men from the vehicle. The officers forced the men to lay face down on the pavement with their arms and legs splayed outward. They handcuffed the men and jerked them to their feet, leading them toward one of the buildings as another man in a tall, Cossack-style cap and green camouflage got behind the wheel of the car and pulled it to the side of the road.

Angelina held Danilo tightly.

After a half-hour pause caused by the chaos, the line of cars and trucks resumed inching forward. It was early evening now, and the light was fading. There was nothing to do except advance toward the checkpoint. To Angelina, it felt like they were riding a canoe toward a waterfall. She kept hearing the yelling of the officers and picturing those men pulled from the car while the officers aimed their rifles at them.

Finally, it was Danilo and Angelina's turn to be questioned at the border.

A Berkut officer in a black mask, black bulletproof vest, blue-grey camouflage fatigues and an AK-74M slung across his midsection motioned for them to stop. They did. Danilo put both feet on the ground but kept his hand on the clutch. Angelina realized the bike was still in gear.

"Where are you from?" the officer asked.

"Donetsk," Danilo answered.

"Where are you traveling?"

"Sevastopol."

"Why are you traveling?"

"We are traveling to take care of my girlfriend's ill sister."

"What's the matter with your sister?" the Berkut officer asked Angelina

"Cancer," Angeline replied. "She's going through chemotherapy and needs help."

"Cancer, eh?" the masked man muttered as he stepped back and surveyed Danilo's bike.

"Then what the hell is that?" he asked, pointing to something on the rear of the motorcycle.

Danilo realized what it was almost instantly, and wanted to smack himself in the forehead for his stupidity.

He and Angelina had been so careful: They had concocted a believable cover story. They had been sure to pack nothing overtly indicative of their activism. They even went so far as to clean up Angelina's laptop and phone, removing anything related to her pro-unity advocacy.

But there was one thing that completely slipped their mind: a sticker — a simple, stupid, forgettable sticker. The decal was a five-pointed star colored in the yellow and blue of the Ukrainian flag that Danilo had affixed to his left pannier several months ago when he had first bought the motorcycle. Before the Euromaidan. Before Angelina.

"What's what?" Danilo played dumb.

"That star!" the officer sternly replied.

"Oh, that. Just some sticker the guy who owned the bike

before me put on there. I've been trying to figure out a way to get it off without scratching the luggage box."

"Bullshit. Get off the fucking bike."

The officer took a step closer and motioned to two nearby Berkut officers to move in.

"What?" Danilo said in a combination of pretend and genuine surprise.

Angelina could barely breathe; the fear was akin to drowning. She fought an instinctive drive to hop off the motorcycle and run like hell toward the Ukrainian checkpoint back up the road.

One of the two approaching officers began circling toward their right side while the other walked forward, reaching out to the motorcycle's handlebars.

"Relax, everyone. Let's clear this up," Danilo said as he moved his throttle hand toward the keys to switch the bike off.

Instead, he simultaneously let the clutch out and jerked his right hand to grab the throttle, letting the bike's forward momentum scoot the seat back under him. Continuing the motion, he twisted the throttle and torpedoed the Versys between the two Berkut policemen. In a microsecond he gunned the bike onto the right median along the outside of the barriers on the road, catching the Russians completely off guard.

"What are you doing?" Angelina screamed.

"Hang on and don't panic!" he yelled.

Angelina clung to his waist like a steel cable.

As the various camouflaged men furiously grabbed for their weapons, Danilo sent the motorcycle down the slope extending off the southern side of the road and caught a pair of dirt tracks that led to the old, concrete causeway road that paralleled the M18 bridge.

They were flying now. The motorcycle screamed. Danilo redlined through the gears at an incredible pace, doing everything he could to keep the motorcycle's front tire on the ground. They were flying across the causeway. Angelina doubted that ten seconds had passed since the moment Danilo gunned the Kawasaki around the checkpoint.

The first shots rang out. They were distant and sounded to Angelina more like factory machinery than guns. The noise echoed off the pavement and against the structure of the bridge above.

Ka-krack-echo-echo-echo! Ka-krack-echo-echo-echo! Krack-krack-krack-krack! Echo-echo-echo-echo!

"Oh my God!" she yelled.

"Don't move!" he shrieked. Their voices were a matched set of pure terror.

Danilo was weaving the bike as they rocketed across the causeway. Angelina didn't dare look back, but she imagined Berkut officers and others scurrying along the M18 bridge above them, pausing to try and get a good shot at the motorcycle that was blazing across the causeway below. While both looked forward, it was impossible not to feel phantom bullets menacing their backs.

After a few more seconds, they had crossed the causeway, and the M18 was sloping back down from the bridge and curving toward them. Danilo leaned the bike left, and they went up the slope, catching a little bit of air before slamming back down on the pavement. The adrenaline rush from the short jump surged through Angelina like a shockwave.

Now, at least for a few quick moments, the array of forces on the bridge had no line of sight to fire at them. Angelina's mind was racing faster than the Versys beneath them. They were now fugitives from just about anyone with a weapon in Crimea. How were they going to be safe? How were they going to get out? Were authorities waiting down the road? Would they be separated and questioned? Threatened? Beaten?

The light was fading fast. Danilo patted Angelina's left leg and flipped up his visor.

"We should be out of range," he yelled over the wind and engine. "Are you okay?"

"Are you out of your mind?" She yelled back.

Danilo let the question hang in the air. He felt equal parts stupid and crazy for doing what he did. He also remembered what happened to Oleksandra Ryazantseva and Kateryna Butko.

"Yes—I guess I'm alright. I'm not shot." Angeline yelled after a pause.

Despite the warm evening air, she shivered with adrenaline.

"We have to get off this road and onto smaller roads before these guys start using their radios. Otherwise, we'll be cornered in minutes. What's the next town?"

"Dzhankoy."

"Alright then, we have to get off the road before Dzhankoy. Once we do that, we can come up with a plan."

Angelina had become almost numb from the uncertainty of their situation. The ground below and sky above felt as foreign as if they were on Mars. She was simultaneously mad at Danilo for panicking, grateful to him for making their escape, and irretrievably in love with him all at the same time. More than anything, she felt dumbstruck—and overwhelmed by the unavoidable feeling that she was never going to get out of Crimea.

Chapter 14
LESSON LEARNED

"The captain will see you now," the aide said to Viktor.

Viktor was waiting in a two-story collection of office suites in an industrial park situated near Dzhankoy's railyards. Most of the suites weren't being leased, so the landlord didn't complain too long, or too loudly when the Russian military silently appropriated the offices to conduct the area command's administrative tasks.

The offices exuded a distinctly non-military feel. Eliminate the camouflage fatigues and the fact that everyone was armed, and Viktor felt like he could have been going to visit an accountant.

Or the school principal. The captain had summoned Viktor for his report on yesterday's foolishness involving Dimitry Lebel and the old Tatar man named Iskandar

Nabiyev. Viktor didn't regret his actions, but he still had to answer for why he left his post to investigate.

Viktor walked across the waiting area and opened the door to the captain's office.

"You wanted to see me, sir," Viktor said.

"Yes, Belov," Captain Lukyanov instructed without looking up from a laptop. "Come in and close the door behind you."

Viktor did so and stood at attention.

"At ease, sergeant," Captain Lukyanov said, continuing to type away.

The captain stabbed at the keyboard for a few moments longer, appeared to look over what he had just written, and clicked the button above his trackpad. The middle-aged officer was shortish, and a little pudgy, and the flanks of his crewcut were starting to gray.

"Okay, you know why you're here, Belov," the captain said. "You left your post."

Viktor nodded.

"Please explain to me why you left your post."

Viktor knew all about the captain's unique approach to dressing down his staff—he didn't. Instead, he made junior officers and NCOs explain precisely why and how they had behaved stupidly. The seemingly benign, almost fatherly approach was agonizing, and in many respects far worse than getting chewed out.

"The civilian Dimitry Lebel alleged a bomb plot, and I felt it best to check out his allegation to determine its validity," Viktor replied. The second he uttered the statement, he regretted it, because he knew any explanation was essentially a dodge from owning up to a major fuck-up on his part.

"Go on," the captain said.

Viktor then related the events of Dimitry Lebel's goose chase and his final instruction to the oafish local supporter to not waste his squad's time and to essentially stay the hell out of the way during the referendum. Viktor tried to keep his retelling concise and factual, much like his report.

Once Viktor finished his account, Captain Lukyanov leaned back a bit in his chair and tented his fingers, looking past Viktor for a considerable bit of time. Then he turned his eyes toward Viktor's.

"Sergeant Belov, why didn't you radio headquarters about Lebel's allegations the moment he told you?" the captain pointedly queried.

Viktor fumbled for the right words.

"I … didn't think his story would pan out, and I didn't want to waste headquarters' time," Viktor finally replied.

"What, are you a human lie detector?" the captain admonished.

"No, sir."

"Are you psychic, sergeant? Can you read minds?"

"No, sir. It's just that …"

"Go on."

"Well, I can't find a better way to put this, except to say that I believe Lebel is a drunk and unreliable. I didn't want to waste command's time on a snipe hunt. And it did turn out that Lebel's story was a bunch of false allegations."

"And what if his story turned out to be true?"

"Sir?"

"A broken clock is still right twice a day, Belov. What if Lebel's story panned out? What would you have done?"

"I'm not sure."

"Well let's take the scenario through its paces, shall we, sergeant?"

Viktor nodded.

"You took Private Markov with you, correct?"

Viktor nodded.

"Is either one of you trained in explosives? Is either of you trained in bomb disposal? What about bomb detection?"

"No, sir. None of those," Viktor said.

"Yet you decided to search a home for explosives. Let's say you found one. What then? How would you prevent the terrorist from setting it off, killing you, the private, Mr. Lebel, and probably himself in the process?"

"I … don't know, sir."

"How would that have looked if the Western media that's crawling around here got hold of that news, sergeant? Right before the referendum?"

"I don't know, sir."

"Correct. You don't know."

Viktor felt microscopic. He was sure he even smelled stupid at this point.

The captain let the lesson sink in a good while. After roughly thirty, very agonizing seconds he spoke up again.

"Sergeant, who gave you permission to leave your post?"

"No one, sir."

"Look, Viktor, I allow you guys a certain level of autonomy out there," the captain said. "I do that because you're all well-trained, smart, capable soldiers. I consider all my men the best at what they do, and I think you are one of the best of the best among them. But you exhibited terrible judgment out there yesterday. Phenomenally terrible. I know your checkpoint is barely trafficked. Hell, I would have been tempted to follow-up on that story out of sheer boredom if I had been in your shoes. But the key word is 'tempted.' I wouldn't have given in to it. Your job is to ensure that checkpoint does what it is supposed to do: check traffic heading toward the radar station. Your job is not to investigate bomb threats—especially ones that are probably false."

"Yes, sir. I'm sorry; it won't happen again, sir."

"I know it won't," Captain Lukyanov resolved. "Now, another thing: Dimitry Lebel."

"Yes, sir?"

"Dimitry Lebel is a fat, drunken asshole."

Viktor fought like Hercules to keep a straight face.

"But he's our fat, drunken asshole. We need the local self-defense groups—or whatever the hell they want to call themselves—to be the public face of order in Crimea. We must support local Russians any way we can to ensure it is clear who is in charge. The Western media are having a difficult time confirming who we are, so we must show that the Dimitry Lebels of the world are in control—regardless of whether or not they actually are. Crimea's separation and referendum must look as homegrown as possible. Do you understand?"

Viktor nodded. "Yes, captain," he said.

"Good," the captain continued. "So when it comes to Lebel, your goal is to keep him appearing in control without making him feel like you're undermining him. Let him strut around in his surplus uniform. As long as he doesn't mess up law and order or interfere with the vote, we should be okay. I don't need him to come whining to me when his feelings get hurt like he did this morning. It was fucking embarrassing."

"I understand, sir," Viktor replied. He'd have to tell Sasha that Lebel tattled like a schoolboy.

"Good," the captain replied. "Okay. Good. ... Look, don't feel too bad about your screw-up and leaving your checkpoint. We all make mistakes. Especially when we're bored. Just stick to your assignments. I'll try to give your squad more opportunities to patrol the town so that you get some more breaks from staring at those fields all day."

"Thank you, sir. I know I speak for the entire squad when I say we'd appreciate that."

"Great. Okay. Now I need to check on something that's an entirely different matter: You're aware of the border checkpoint breach at Chongar, correct?"

"Yes, sir. We received the update—a man and a woman on a green and black motorcycle with Ukrainian flag stickers on it broke through yesterday evening."

"Correct. I have no idea what that is. It could be serious trouble, or it could be that they got spooked by the Berkut or Cossacks. Those guys can be pretty heavy-handed. Either way, you're manning a checkpoint, so you need to have your squad keep an eye out for fugitives."

"Yes, sir. Absolutely, sir."

"Good," the captain replied. "If you come across them, the orders are to arrest, detain and report at all costs. Do not fire unless fired upon. ... Okay, before you take off, you and your team are clear on your duties for guarding the polling station tomorrow, correct?"

"Yes. Set up a wide perimeter around the station and keep an eye out for trouble," Viktor said. "The goal is to not obstruct the flow of foot traffic in and out of the poll but to observe for actual security problems. Local authorities will have control of the actual polling station and are responsible for quelling any protests or anything like that."

"Correct. Excellent. Okay, sergeant, it looks like by the end of tomorrow, you and I will be one step closer to being back home. You're dismissed."

"Yes, sir. Thank you, sir."

Viktor left the building and began his trip in the Tigr back to Checkpoint Anna. As he drove through Dzhankoy proper, he wondered about tomorrow's vote. It was a certainty that Crimea would vote to separate and become part of Russia—especially considering who was in charge of the referendum—but how would things change once Russia tallied all the ballots? Would the buildings and fields look or at least feel any more Russian than they did now? Would the people act differently?

Viktor decided to put those musings in the back of his mind and concentrated on the drive. The roads felt simultaneously familiar and foreign, and all this talk about Russia was magnifying his desire to get back to his wife and his home.

Chapter 15
HOSPITALITY WITH A HATCHET

Danilo blinked into the slice of blue-crystal dawn light that was streaming through the crack in the doorway and cutting across his previously sleeping face. He was completely confounded as to where he was until he stretched his hand out to block the early morning sun so that he could survey his surroundings. He and the still-sleeping Angelina lay on a half-unrolled canvas tarp that protected them from the dirt floor of a small structure built of wood. The panniers from the motorcycle were stacked next to a bag of potting soil and some gardening tools.

Danilo's memory returned to him. The structure was a small shed that stood behind an old farm on the outskirts of Dzhankoy. As they were escaping on the motorcycle, he concluded that if they took the smaller and more remote roads, they'd more likely go undetected. While the Berkut and Russian forces would be looking for a man and a woman flying down the M18 on a green Kawasaki, he and Angelina would find a spot to hide and determine their next steps. So he kept turning onto smaller and smaller roads.

Eventually, they ended up riding south on a half-dirt, half-gravel road in the middle of a network of farms to the west of Dzhankoy. There was enough grass growing in broken spots in the old lane that Danilo figured they were as off-the-map as they could get. When they neared a tangle of half-dead olive trees situated about twenty yards to the west of the road, Danilo decided to cut the engine and coast along in the moonlight until they were parallel to the knot of scrubby old trees.

Danilo steadied the bike while Angelina hopped off. She removed her helmet and finally let out the fear and frustration that she must have been overcome with since he raced out of the checkpoint.

"What the hell were you thinking?" She demanded.

"I'm sorry. I panicked," he said. "As soon as the guy told me to get off the bike, I started thinking about what happened to those guys in front of us, and I remembered what happened to Oleksandra Ryazantseva and Kateryna Butko, and I didn't want that to happen to you."

"Well, now we're fugitives, which is even worse! The Russians and the Cossacks and all these other armed thugs probably think were spies now."

"I know… I know… I fucked up."

"Danilo — they were shooting at us!"

"I know. I don't know what to say. Weren't you scared when he told us to get off, too?"

Angelina paused to consider the question.

"Yes … Of course," she said. "I have to admit that I was

thinking the same things you were. I wanted to run, too. But that doesn't mean we should've, Danilo."

"I'm sorry. Please forgive me. I'm crazy about you. I'm feeling like the world's biggest moron for putting you in this danger. Please forgive me. Please. I'll figure out a way to get us out of this."

"I forgive you, but understand this: we will figure out a way out of this mess together. Save the unilateral decision-making for guys like Putin."

Danilo let out a laugh and smiled at Angelina, but she wasn't going to let him off the hook so easily.

"Now, is there a reason you pulled off the road? Did we run out of gas or something?" she asked.

Danilo's face resumed a more chastened expression.

"Well, look over there, to the east," he said. "I don't know if you can make it out, but beyond the field, there are a few small structures over there. I thought we could hide the bike among these trees over here, and then see if we can hide there at least for the night."

"Won't someone find the motorcycle?"

"I don't think so. It doesn't look like anyone uses this road much."

"Why not just keep riding?"

"Well, I think if we can get off the main roads for at least for a few hours, we will confuse our pursuers. There are a probably a hundred different farm roads crisscrossing this part of Crimea, so the Russians and everyone else will have a tough time determining where we were headed and which road we picked to get there. And in the meantime, we can use the GPS to figure out a way to get home. It might even be a good idea to ditch the bike and helmets and find some other way back. Maybe a train?"

"Leave the motorcycle?"

"Well, it's not ideal, but if it gets us out of trouble … yes. I can leave it." Suggesting that they leave the bike behind made Danilo die a little inside, even if he knew it was the right thing. "What do you think?"

"I think it's a good idea, as long as no one realizes where we are hiding. Dzhankoy is a pretty big town. I'm sure they have a train station or a bus line or something, but I think we'll need to lay low. They're going to be looking for a young man and young woman from Ukraine, won't they?"

"Good point. Well, why don't we hide the bike and rest for a bit? Then we can figure out our next steps."

"Okay. I actually think we'll get out of here."

And with that, Angelina walked over to Danilo and gave him a hug and a peck on the cheek. Despite the terrifying situation in which they found themselves. Immense relief washed over Danilo.

They pushed the trusty motorcycle over the rough ground toward the small grouping of trees; Danilo with his hands on the bars and Angelina pushing from behind. The darkness, washboard-bumpy earth, the overgrown grass, and the weight of the motorcycle made the trip to the cluster of olive trees the longest twenty yards either of them had ever walked, but eventually, they found themselves standing in the midst of the tree trunks.

Danilo turned off the gas on the motorcycle and ran the engine until it faltered so that he was sure he had run the gas out of the fuel line. Then he killed the bike and walked into the thickest part of the overgrown grass and tree trunks. There, Danilo and Angelina removed the panniers, carefully laid the Kawasaki on its side and set the helmets beside it. Then they collected some branches and clumps of dead grass and covered the motorcycle and helmets. Despite the lack of decent light, they decided the bike was well hidden and set out across the field toward the farm buildings, carrying the panniers with them.

Quickly jogging along a low stone fence and the edge of a field, they made their way as discretely as possible until they came upon a small barn, some kind of chicken coop or animal cage, and a green shed. The three structures sat behind a small farmhouse and were bordered to the north by a stand of trees.

Danilo tried to open the barn.

"It's locked," he whispered to Angelina.

"This shed is open," she replied and motioned him to come to her.

She opened the door and they both went in. Danilo carefully closed the door behind him.

"Well, the inside looks okay," Angelina said. "Let's sleep here for a few hours and come up with a plan."

"Okay. If something happens, we should make for the motorcycle."

"I'd rather not think about that, but … okay."

They tucked the panniers in the corner. Danilo found a green, plastic tarp and rolled it out on the ground carefully and quietly. They lay down together, spooning for warmth despite their leather jackets and sweaters.

"Don't get any ideas, Cassanova," Angelina said. "I'm still pretty mad at you."

"I'm too tired to have any ideas."

And with that, they both fell utterly unconscious.

*

A blinking Danilo realized he was still in the shed, but that it was now morning. He tried prodding Angelina awake. After a few tries, she began stirring and sat up.

"Where—mmmph?"

Danilo had put his hand over her mouth.

"We are in the cabin we found last night," he whispered into her ear. "If you need to say something, talk quietly."

They looked around at the shed in the morning light. It could be a backyard shed anywhere in the world: rakes, shovels, tools, hand trimmers, paint cans, planting supplies, and the like. All were well used. Angelina stood up and peaked through the crack in the door.

"I don't see anyone out there," she said. "The sun's barely up. We should get out of here."

"Right," Danilo agreed. "We should roll up the tarp to hide the fact that we've been here."

As they rolled the plastic sheet, Danilo thought out loud. "I can't decide if we should ditch our jackets or not. We can be easily identified wearing them, but they sure kept us warm last night."

"Let's hide them with the motorcycle," Angelina suggested. "We can double up on sweaters. We should probably get rid of the panniers, too."

"You're right. I have a backpack rolled up in there," Danilo said, kneeling down to open one of the luggage boxes. "We can carry the necessities in that."

"Good idea—hold on. Shhh," Angelina put her finger to her mouth. The sound of a creaking door spring came from the house. They heard footsteps coming toward the shed. Angelina froze. Danilo quickly scanned the structure and grabbed a hatchet. They exchanged worried glances and then fixed their attention on the door.

The footsteps grew louder and then stopped. The door shook and then quickly opened. Danilo and Angelina tried to get a good look at their foe, but the morning light blinded them.

"Ah, I thought I heard visitors," a small voice said as

Danilo and Angelina's eyes adjusted. "This shed certainly is getting a lot of company these days." They could make out the figure of an old man, very lean and wearing a grey jacket and brown pants. He had a slight mustache and grey hair at the temples of his balding head.

"I'll be needing that hatchet, young man," the old man said. "That is, if you want to have any tea."

Danilo and Angelina were dumbfounded.

"You look like you're afraid," the old man continued. "My guess is you're in hiding."

The old man was pointing to one of the panniers; the one labeled with the blue-and-yellow sticker. Danilo hadn't noticed before, but it had a bullet hole in one corner. He immediately felt his stomach sink. That was much too close for comfort. Angelina could have been shot.

"You can relax," the man in the doorway advised. "I can assure you anyone being pursued by the Russians is safe with me. You should have knocked on my back door. I have an extra bed and a sofa you could have used. Anyway, I should introduce myself. My name is Iskandar Nabiyev, and you are in my shed, on my property, and are still holding my axe. I'll have to ask once more you to give that back. My hospitality only goes so far."

The old man held out his hand to Danilo and gestured for the hatchet. Danilo shook off his fear and confusion and offered the hand axe handle-first to Iskandar. Iskandar smiled and took it.

"I'm sorry," Danilo said.

"No need," Iskandar replied. "Now tell me your names and join me for tea."

Danilo and Angelina introduced themselves and followed Iskandar out of the shed and up the stairs at the back of the farmhouse. An old, yet well cared-for samovar sat on the stoop. The aging farmer handily used the hatchet to chop small bits of kindling from a log and place them into the samovar.

As Iskandar started the fire to boil the water and prepared the teapot, the couple related their story. They told him about the riot in Donetsk, the snap decision to go to Crimea, the fiasco at the border crossing, their panicked ride through the farm roads, and how they came to sleep in his shed.

Eventually, they moved inside, and sat around Iskandar's dining table. He told them about the recent events in Crimea, the strange Russian soldiers who refused to acknowledge they were Russian soldiers, the increasingly aggressive Dimitry Lebel, and how many Ukrainians and nearly all Tatars were refusing to participate in the sham referendum.

After a while, the conversation paused and they continued sipping their tea. This was the first time Danilo felt genuinely relaxed since lazing in the afternoon sun at that café in Melitopol. Angelina smiled and spoke.

"You have been too kind," she said. "Thank you. We'll try to be out of your house after nightfall."

"Yes," Danilo agreed. "We shouldn't be putting you at risk. You've been unnecessarily generous."

"Nonsense," Iskandar replied. "This is my house and my hospitality. I'll decide when you've worn out your welcome."

"But—" Angelina tried to reply.

"No, I insist," the old man cut her off. "Truly, I insist. I am not happy the Russians have invaded. I have been at the sharp end of Russian 'hospitality' before, and it ended in decades of misery for me, my family, and hundreds of thousands of people like us. So, to see two young people put themselves at risk to come here and protest what the Russians and their collaborators are doing in Crimea gives me much hope—and much heart. I admire your spirit. You are my guests and I am honored to have you."

The old man freshened everyone's cup with more of his potent brew. Danilo noted that the small cups gave off steam that smelled like the region's history—a natural mingling of east and west.

Iskandar continued talking.

"You will need to stay out of sight for a while. The longer you can do that, the more likely the special police and the Russians will get distracted from the search. Then, when enough time has passed, you should be able to leave for Ukraine in relative anonymity. How you'll pass the border is another question, but I suggest that you stay with me for the next few days."

"Are you sure?" Danilo asked. "You're taking a significant risk."

"No, I don't think that I am. I'm an old man who lives on his own. No one is going to think that I'm harboring any fugitives—especially a young couple in leather jackets riding a motorcycle. ... You're not exactly my style."

The three of them chuckled.

"Don't people visit your home though?" Angelina asked.

"The only people who look in on me from time to time are my Imam and his son, and sometimes my children. Also, as I mentioned, that drunken oaf I told you about comes by to harass me every once in a while until I make him feel foolish enough, but then he goes home to drink some more."

"I wouldn't want to risk running into him," Danilo replied.

"Don't worry about him. He's mean, and he has his

craftier moments, but he's already made a recent visit to harass me, so I don't think he will return for several days."

"I think the idea of hiding for a little while to confuse the Russians makes a lot of sense," Angelina said. "I think this is safe, Danilo. Let's do it."

"Agreed," Danilo replied. "Mr. Nabiyev I have to admit that I worry about getting you in trouble."

"Don't. You are safe and so am I, and I am only too happy to know that in some small way, I am driving these dogs crazy with frustration. ... So it's settled then? You're staying?"

Danilo and Angelina nodded to Iskandar.

"Excellent. You're doing the right thing. Later, tonight, we shall go to the old road and collect your motorcycle, and hide it in the barn. In the meantime, who's for more tea?"

Chapter 16
VODKA AND WORRY

"I'm all right."

That's all Danilo's text message said.

How could three words so forcefully and completely convey the exact opposite of their intended meaning? No one ever texts the statement "I'm all right" when they're truly all right. Something was very clearly wrong—all wrong.

Veronika was convinced of that by the second text she received from her little brother: "Do not try to call me."

Veronika's spiral of worry only deepened upon reading Danilo's third and final text: "Do not try to contact me or respond to this message. My phone might be monitored. Watch your phone instead. I will send messages when I can. Do not do anything to reach me. I will be okay."

What the hell was going on? Who sends cryptic texts with instructions about contacting them — let alone the fact that the Berkut or Russians might be monitoring his phone — unless he was in serious trouble?

The messages made her feel even worse than when she watched her brother ducking sniper fire during the February 20 sniper attacks. The danger that day in Independence Square was known — terrifying but at least comprehensible. But these vague messages? Who knew what was happening to Danilo?

Fifteen minutes after the third message, Veronika now sat up in bed, staring at her phone, waiting for another message. It never came. She turned and looked out of her bedroom window at the lights of Kyiv. Though the referendum happening the next morning in Crimea was far away, there was still some bustle below her apartment in Independence Square — there was always activity in what had become such an important place. While there was an effort to clean up the barriers, many shelters and stands still stood as testimony and celebration to the Euromaidan protests.

Often, an old, upright piano painted in the yellow and blue of the Ukrainian flag with a semi-circle of EU-style stars emblazoned on the fallboard would attract some late-night pianist. On those nights, music would rise up from the rickety instrument and swell across the square, evoking those nights when musically inclined Euromaidan activists — often with their faces obscured by balaclavas or kerchiefs — would peel off their gloves, sit in front of the faithful instrument, and serenade their fellow protestors in the face of Yanukovych's menacing special police.

But no one played that night. Veronika's phone was quiet as well; it offered no vibration, no beep, no alert, not a single whisper from her brother. What had he gotten himself into?

After several more minutes of staring at her phone in vain, Veronika got up from her bed, put on a robe and strode into the kitchen. She opened up her freezer and pulled out a frosted bottle of Slava. The vodka poured into a shot glass with an almost silken quality. She held the small glass in her hand to warm the ice-cold spirit ever so slightly before quickly slinging the contents in her mouth. She let the drink linger on her tongue for a moment before swallowing.

Tonight was unquestionably one of those moments where a drink might calm her nerves enough to help her think straight.

Or not. After sitting at the table for a few more minutes and another slug, Veronika was still at a loss as to what to do. She needed help, and it wasn't long before her fingers flicked across her phone. She knew she shouldn't be calling anyone at this hour, but she had to.

"Hello?" a voice on the other end of the line groggily muttered.

"Alina, it's me, Veronika. I'm sorry to be calling — I know it's late — but I think Danilo is in trouble and I don't know what to do."

"What? Who's this?" It was clear Alina was still partially asleep.

"It's Veronika. I think Danilo is in trouble. Can you help me, Alina?"

"What? ... Oh! Veronika. I'm sorry. It's just so late. ... Or is it early? I wasn't expecting a call. What's the matter?"

"I need your help. I'm worried about Danilo."

"Is he okay? Has he wrecked his motorcycle?"

"No crash I don't think, but I don't think he is okay. He's

been sending me strange text messages. Can you come over?"

"I'm on my way. Give me a half-hour or so."

Within 30 minutes the two women were sitting on Veronika's couch. Veronika was sobbing into Alina's shoulder.

"It's okay," Alina reassured. "We'll figure this out."

"I don't know what to think — what could be happening to Danilo?" Veronika said in a breathless rush of words.

"Don't worry. We'll figure this out. Tell me what you know."

Veronika told Alina how Danilo had informed her that he was heading to meet Angelina in Donetsk. She recounted how she had scolded her brother for walking into what was undoubtedly a dangerous situation, and that there were sure to be pro-Russian thugs gearing up to attack the protest. And, sure enough, as she had found out in a phone call later that night, they had been involved in a street battle. Fortunately, they were able to escape to Angelina's apartment.

But that had been on Thursday, and then she hadn't heard from him until the cryptic texts that had arrived forty-five minutes ago.

"I agree that the text sounds bad," Alina said. "You only try to reassure people when you know they're going to worry about you. You don't pile it on."

"Exactly," Veronika said.

"And the bit about being monitored and not to contact him …"

"I know! I don't know what to do."

"Well, let's think. Where could Danilo be?"

"That's just it. If they were in Donetsk, he wouldn't be texting like that. No one in Donetsk would be monitoring his phone. It doesn't make sense."

"He has to be someplace where he isn't safe and where someone would have the capability to tap into his phone."

The two sat quietly for a minute, both women weighing the possibilities and mentally mapping Danilo's probable whereabouts.

"Crimea," Veronika said after a long pause.

"Why would Danilo go to Crimea?"

"Well, he and Angelina are pretty idealistic. The Russian referendum is tomorrow. Maybe the two of them thought they could do something about it."

"That's insane."

"My little brother's head is at least fifty percent full of bad ideas. Maybe even one hundred percent."

Alina tried to suppress a laugh, but a giggle sputtered out. Veronika immediately gave her a cross gaze, but it was no use; she couldn't contain her laughter, either. Still, while Veronika laughed, her eyes filled with tears.

"Look at me," Veronika said. "I'm a mess. I don't know whether to laugh or cry about my silly, stupid little brother."

"It's okay, dear. Look, we know Danilo hasn't been arrested or seriously hurt, because then he wouldn't have been able to text. It's obvious that he's in a bad situation, but he doesn't want you to worry, because at least at some basic level he is okay."

"That's true," Veronika acknowledged. Alina's point helped a little.

"And," Alina continued. "I think you could be right about Crimea. Of the all the places where he might be concerned about the use of his phone, that would be it. The Russians control nearly all of Crimea at this point, and once they've pretended to count the phony votes in their made-up referendum, they will control it entirely. Who else would be monitoring people's calls?"

"Crimea," Veronika said to herself, internally confirming her brother's location.

"Crimea," Alina echoed.

"If he's there and he has Angelina with him, I'll wring his scrawny neck. He should not be jeopardizing that girl. She is far too sweet for my lunkhead brother to be putting at risk."

The two women laughed again and then sat quietly on the couch for some time. Veronika poured them each a shot of Slava, and each sipped at her small glass and considered what to do next. Down in the square, someone began playing the old piano. The tune wasn't familiar, but the melody was soft and serene. Veronika wiped her eyes with a tissue and spoke up.

"Alina, I need to borrow your car. Will you lend it to me?"

"My car? To fetch Danilo? You want to drive my car to Crimea?"

"Yes. Well near it, at least."

"Veronika, you're my friend. You know you can borrow my car any time you like, but this is crazy. How are you going to find your brother in all of Crimea? You don't even know for sure that he's there."

"But maybe if I can get close to Crimea—and perhaps inside—he'll text me again so that I can get a better idea of where he is. Then I'll be close enough to rescue them. Chances are he—or they, if he's brought Angelina along—will be on that motorcycle and need some less recognizable form of transportation."

"Oh Veronika, this doesn't feel good to me. It's not the car I'm worried about; it's you."

"I don't feel too great about it, either, but unlike my brother, I will keep my phone on at all times so that you can contact me. And if you get too nervous about your car, or about me, I'll give you veto power. You can call me home if you ever get too worried."

Alina mulled over the idea for a few minutes. She signaled her agreement with a nod. Veronika leaned forward and hugged her.

"Thank you," she said, her eyes getting wet again. "Thank you. I don't know what else to say except thank you."

"You don't have to say it," Alina replied. "Find your brother and his girlfriend and get back to Kyiv before Putin locks up the entire Peninsula. I predict bad things for Crimea—soon."

"They're already happening, I'm afraid."

Less than two hours after packing and dropping Alina back at her place, Veronika was heading south on the M05 in Alina's Hyundai. It would be dawn soon, and a grueling, eight-hour drive stretched ahead. Veronika kept her phone plugged into the charger and glanced at its screen in hopes of seeing a new message every time she checked the dashboard. When would Danilo text her again? Would he text her at all?

There was nothing left to do but drive and hope.

Chapter 17
REFERENDUM MORNING

On March 16, 2014, slightly before 6 a.m., sunlight spread across Crimea from the east and reached between the hills and the buildings of the port city of Sevastopol like great fingers, illuminating the bay until it turned into a radiant cauldron—as though swirling, undulating light had replaced the water. Windows facing the sunrise lit up like sheets of gold, pink and orange.

Stewart had found the sight nothing short of spectacular. Unfortunately, as the day continued, neither he nor Ken saw an equally dramatic story coming from the day. They had thought drumming up something newsworthy on such a pivotal day would have been a cakewalk, but so far their efforts had yielded only crumbs.

That was surprising, given that the entirety of Crimea

was caught in the fervor and activity of Russia's hastily assembled referendum, which would determine whether or not the Black Sea peninsula would become part of Russia. Instead of the usual election day excitement, only half of the population was caught up in patriotic enthusiasm, while the other half was shrugging off the occasion with a sense of resignation.

"Half of this place is waving flags, and the other half has given up," Ken said to Stewart as they stood out front of the second polling station they had visited that morning.

Voters were streaming in and out of the post office where residents of the city could cast their ballot. Out front, several men in mismatched camouflage fatigues with Ribbons of St. George wrapped around their arms stood guard. Off to the side, several city police officers kept watch, and in a much wider perimeter, the disguised Russian soldiers maintained watch over the whole thing.

"The funny thing to me is that all the flags being waved are the same," Stewart replied.

No Ukrainian or Crimean flags were flying. Only the Russian Federation's tricolor was on display in economy-sized portions this morning. Voters were carrying small versions of the flag, and cars had plastic versions clipped to their windows. The Russian flag was even flying over the post office. To the right of the main entrance, a three-man work crew was already working at removing an emblem of the Ukrainian trident from the building.

"Seems a tad premature," Ken observed.

"I guess they figure there's no sense in pretending. We both know Crimea will be a part of Russia once all the ballots are counted."

The Tatars were boycotting the referendum, as were the majority of those who wished to remain part of Ukraine.

The general opinion of those who were opposed to becoming part of Russia was that the election was rigged and that participating in the process would lend it an air of credibility.

"Yeah, I guess it was decided the moment these guys arrived," Ken said, gesturing to the Russian soldiers, some of whom were having their photos snapped with grannies, young women and men waving Russian flags and orange-and-black striped pennants.

"Well, let's see if we can get any comments from these people," Stewart suggested, and they wandered over to voters exiting the post office.

"Excuse me, madam, may I ask you how you feel about today's election?" he asked a woman, her gray hair neatly contained by a floral headscarf. Ken stepped back a few paces to get a good shot and raised his camera.

"I feel wonderful!" The old lady beamed. "We are finally coming home—home to Russia!"

"Is that something you've always wanted?" Stewart asked.

"Well ... not necessarily. But when those fascists took over in Kyiv, I knew something had to be done. They are monsters. Do you know what the news is saying? They shot their own people and then claimed it was Russia!"

Stewart had heard about the conspiracy theory-turned-Russian propaganda that the snipers that had cut down roughly one hundred Euromaidan protesters were not Berkut police, but actually members of the Euromaidan themselves. The suggestion was that the sniper fire was a "false flag" operation designed to undermine the last remaining shreds of legitimacy the Yanukovych administration could claim so that his detractors could finally depose him.

Of course, the conspiracy story flew in the face of video evidence showing Berkut police firing rifles at Euromaidan protestors, and protestors dying, and it flew in the face of testimony from everyone that was near Independence Square that day. But the tale sounded good to those who wanted to believe it, and that's all that counted.

Thanks to Russia taking over all television on March 9, it was the only story that Crimeans, such as this older woman, were hearing. He had to hand it to the Russians; they knew the power of the press.

Worse, some of Stewart's peers in the western media were honestly buying into the rumor and regurgitating it. In the 1930s, these individuals would have been known as "useful idiots," a term allegedly coined by Lenin to describe Western journalists who were relying on Soviet sources and in turn disseminating the Soviet propaganda line to their audiences without any real fact-checking, and usually because the stories meshed with their personal biases.

Stewart preferred the expression that his Canadian partner in crime used: "a bunch of tools."

In any case, the conspiracy-theory story had resonated with the Pro-Russia camp and was bolstering the referendum's bullshit premise that voters could only pick between being ruled by fascist tyranny or Mother Russia's warm embrace.

Stewart thanked the woman, and they turned to another voter, a middle-aged man in a green down jacket with a ribbon of St. George pinned to his collar.

"Excuse me, sir, may I ask for your opinions on the election? How did you vote?"

"To join Russia, of course," the man answered. "Who wants to know?"

"I'm sorry. I'm a reporter for European media—ETN."

"Well then, Mr. Western Reporter, I will tell you why I voted: to get out from under the repression of the EU and the Americans. We must be part of Russia if we want to be free."

"Why do you feel Western governments are trying to repress Crimea?"

"They are trying to control the world! They want our gas. They want our ports. They want to trap us in IMF loans and keep us beholden to the Jew bankers who control everything in the West."

The man's tone grew louder as he continued to speak. As he did, Stewart noticed three of the men in camouflage that had been standing in front of the post office were now striding toward them.

"The West is mired in greed and perversion," the man continued. "They openly permit homosexuals to try to convert children to their disgusting ways. We cannot live like that. Someone must stand for civilization and what is right!"

Before Stewart could ask another question, one of the camouflaged men stepped between Stewart and the voter. The other two stood to Stewart's right, leering menacingly at him.

"What's the problem?" The militiaman asked. "Are you trying to disturb our polling station?"

"Not at all," Stewart replied. "I'm trying to get voters' opinions on the referendum."

"Why, so you can turn it into propaganda against us? Against Russia?"

"No, I'm just trying to cover the news."

"Cover it somewhere else, foreigner. I don't know where the hell you're from with that accent, but it's clear you're here to cause trouble."

"They want to use our words against us," the man in the green jacket charged.

"That's not true," Stewart said. "I'm just a reporter doing my job."

"Well do it elsewhere," the camouflaged man said. "Otherwise we'll smash your camera or worse."

"Come on, Ken," Stewart said. "It's time to go."

"Got it," Ken replied.

The two walked away with the pro-Russians yelling insults at their backs. Ever since the nightmare at the strange checkpoint outside the city, the two took any threat or menacing from the militiamen seriously.

"Well, whaddya wanna do now?" Ken asked.

"Let's check the next polling station," Stewart said. "I believe there is one at a city office about three blocks north."

"Sounds good."

As they trudged along the sidewalk, they encountered a familiar face: Bill Lowry, who they hadn't seen since the aftermath of the checkpoint horror show.

"Going to the polling station?" Bill asked.

"Yes," Stewart replied.

"Don't bother. The pro-Russian goons are feeling particularly surly. I almost got my ass kicked."

"Where's Vasyklo?"

"He's getting shots at a polling station over by the Admiral Hotel. I figured why bog him down with my interviewing when he can get way better shots over there."

"I hear you," Ken said.

"What about you guys? Coming from the post office? How is it down there?" Bill asked.

"Not so hot," Stewart replied. "We got a couple of good replies, but the goon squad stepped in and shut us down."

"Yup," Bill said. "These guys in camo are a real problem.

Honestly, I'm thinking about heading to a smaller town. It's easier to get out of the city now that things have calmed down, and I'm thinking Simferopol might be better. There might even be some people in the opposition willing to get out and protest in a way that would be impossible here."

"That's an excellent idea," Stewart said. "I think anyone who is still pro-Ukraine would be too scared to show themselves with all this going on." He gestured to the passing cars and people decked out in Russian tri-colors.

"Well, maybe I'll see you up there, then," Bill said. "In the meantime, I gotta go pick up Vasyklo."

"Got it. See you there," Stewart replied.

Stewart and Ken started walking back to the Best Western to get the rental car so that they could head north. They decided to check out in case they had to stay the night, but the manager assured them he'd keep their room since they had been good guests and made it a point to tip extra at the bar. After packing their gear in the back seat and stopping to get some coffee and gas up the Geely, the pair drove out of the city and headed up Highway 6.

"No checkpoints so far," Ken observed while driving.

"I think the Russians must be cracking down on that stuff, or at least giving the police and militias strict rules on how to conduct stops," Stewart replied. "Things were getting out of hand."

"Out of hand? Are you fucking kidding me? I'd say things were well beyond 'out of hand' five days ago, if you'll recall."

"Sorry. You know what I mean. The Russians had to bring these guys to heel before any more stories got out about Ukrainian women being detained and beaten, or journalists getting shot. The Kremlin can only control so much news."

"Sorry back at ya. I guess I'm still a little edgy from getting shot at."

"Why's that?"

The two laughed.

"Should we keep going north to Simferopol?" Ken asked.

"No," Stewart flatly replied.

"How come?"

"On further reflection, I think Bill's making a mistake. He's right about getting out of Sevastopol. It's too big, and the pro-Russians are dominating the day. But going to Simferopol seems like it will be the same," Stewart continued. "It's the capital city. There is no way Russia is going to allow a single Ukrainian flag to be flown there. I think we should head farther north—to Dzhankoy."

"Dzhankoy? There can't be much going on there. It's pretty small."

"Kind of small, but big enough to generate some news. That's the town where we saw that church group protesting. Remember that? Maybe it's far enough off the Russian propaganda radar that we might see some protest or dissent."

"That's a good point," Ken agreed. "Okay, let's do it. To Dzhankoy. One thing though …"

"What's that?" Stewart asked.

"I just hope we get back to Sevastopol before the hotel bar closes. This is going to be a long day."

Chapter 18
DZHANKOY GETS DICEY

"You shouldn't have sent your sister those texts," Angelina said.

She and Danilo were sitting at Iskandar Nabiyev's table while the old man was out back trimming a stand of gnarled apple trees that had seen many harvests.

Given the humdrum activity at the old man's house, one would never know it was the morning of Crimea's referendum. Iskandar explained to them how Tatars across Crimea were boycotting the vote since the referendum's outcome was a foregone conclusion.

"If I had received a text like that, I would have gone out of my mind with worry," Angelina scolded.

"I just didn't want her to start worrying if I had crashed my bike, or if I had been beaten up back in Donetsk, or something like that," Danilo explained. "I had to tell her something."

"I understand that, but I'm positive you did more harm than good. Seriously, 'my phone might be monitored?' That's a terrible thing to text someone. And besides, if you genuinely believe your phone is being monitored, don't you think that maybe you shouldn't use it at all?"

"Ughhhh ... You're right, you're right. It's just that if we go dark, my sister will go crazy over that, too."

"You're forgetting that no news is good news. If your sister wanted to know your status, she'd call or text."

Suddenly the back door in the kitchen opened.

"Danilo," Iskandar called. "I'd like your help, please. Angelina, while Danilo is helping me, could you make some lunch? There is kindling for the samovar on the back steps."

Angelina would usually be insulted by the implication that she was the natural one to cook, but Iskandar was from an entirely different era. Besides, he was giving them a safe hideout while they plotted a way to get out of Crimea without raising suspicions. But most of all, she liked the old man. He was sweet and humble while being hardy despite his years. She hoped that Danilo's aging might take a similar trajectory over time. Also, she'd be lying if she said that she didn't like to cook.

"Absolutely, Mr. Nabiyev," she replied, hoping she didn't sound too self-consciously formal trying to match his proper tone. "It would be a pleasure."

She meant it.

*

"She's a sweet girl," Iskandar remarked to Danilo as he shut the back door behind them. "You're a lucky lad to have her, you know."

"Oh, absolutely" Danilo enthusiastically confirmed. "She's marvelous."

"She reminds me of my Aysilu — my wife. She passed away seven years ago."

"I'm sorry."

"Thank you. So am I. I miss her as much today as I did when she passed. The grief is gone, but the longing remains. I know we'll be together again."

"That's a good way to think about it."

"It's the only way to think about it. Do yourself a favor, young man, and heed what I am about to tell you."

"Of course."

"Make every moment count and make every moment last. A lovely girl like that is a gift from God, and you should demonstrate your appreciation for God's gifts by treating them well. Do that, and you'll both have memories to last into the hereafter."

"I like that. I'll do it."

Iskandar stopped for a moment and looked Danilo over, which made the young man momentarily self-conscious. Satisfied with his assessment, Iskandar nodded and smiled slightly, his mustache curving upward.

"Yes, I believe you will. You strike me as genuine, Danilo. That's a good quality."

"Thank you, sir."

"You know what's another good quality?"

"What's that?"

"Industriousness! I need your help cutting up the branches I've removed from these old apple trees. My small orchard has served me well over the years, and that longevity is due in no small part to regularly pruning limbs that are no longer producing. Will you help me?"

"It's the least I can do."

Iskandar and Danilo set to their work, cutting up the various limbs the old man had removed. Much could be salvaged as kindling.

While the two worked, Danilo pondered how he and Angelina might get out of Crimea. The hope of engaging in any activism had evaporated the second the two of them had jumped the border checkpoint, and their fugitive status had him worried. Angelina had told him the notion that the Russians or any other authorities in Crimea would be monitoring cell phone traffic was far-fetched to the point of paranoia, but he wasn't so sure.

If Russia had taken control of Crimea's infrastructure, Danilo assumed that it could, and probably would, monitor texts being sent to and from Ukraine—especially if a pair of Ukrainians had broken their way through a checkpoint and were currently in hiding. *Won't the Russians want to know what a couple Ukrainian super spies are plotting? Even if all we wanted to do was wave a couple of flags during the referendum?*

So, if Russia monitored for that kind of activity, then it could probably track down their general location using either information from the mobile phone network or Internet addresses. It made him worry that Angelina was right that even messaging his sister a few times might have been enough to tip them off.

Of course, this presumed that Russia could mobilize a substantial "big data" analysis infrastructure on the turn of a dime. Besides, paranoia wasn't getting them out of Crimea, either. They still needed a plan, and Danilo was drawing a blank.

The backdoor to Iskandar's house opened.

"Lunch is ready," Angelina called.

"That girl is a peach," Iskandar remarked to Danilo as he set his shears down in the grass. "Let's eat."

"How are my two farmers?" Angelina asked as Danilo and Iskandar trotted up the back steps.

"Hungry," Danilo announced. Although he was no stranger to labor, this had been the first yardwork he had done since he lived with his parents. He had no garden to care for at his apartment and savored the feeling of coming in for a meal after working in the country air.

"Yes, hungry," Iskandar agreed.

"Well good, because I whipped up a little of everything," Angelina said. "I wasn't sure how much to make."

Iskandar looked at the spread Angelina had laid on the table. She had reheated some borscht that Iskandar's daughter had brought to him earlier in the week, made some meat-filled nalisniki pastries from scratch, and laid out a vinaigrette salad with bread. As the two men sat, Angelina poured three cups of tea.

"A feast!" Iskandar exclaimed. "I don't usually eat this much, but I've worked up a good appetite. We'll nap all afternoon at this rate, but let's eat!"

As the three took their time enjoying the lunch, they chatted about how they could solve Danilo's and Angelina's problem of leaving Crimea.

"You must not take that motorcycle," Iskandar said. "It is too recognizable."

"I know," Danilo said. "It's sad ... I'm going to miss that bike. The Versys and I have been through a lot together."

"Material things come and go," the old man replied. "When I was young, in the Uzbek village we were forced to live in, there was a horse I used to ride. I named it Wind. I loved riding that horse, but I would have traded him for return passage to Crimea in a heartbeat. Don't get attached to things. Home and family are more important than things."

"Maybe we could trade the motorcycle for a car," Angelina said.

"Now you're talking," Iskandar replied. "That's a good idea."

"That is a great idea," Danilo agreed, "but we don't know anyone with a car looking for a motorcycle in exchange. Do you know of anyone who might help us make such a trade?"

Iskandar paused to think.

"Well, I could ask my Imam's son, Musa, if he knows of anyone," he replied. "In fact, he might be interested in it. He's young; about your age. Young men like motorcycles."

"That'd be terrific," Angelina said.

"If that pans out, we're off to a great start," Danilo said. "Still … it doesn't get us through the checkpoint. They'll be on the lookout for us. Do we try and change our looks? Dye our hair? Maybe we need to exit Crimea separately."

"I think you're overly paranoid," Angelina scolded. "Let's not forget we were wearing helmets."

"I'm not sure I'm paranoid enough. I think the Russians and especially all these pro-Russian separatists are so 'on alert' that they are overreacting to everything. Just think of those three guys we watched getting detained at the border. That was nuts. So if they are yanking people out of cars, or shooting guns, who's to say what else they are doing?"

"Okay, 'paranoid' was a poor choice of words on my part," Angelina said. "But we are going to have to take some risks to get home, and hair color is not a concern."

"You're right. I don't know what to think. I don't know what's safe and what isn't."

"The car is the best idea so far," Iskandar advised. "So let's focus on that first. Why don't you two please clear the table while I go get something?"

Danilo and Angelina collected plates and silverware and brought them into the kitchen. As Angelina started to fill the sink, Iskandar returned to the table and called for Danilo to join him. Danilo looked to Angelina for direction; he felt uncomfortable leaving her with all the work.

"Go ahead," Angelina said to Danilo in a hushed tone. "He's a sweet old man, and I don't mind washing the dishes. Go talk with him."

Iskandar was sitting at the table sipping tea with what looked like a small, textured leather briefcase. He unclasped the little brown case and opened it, revealing a backgammon set.

"Do you play?" he asked.

"Not really," Danilo replied. "I played some with friends when I was in school, but that was years ago. I'm not sure I remember the rules."

"You'll pick it up quickly if we start playing. Here, let me show you how to set up the board."

The old man then laid out the round tiles in mirror-image patterns on both sides of the board.

"Ultimately, you want to get all your pieces in your 'house,' and then start moving them off the board," Iskandar explained as he rolled the dice. "But how you go about accomplishing that is another thing entirely. You shape your strategy, carry it out, and attempt to see it to fruition."

Danilo figured the best way to start was to play it safe. The old man was an experienced player, so a defensive approach was warranted. But he soon noticed that the old man was moving his pieces quickly around the board. Moreover, in the rare moments when Danilo sent one of Iskandar's pieces to the "bar," the old man quickly regained his momentum. It wasn't long before Iskandar had amassed all his tiles into his house and was moving them off the board while Danilo was still moving his tiles home. Iskandar's victory was swift.

"You're playing too conservatively," Iskandar advised as he set up the game again. "You need to be willing to take risks if you want to win."

"Okay," Danilo said. "Got it. I'll be a little more aggressive."

Soon they were playing again, but Danilo's riskier, more offensive strategy didn't work any better. The setbacks were getting increasingly frustrating as Iskandar brought more tiles into his house, and doubling them up so that Danilo couldn't land his tiles that were on the bar back onto the board. Iskandar's victory came even more quickly than in the previous game. Danilo exhaled in mild annoyance, as Iskandar moved his last tile off the board.

"Heh-heh," Iskandar chuckled. "Don't get vexed. Remember you're re-learning the game, and I am a crafty old man who has played his whole life."

Danilo grinned. It was nice to see the old man have a good time.

"Sorry, Danilio said. "Didn't mean to let it get to me. I just can't seem to make much progress one way or the other. I'm either taking too much risk or not enough. I can't seem to strike a balance."

"Well … ," the old man began to say something, but then trailed off as he set up the board for a third game.

Danilo waited patiently for the old man to continue his thought.

"Odds," Iskandar finally continued after the board was set up for a third round. "It comes down to odds."

"Odds?" Danilo.

"Yes," the old man confirmed as they started playing

their third game. "You need to look at the possible moves you could make, and then start calculating the likelihood of different rolls of the dice based on those moves, as well as the rolls and moves of your opponent."

The old man pointed to some pieces on the board to make a point:

"For instance, if you move your tile to that spot that is four spaces away from my tile, I have a wide variety of possible rolls that will let one of my pieces hit your tile and send it to the bar," he said. "I could roll a one and a three, two twos, or two ones, which would give me four. That's a lot of chances.

"But," Iskandar continued, "if you move it over here, I can only hit that tile with a one. That's it. I only have two chances of rolling a one to hit him. That's much less likely. Odds, Danilo. This game is about odds as much as it is about strategy. In chess, you rely solely on your ability to strategize and think ahead to win. In card and dice games, you are mostly at the mercy of random chance. But in backgammon, you must deal with both factors: You set a strategy, but fate influences its outcome. So you must constantly shift and adjust based on the odds."

"Now I get it," the young man replied. "It's much more appealing when you explain it that way."

"It should also get you thinking."

"How so?"

"It should remind you of something."

"What's that?"

"Life. Backgammon is about life, which is also about odds. In life, you set a strategy to accomplish something, but fate can send all your effort and enterprise crashing down — or it can help raise it up. So, you must assume some risk, but at the same time, you must only risk so much. Life is about measuring risk as it relates to your plans. Understand?"

"I do."

Danilo jumped when a loud voice thundered suddenly from outside.

"Hey, rabbit! Come out of your hole, rabbit!"

"Who's that?" Angelina asked in a quiet voice, stepping out of the kitchen. "What's going on?"

"Are we found out?" Danilo asked in a similar hush.

"Not yet," Iskandar said. "You're okay. But, go to the bedroom and keep out of sight as a precaution."

"What's going on?" Angelina repeated.

"It's the man I mentioned, Dimitry Lebel," Iskandar explained. "The drunk who doesn't like me. Whatever you do, do not show yourselves. I have handled him many times before. Like all bullies, his bark is far worse than his bite, and I can usually frustrate him into leaving."

"Okay," Danilo said and turned to Angelina. "Come on, let's go."

*

After Danilo and Angelina were safely in the guest bedroom, the old man poured two cups of tea and headed out the front door to confront Dimitry, who was standing in the road, wearing his new military clothes.

"Ah, General Dimitry, is it? What a pleasant surprise. Would you like a cup of tea?"

"Where are they, you worn out old Tatar?"

"Where are who?"

"We've received word there are fascist, Euromaidan agents in the area. I bet you're hiding them."

Iskandar kept his face calm.

"Who is we?"

"Who do you think? The Russian defenders of Crimea,

that's who. Where are the Ukrainians?"

"There are as many Ukrainians in my home as there were bombs the other day, Lebel. Don't you have anything better to do than harass old men? Don't you have your land to work?"

"I do, but I have to admit, I like yours better, Nabiyev. That's a nice house. Maybe I'll live there … when you're gone."

"Oh, I like my home fine, and I don't think I'll be leaving it any time soon," Iskandar said, stepping through his red gate and into the road to meet Dimitry face-to-face. He offered a cup. "Why don't you enjoy its hospitality and have some tea?"

"Screw your tea, old man!"

Dimitry batted Iskandar's hand and sent the cup crashing to the pavement.

*

Back in the bedroom, Angelina and Danilo exchanged worried looks upon hearing Dimitry's yelling.

"I think we better peek out the front window and keep an eye on things," Danilo said. This doesn't sound good."

"He could see you," Angelina warned.

"I know, but I can't ignore what's going on out front. Iskandar might need our help."

"Don't let that guy catch a glimpse of you."

"I promise I won't."

Danilo crouched down and padded to the front window, where the curtains were drawn. He pulled the tiniest possible corner of the drapes back so he could monitor Iskandar's exchange with the angry Russian.

"Oh dear," he heard Iskandar say. "You've dropped the cup. Here, have mine."

Danilo watched Iskandar offer the other cup to the big man, who swatted it away, as well, sending it shattering on the pavement. Iskandar took a step back and raised in his hands in mock surprise.

"You are really clumsy today, Dimitry. I'll run out of teacups at this rate."

"That's it!" the big man said. "I'm sick of your smug bullshit!"

Dimitry assumed a fighting stance. It was clear he was going to attack the old man.

Danilo felt the hair on the back of his neck stand up. Angelina now crouched behind him.

"What should I do?" he asked her. "That gorilla is going to beat the hell out of Iskandar."

"Don't do anything—yet," she replied. "Iskandar has said that he's handled him before."

They watched Iskandar look his adversary up and down with a neutral expression.

"Take it easy, Dimitry, I have offered you nothing but hospitality," the old man advised. "You have offered me nothing but scorn. And now you've broken two of my teacups. If your goal is to scare me off, it's not working. I'm here to stay."

"Not if I can help it," Dimitry growled back.

The scene in the middle of the road quickly horrified its hidden spectators. The big Russian wheeled his arm back and sent his fist rocketing forward, twisting his body as he did to put as much force behind the blow as possible. The old man rolled his head sideways as he rotated his hips and stepped to the side, dodging the swing. The old man kicked the back Dimitry's knee and pushed the big man's frame in the same direction as the blow with all his might, sending him toppling to the ground among the shards of broken cups. Iskandar turned and hurried through the gate back to his front door.

He popped through the front door and quickly closed it behind him. He shot the young couple a surprised expression and made his way to the front closet.

"I thought I told you two to stay in the bedroom," he said calmly and quietly as he opened the closet door and rummaged for something. He turned holding an almost antique-looking double-barrel shotgun with an ornately engraved receiver and polished stock.

Danilo and Angelina didn't reply, staring at the old man with their mouths agape.

"You must stay hidden," Iskandar continued. "If you are discovered, I won't be able to live with myself. Stay hidden! Do you understand?"

Danilo and Angelina nodded.

"Good. Lock the front door and escape out the back if Dimitry gets the better of me."

Danilo and Angelina ignored Iskandar's entreaty to hide and kept watching at the window. They watched Iskandar go back out the front door to confront the drunk Russian, who had by now passed through the gate and traveled halfway across the yard. Lebel's now-red face featured a scratch on the left cheek, and the left knee of his camouflage fatigues was ripped clear across. The enraged man stalked across the yard. Iskandar cocked back one of the hammers on his shotgun and leveled the weapon at his foe.

"Not a single step further, Dimitry Lebel."

The Russian froze.

"Listen to me carefully," Iskandar calmly continued. "I have been ignoring your insults and foolish behavior for years, but ever since the Russians came, you have become bolder, more abusive. I've tried to make peace with you, but you've only insulted me. You even brought those soldiers to my door with your accusations. Now you say you want to steal my home? You have taken things too far, you fat drunk. Are you listening to me, Dimitry?"

Dimitry nodded.

"Good. If I catch you on my property again, I won't hesitate to fill your belly with buckshot and leave you to bleed out slowly until you die. I'm an old man, Dimity, and I have difficulty falling asleep. Maybe your soft moaning will lull me into a deep, untroubled slumber."

Dimitry Lebel's eyes grew wide with fear-induced sobriety.

"Tell me, do you understand?"

Dimitry nodded again.

"Good. Get off my property, and stay far away. I don't want to see or hear you around here again. Come back, and you die."

Dimitry turned, walked through the gate and headed up the farm road. He didn't turn back.

Danilo and Angelina held their breath until the old man lowered the hammer gently back into place, opened the breech, removed the two shells, and dropped them into his jacket pocket. He then went back inside.

"I don't think he'll be back," Iskandar said as he entered his home.

"I'm positive he won't," Angelina replied.

"Remind me never to get on your bad side," Danilo said.

Iskandar smiled and headed back to the closet to stow the gun. He traded the weapon for a broom and dustpan.

"I better sweep up the broken cups," the old man said.

"I'll help," Danilo said.

"I think I'm going to sit here for a moment and catch my breath," Angelina announced.

"That's a good idea," Iskandar said, following Iskandar outside. "You've been through too much as it is, a nice young woman such as yourself."

"That was amazing," Danilo said.

"It was risky," Iskandar replied. "But I think it was the right risk. I didn't stand a chance without the gun. Dimitry would have beaten me into a coma with just a couple of punches. Then he would have found you two, which would have been a disaster. My dodge was a lucky move. I haven't been in a fight for decades — generations, in fact. My back is going to be killing me for weeks."

"I feel terrible you had to go through that on our account."

"My hospitality is not obligatory, Danilo. I happily and freely give it to you. It is lovely to have the two of you here. Your enthusiasm and optimism are sorely needed qualities these days. And very infectious, too."

"I don't know what to say," Danilo said, crouching to place the dustpan on the road next to a small mound of broken earthenware that Iskandar had swept.

"Well, don't say anything," Iskandar said, sweeping the shards into the dustpan. "Just keep thinking about how you and Angelina are going to get home. I will call Imam Mustaffa to see if his son might be able to help arrange a trade of the motorcycle."

"The sounds good. And I think it would be a good idea to make a call myself."

"Oh? I thought you were worried about using your phone. Who are you going to call?"

"I've weighed the odds, and I think I should call my sister."

"There's a good lad."

Chapter 19
THE HUNTING PARTY

"Now I know how a roasted pig feels," Viktor said to Sasha. "He slow-cooked me in there."

"The Captain does have a way of doing that to a person," Sasha replied.

"Indeed."

Squad B had fanned out around the railway depot, where a polling station had been established for today's referendum. The three privates, Albert, Boris, and Pavel, along with Sergeant Sasha, were spaced out roughly twenty meters apart. Viktor walked from man-to-man to check how each was doing, and to beat the mind-destroying boredom that resulted from four hours of standing in front of a train depot. No one was talking to the soldiers much that day — either the novelty had apparently worn off, or Dzhankoy's populace was focused on the referendum — so he decided to chat with Sasha.

Officially, Squad B was at the polling site to provide "general security." Unofficially they were there to ensure there were no protests or other outbursts that could provide news fodder for any Western media. The goal was clear: no debate, no bad news, and only a perfect election with nothing of note occurring besides a substantial turnout that overwhelmingly approved of Russia's annexation of Crimea.

The more hands-on security was being carried out by members of a local group of pro-Russia militiamen who Viktor had expected to be led by Dimitry Lebel. However, the hulking, obnoxious Russian was not to be seen this morning.

"Speaking of your best friend, have you noticed the savior of Dzhankoy's Russian speakers isn't around today?" Sasha noted.

"Yeah, I did notice that," Viktor replied. "You'd think he'd be rushing over here."

"Anything to feel important."

"Exactly."

"Well, what exactly the Captain say?"

"First of all, he made clear I shouldn't have left the checkpoint. That much is obvious. Now that I look back on it, I'm glad he's not going to court-martial me. I don't know what the hell I was thinking, to be honest. That was a fuck up."

"Don't beat yourself up. We got too stir crazy and stuck in a rut to make good decisions. ... What else?"

"That this Dimitry Lebel character is untouchable. He's on our side — whether we like it or not — and we have to support him."

"That's gonna be a tall order. The guy's a drunk and a bully."

"I don't like it either. That foolishness with the old Tatar man was ridiculous."

"And don't forget that old woman. Notice that she was completely cowed when we saw her a week or so back. I don't want to think about what those assholes did to put the scare into her. And make no mistake, they're going to get worse."

"True. ... Anyway, that's basically what the captain said to me. That and a reminder about the couple on the motorcycle."

"Oh yeah. Did he say anything interesting about that?"

"That there's no change from what we already knew. He told us to keep an eye out for them while we guard the polling station."

Sasha snickered. "As if Euromaidan activists that are in hiding are going to show up in Dzhankoy," he quipped.

"I know, but we still have to keep an eye out," Viktor reminded him. "It goes to show how keyed-up the locals have become."

"Case in point," Shasha said, nodding his head toward the five pro-Russian militiamen strutting around the polling station.

"Oh great," Viktor said, motioning to a little car that had pulled into the parking lot. The two Western journalists from several days ago were visible through the windshield. "The paparazzi have arrived."

"I have to have a serious talk with my publicist."

*

"This is it," Stewart said.

Ken steered the Geely around the traffic circle in front of

the train station and found a parking spot in the adjacent lot. A Russian flag was flying in front of the depot.

"This is the polling station?" Ken asked as he checked his camera's battery life.

"Correct," Stewart said. "Let's head over there."

"There doesn't seem to be much at all going on. I'm afraid this story is a bust; just a bunch of people in coats going in and out of a building. At least Sevastopol had a mess of flag waving. I'm sure Simferopol would have been the same."

"It would have been. I do think this was worth the risk, but we might've crapped out."

"You can say that again. What do you want to do?"

"Well, let's try and get some exit interviews and maybe we can play up the rural angle or something like that."

"Sounds good. I'll take a sleepy non-story over the potential ass-kicking Lowry warned us about back in Sevastopol."

"I'm not too sure about that."

"You're deranged," Ken observed.

"I'm not too sure about that either. ... Hey, maybe we start with those two," Stewart said, motioning to the soldiers standing in front of the depot.

"Okay, but I bet you they give us the silent treatment," Ken replied.

"Hey, those are the soldiers from the church protest," Stewart said as they approached the soldiers. "I'm positive of it. I think the taller one is in charge. Start rolling when we're close. I'll see if I can get him to say anything."

"Good luck. These guys are mannequins."

"I know, but it's worth a shot."

And with that, Stewart began interviewing the taller soldier.

"Hello there," he said in Russian. "You might remember me from a week ago. My name is Stewart Cooper. I'm a reporter with ETN. I was wondering if you could tell me what you gentlemen are doing here today."

The soldier paused for a moment before speaking: "We're here ensuring general security for today's referendum."

"What kind of security threats are you expecting?" Stewart asked.

"None really."

"And what part of Russia are you soldiers from?"

The Russian soldier didn't say anything but greatly appreciated that his balaclava was hiding his wry smile. Despite Russia's official statements to the contrary, there were Russian soldiers in Crimea, and he was one of them. He knew. The reporter knew. Everyone knew.

"Hey, I had to ask. Can you share your rank or name?"

The soldier remained silent.

"Well … Thanks for your time. I think we had better go and speak with some of the voters."

Stewart walked back to his partner and switched back to English. "Okay, Ken, let's get some other comments."

"Got it."

*

The two Russian sergeants observed the scene as Stewart and Ken walked to the train depot to interview voters.

"You know those local militia guys are gonna hassle those two," Sasha said.

"Let's hope not," Viktor replied. "As boring as this is, I'd appreciate it if things didn't get exciting. The last thing I need is another talk with the Captain."

"No kidding."

"Come to think of it, I'm going to walk around and tell the guys they should not speak with those reporters — any reporters, in fact."

"Sounds like a plan."

*

As Viktor walked from Albert, Boris, and Pavel to advise each on media relations, Stewart and Ken began soliciting comments from voters as they exited the polls.

"How did you vote in the referendum?" he asked a middle-aged woman with large sunglasses perched on the top of her head despite the grey, not-truly-spring weather.

"Elated," she said. "Finally we will be part of Russia — as we should be."

"So you're sure of the outcome?" Stewart followed up.

"Absolutely," she said. "I don't know a single soul who is voting against it."

"But there are people in Crimea who would prefer to remain a semi-autonomous region of Ukraine, correct?" he probed.

"I believe most of the people waving the Ukrainian flag are extremists who do not live here," she responded.

"I see. Do you — "

The woman cut him off.

"Thank you very much," she said. "I must be going."

Before Stewart could thank her back, a man interposed himself between Stewart and his ex-interviewee, who was now hastily stepping away from the railway depot in clattery red heels. The man was in his thirties, sporting a mustache and a Ribbon of St. George pinned to his warm-up jacket.

"Who are you?" The man demanded.

"Stewart Cooper, reporting for ETN," Stewart replied.

"Did you vote?"

"What business is it of yours?" the man asked, his voice getting louder. "Are you foreign propagandists? I don't recognize your accent. Where are you from? Are you Americans?"

"I'm English. My cameraman is Canadian. We're interviewing people on how they voted and what they think of the referendum."

"Well, I'll give you a quote: The referendum is the best thing to happen to Crimea since the Battle of Balaclava. How's that? Now, why don't you go back to England, Mr. Reporter?"

Stewart shrugged off the jab regarding Russia's Crimean War-era rout of Britain's Light Brigade. Belligerent as he was, the guy was smart and might produce a compelling sound bite.

"How do you think the referendum will go — will Crimea become part of Russia again?"

"Of course it will," the mustachioed man replied. "Repatriation is a foregone conclusion. Why would anyone not want to be part of Novorossiya? It is time for us to reclaim our greatness."

Novorossiya — "New Russia" — was a phrase that Stewart had heard being repeatedly used by Putin and other Russian politicians in recent days. In historical terms, Novorossiya referred to a geographic region roughly consisting of the Ukraine, the Black Sea and Azov Sea regions that the Russian Empire had conquered and annexed in the Eighteenth Century. Now the phrase had been resurrected as a battle-cry by pro-Russian militia groups hoping for Crimea and Eastern Ukraine to become part of Russia.

To Stewart, the notion that Russia could dubiously allege

that Western imperialism had fomented the Euromaidan, while at the same time invade and annex Crimea in the name of "Novorossiya" — and without a scintilla of irony — demonstrated Putin's total political control. Russia was directing the narrative for sure: it would be mighty once again.

Stewart kept those observations to himself.

As Stewart and Ken conducted the interview, a couple more men skipped down the train depot steps to join the conversation. One was wearing camouflage and the other jeans and a black jacket. The one in camouflage also wore a balaclava and a ribbon of St. George. Stewart didn't like the look of them, and he felt Ken tense up next to him.

"What's going on here?" the camouflaged man demanded.

"They are interviewing me about the vote," said the man with the mustache. "I'm sure they will twist my words around."

"Not at all," Stewart said. "We're here to report what people have to say."

"Yes, but we know how you do things," the man in the black jacket interjected. "You twist meanings to make lies about Russia."

"I don't do that," Stewart said, keeping his voice calm. "I'm just interviewing about the referendum. How did you men vote?"

"Never mind how we voted," the camouflaged man said from behind his balaclava. "We're here to ward off troublemakers, and I'd suggest you two move along."

Before Stewart could reply, a voice boomed out from across the parking lot.

"Hey, you louts! It looks like I can't take a break for one second without you getting into trouble!"

It was a big man, who Stewart recognized from the church march they had covered. Dzhankoy was a small town indeed. The man strode up to the scrum of three pro-Russians and the two reporters. The knee of his fatigues was ripped, and he wore a Band-Aid on his cheek.

As Dimitry drew closer, both the man in the black jacket and the camouflaged man sloppily saluted him.

The man in camouflage took a step back and looked over Dimitry.

"What happened to you? Your face? Your pants? Is your wife beating you, Dimitry?" he joked.

The man in the black jacket slapped his back and guffawed. Stewart remembered more about this man Dimitry, and how he was trying to stir up trouble at the checkpoint as well.

"Haha, very funny," Dimitry replied. "I tripped while getting off my tractor. I didn't have time to have the wife mend my pants. Anyway, what's going on here?"

"These two Westerners are bothering voters here at the poll," the man in the black jacket reported.

"Look," Stewart began, "we're simply here to report—"

"Enough," Dimitry said, cutting him off. "I don't need to hear one word. Here's what's going to happen. You're going to leave the polling area and quit bothering voters, or we will make you leave. Do I make myself clear?"

"We're just —"

"I'm not kidding. Quit disturbing this poll, or we'll arrest you."

"And who are you? Are you the police?"

"We are the Dzhankoy Self Defense Force, and we're in charge of maintaining order at this poll. Do you understand? You need to leave this poll, now, or we arrest you and hand you over to the police." As Dimitry made his warning, he gestured with his head toward a police car that was sitting in the parking lot.

"Okay, okay, we'll leave," Stewart replied. He turned to Ken and spoke in English. "This big bloke is threatening to have us arrested for disturbing the poll. I'm pretty sure he was the guy driving the flag-covered tractor from a week ago. Seems like he's in charge of these men. We have to clear off."

"Okay," Ken said as he lowered his camera. "It's not like we are striking any gold anyway."

"No," Stewart said as the two walked toward the parking lot, "but the guy with the mustache gave me a couple of good sound bites, and I think that, along with the stuff with the Russian soldiers and that woman, we can stitch together something decent enough to file. I can put together some narration to tie it together."

"Okay, let's get some establishing shots," Ken replied. "We better hope that Bill and Vasyklo didn't get their asses kicked in Simferopol, or get shot at, or something sexy like that. We'll never compete."

*

"I'm glad that deescalated on its own," Viktor said, watching the scene resolve.

"No kidding," Sasha agreed. "Being on the evening news would cramp my style. It goes against my philosophy of keeping a low-profile."

"You and thirty-thousand other nameless guys in the same patchless uniform."

"Our friend Dimitry didn't look too hot. Did you see his face? Looks like he got clocked or cut or something."

"Well, let's hope he and his private army keep to themselves."

The two sergeants continued to chat while the polls remained open. At one point, Sasha jogged back to the Tigr on a break and grabbed a container of tea that he and Viktor shared. The privates also took short breaks to eat or kill the boredom. Squad D would soon relieve them. As evening drew near and the polls were closing up, Viktor took one more walk from man to man to make sure all was well, and then rejoined Sasha to keep an eye on Dzhankoy's self-appointed militia from across the lot.

Dimitry was speaking excitedly to his crew of five men. As he gesticulated wildly and his voice increased both in volume and cadence, Viktor was sure something was up.

"What the fuck is going on over there?" Sasha wondered.

"I have no idea, but I am sure I don't like it, whatever it is," Viktor replied.

"Tell me about it," Sasha said.

In all the yelling, Viktor heard one word; just one single word that instantly clarified what was going on: "Nabiyev."

Dimitry and his men sauntered to the parking lot and began to load into two cars.

"Something's going on. How much time do we have left before we can leave here?" Viktor asked Sasha.

"About half an hour," his stout counterpart stated.

"Shit. Any tea left?"

"Not a sip."

"This is going to be a long thirty minutes."

*

Stewart and Ken watched Dimitry's crew assembling from inside the parked Geely, where they had been reviewing some of the footage on the laptop.

"Those guys look like they mean business," Ken observed.

"They certainly do," Stewart chorused. "I wonder where they're going?"

"Only one way to find out," Ken said as the two watched the Dzhankoy's Self Defense Force pull out of the parking lot and head toward the traffic circle.

Chapter 20
SPEAKERPHONE SONATA

Southern Ukraine's landscape scrolled past Veronika's view like the credits of a movie. Worried sick, she hurtled through the countryside in Alina's immaculately kept white Hyundai on a trajectory that would see her get to the Crimean border crossing at Armyansk in two hours. If she could get close to the border, perhaps she could assist Danilo's and Angelina's escape. Crimea was still in a state of confusion and Russia would still be working to implement its control over the area. Russia had bigger fish to fry than two young Euromaidan activists, didn't it?

Since she had set out early that morning, her mind had been racing as fast as the little hatchback was flying down the M17. Music was playing on the radio, but she couldn't focus on anything but Danilo.

The car stereo, along with Veronika's agonizing, was interrupted by a chorus of chirping crickets signifying that her phone was ringing. She looked at the display—Danilo! She practically lost control of the car as she fumbled to answer the call on speakerphone.

"Yes? Hello?" Veronika answered in nearly breathless excitement; she felt like she had just sprinted around a city block. "Danilo?"

A voice answered back.

"Big sister?"

It was him.

"Danilo, I've been so worried. Are you okay? Where are you? What's going on?"

"Yes, I'm okay. That's why I'm calling. Let me explain."

"Well hold on. I need to pull over. I can barely think straight now, let alone drive. Give me a moment."

Veronika found a safe spot to pull off the road and put the emergency blinkers on. She continued the conversation with the *click-click* of the signal lights in the background.

"Okay," she said. "Tell me what happened."

Danilo methodically told the story of the Donetsk riot, the decision to ride into Crimea, the panic at the Chongar border crossing, hiding in the field and then the shed, the helpful old Tatar man named Iskandar Nabiyev, the angry drunk Russian, and the foolishness he felt over his misguided text messages.

"I'm so sorry," he said, wrapping up his report. "I was freaked out and wasn't thinking clearly. I should have never sent you those messages. Can you ever forgive me?"

"You're a fucking idiot," Veronika replied.

She let that sink in for a while before she continued.

"Do you know where I am?" she asked her little brother.

"No ..." he replied. It was clear he was bracing himself

for a big sister-style scolding.

"I'm in Alina's car, two hours outside of Crimea," she replied. "It didn't take Alina and me long to figure out that just about the only place in the world you'd be worried about having your phone 'monitored' was if you had gone into Crimea for some stupid reason. I just can't believe you brought Angelina with you."

There was a pause as Danilo stumbled for a reply.

"I'm going to strangle you," Veronika stated plainly. "I'm honestly going to murder my little brother. I mean … I love you, you mean the world to me, and I want you to have a long and happy life, Danilo, but I am going to choke the life out of you. At what point did you think it was a good idea to bring that nice girl into that shitstorm, little brother? Did you think you two were Bonnie and Clyde? Were you going on an adventure? Danilo, the Russian army just invaded Crimea! These people are not screwing around. Why else do you think you got shot at?"

"It was idiotic," he replied. "We just wanted to help. We wanted to remind the world that the referendum didn't erase the invasion or the fact that Russia was silencing the Ukrainians and Tatars here."

"Danilo, the world already knows all that; it's hard to ignore tens of thousands of Russian soldiers. Everything about your little scheme was a bad idea."

"Believe me. I know that—now."

"So what are you going to do?"

"We're trying to figure a way out. We're thinking of trading my Kawasaki for a car and then driving back through Armyansk."

"It's not a bad idea. I'm sorry about your motorcycle."

"So am I, but I figure it's the price I have to pay for my idiocy."

"You took the words right out of my mouth."

Danilo sighed.

"Look," Veronika continued, "you need to keep your phone on. Think about it: If the Russian army or its agents were trying to locate you by your telephone, they would have already been able to find your phone's last position or the last cell tower you used or something—they must have a way. Here's the reality: you don't matter. The Russian army is too busy to devote its intelligence apparatus towards finding a couple on a motorcycle."

"I know," her little brother said. "You're right. I was being overly cautious to the point of paranoia."

"And then some. Anyway, I'm approaching Kherson. That's about 90 minutes from the border. I'm going to try and find a room there. I want you to stay hidden and keep me posted in case you need my help. We're going to get you out of Crimea."

"I know. Okay, I better go. I love you, sis."

"I love you too. Be safe and be smart, okay?"

"Okay."

*

Exhausted and in need of a place to stay as close to Danilo as she could reasonably get, Veronika found an economy room at the Diligence Hotel in Kherson. The Diligence was an old hotel that had been renovated to accommodate business travelers with tidy, quaint rooms. After enduring the past twenty hours' stress, the hotel stay felt like a spa. Decorated in whites, creams, and browns, Veronika's room felt warm and inviting and helped her wind down from the trip.

Following a hot shower and a brief nap, Veronika took an early supper in the hotel restaurant and decided to drive to the border to check out the crossing before the sun had fully set. She didn't want to cross into Crimea, but she couldn't help being curious about what the border — a place she had been to in the past — would look like now that the Russians had closed it off.

Her trip through what was mostly farm country was uneventful and oddly therapeutic. Perhaps she merely needed a drive that didn't involve ulcerating over her brother. Veronika was beginning to feel somewhat reassured regarding Danilo's and Angelina's situation and rolled down the windows to take in the rich, loamy scents of the countryside. She inhaled the late afternoon air, which was unseasonably sultry for early spring.

Approximately fifteen minutes from Armyansk, the M17 curved along a rise in the landscape that overlooked the border. Veronika pulled off the road to look across the border and the land bridge that connected the Crimean Peninsula to Ukraine. Across the vista, lights began to switch on here and there in the fading light of evening.

Veronika had driven this route to Crimea for summer beach holidays several times, but as she gazed across the broad view, she realized that she was seeing it differently now. While she had driven here to help her brother, she also had felt an instinctive desire to come here. Forces far beyond her control had disturbed her sense of place, and she had to witness the physical manifestation of this disruption for herself.

Previously, Crimea felt like another part of Ukraine. Politically, it had been considered semi-autonomous and treated slightly differently, but to Veronika and practically any Ukrainian, Crimea seemed like another oblast. It was Ukraine. But that was before February 28. Now, all of a sudden, Crimea seemed almost foreign.

Moreover, she felt great empathy for Crimea. The past few hundred years had not treated the region well, but over the last twenty years or so, Crimea had started to see some relative normality. Now that quasi-normality had disappeared in one night. *How long until the Tatars start suffering mistreatment? Maybe they are already being abused. How about Crimea's other non-Russians? What about my brother and Angelina?*

As Veronika stood in the warm breeze and tried to make sense of this mishmash of confused emotions and motives, something caught her attention: All along the length of a newly installed fence that closed off the border, crews of Russian soldiers were digging regularly spaced holes of the same dimensions and posting signs. The rows of perfect holes simultaneously looked at home in such an agricultural area and utterly alien, as though intergalactic farmers had landed and started sowing strange seeds.

That's when Veronika realized what the Russians were doing: They were laying a minefield. The signs must have been warnings to Ukrainian civilians and military personnel to stay out—out of what used to be Ukraine. Moreover, it was forcing Crimeans to remain in Crimea.

Veronika got back in the car as the final light of evening disappeared into murky twilight. It would be dark in minutes. She hung a U-turn and started driving back to Kherson, unsettled. As she reached the outskirts of the town, it dawned on her what the holes the Russians were digging also looked like—graves.

It took some will on Veronika's part to ensure her recently regained reassurance over Danilo's and Angelia's circumstances didn't falter or fade. She wanted them out of Crimea, she wanted them back home in larger Ukraine, and she wanted them back home now.

Chapter 21
DECISIONS

Squad B pulled into Checkpoint Anna to relief Squad C shortly after sundown. As Sasha brought the Tigr into position behind their mini citadel of sandbags and boredom, Viktor instructed Albert, Boris, and Pavel to take their positions, with Boris manning the Pecheneg machine gun. Then he motioned to Sasha to join him for a private chat behind the truck.

"I gotta go," Viktor told him.

"What are you talking about?" Sasha asked.

"I gotta go."

"Ok, I'll repeat my question then: What the hell are you talking about, Sergeant Viktor Belov?"

"You know where that goon squad was heading. I heard that fat fool Lebel very clearly state that old Tatar man's name. They're heading over there to kick ass. I have to see if I can stop it."

"For a third time: What the fuck are you talking about? Did you not just get grilled by the Captain for leaving your post without orders to check in on that old man?"

"I know. I don't know what to say. I've been thinking about it the whole drive over here. I don't think the local cops will get involved if I warn them—they barely looked alive back at the polling station. So, it's up to me. If I let that drunk and his goons go after that old man, I know for sure that it will haunt me for the rest of my life."

"I hear you. I really do. But, you could wind up in the stockade for that kind of bullshit. I can't let you go over there, Viktor. You have a wife to think about."

"I have to. There is no doubt about it. I must. Sasha, there is no doubt that they'll kill him."

Sasha stared at Viktor, clearly furious with worry. His nostrils flared, and his eyes flicked back and forth, scanning his friend in angry disbelief as he tried to parse the situation.

"Okay, go," Sasha finally said. "But if something goes down, do not get in involved."

"I can't promise that," Viktor replied.

Again, Sasha paused and glared.

"You're gonna give me a fucking heart attack," Sasha hissed, trying to contain his irate frustration. "Can you promise to keep this as low-profile as possible?"

"Absolutely. I plan to stay in the shadows unless I'm absolutely needed," Viktor said.

"Fuck me. You are an idiot. ... Okay, we'll hold down the fort then. Just be careful—and quiet."

"Absolutely."

Viktor checked his water and night vision goggles, ensured his weapon was in order and headed out on foot toward Iskandar Niabiyev's modest farm in the light of the full moon.

"Where's Sergeant Bel—I mean Viktor headed?" Albert asked.

"Viktor isn't going anywhere. He's right here with us," Sasha replied.

"What do you mean? He's heading out across the field."

"No, he's sitting in the cab of the Tigr. Don't you see him?"

The three privates stared blankly at their large and clearly pissed-off sergeant, who repeated his question:

"I said, don't you three assholes see Viktor in the fucking Pav Tigr parked adjacent to our checkpoint?"

Again, the three privates appeared confused.

"Albert, do you see Viktor in the Tigr?" Sasha asked, nodding his head as he did so.

"Uh, yes?" the private shakily confirmed.

"Good. Boris? Pavel?"

"Yes, Sasha," they chorused.

"Good. I'm glad we have that straight. Viktor is right here and hasn't gone anywhere. Is that clear?"

The three privates nodded.

"Good. Because if it isn't clear, I will make your lives hell. Forever."

The four Russian soldiers stared out across the crossroads, woods, and fields, which were bathed in grey-blue lunar light, each quietly mulling the same worry: What the fuck was Viktor doing?

*

Angelina and Iskandar sat at the dining table amongst stacks of paintings and sketchbooks. The old man had brought the Samovar inside and placed it on the table. They were using it to keep the teapot warm. The old Tatar was delighted to share his work with the young woman while Danilo was out back talking to his sister on the phone.

"Your work is beautiful," Angelina said. "I'm no artist — not like you — but I have taken some classes, and I have to say that I'm amazed at the number of styles and media that you use. I see Conté crayon, pencil, charcoal, watercolors, acrylics, pen and ink ... how did you get so good at all of them?"

"Practice ... and desire," he said. "When I was a boy, after the Russians had deported us to Uzbek, I drew all the time, but I had very little in the way of art supplies. I would use mostly bits of charcoal on scrap pieces of wood, bark, or cast off packaging or parcel wrap. A pencil and some paper were a rare treat. So when I was older and could earn some more money, I would buy decent drawing or painting supplies. But regardless of supplies, I always kept practicing; even after I was married; even after my wife and I returned to Crimea with our own family; always practicing. My wife, Aysilu, would tease me a little — a farmer who wished he was an artist — but she also liked what I did. To her, I was a real artist."

Angelina nodded and smiled.

"But it's practice that gets you where you want to go," the old man added. "You start out doing poorly, but then you begin to develop a relationship between your subject matter and the tools you are using and your abilities. Eventually, you start surprising yourself."

"You're surprising more than yourself, Mr. Nabiyev. I believe you saved our lives."

"I could say the same thing about you two."

They both sipped some tea.

"Why rabbits?" Angelina asked. "Nearly everything

you've done depicts them in some way. Why?"

"I like rabbits," he said. "They're survivors when they shouldn't be. God designed the rabbit to die."

Angelina laughed a little.

"It's not a joke!" Iskandar dramatically chided in a mock scolding. "Seriously though, the rabbit seems designed to die. For instance, their back legs are so powerful they can use them to kick at a predator or thump on the ground to warn other rabbits, but their backs are so weak that rabbits can break them if they kick their legs too hard. Or, their stomachs—rabbits lick themselves to keep clean, but they cannot digest their hair, so they get hairballs like a cat, but they cannot cough them up. Unless they consume specific enzymes in their diet to help them break down that hair, rabbits will develop stomach obstructions and die.

"Their ears are another example. When rabbits get hot, they cannot sweat or pant like other animals do to get rid of excess body heat. They can only radiate body heat off of their ears. So, if they cannot find a shady place to keep their body temperature down, they will quickly die in the sun.

"And think about all the predators that prey on rabbits," Iskandar continued explaining. "The whole world seems to be against these creatures, yet somehow, they persist. They burrow, they run, they wait out danger, they patiently bide their time. Despite the world and God's design, rabbits live. So, you see, it is easy for me to admire them."

"I see," Angelina.

"Plus there are a ton of them trying to eat what I grow, so I figure they owe me their services as free life models," the old man deadpanned.

The two shared a chuckle before Angelina turned to the kettle keeping warm on the samovar. She warmed up her and Iskandar's cups and returned the pot to its platform at the top of the boiler.

"This is a lovely old samovar," she observed. "Have you had it long?"

"Aysilu and I received it as a wedding gift," Iskandar recalled. "A woman who was a friend of the family gave it to us. She had always intended to give it to one of her children, but they all died in the Sürgünlik—our exile—so she gifted it to us. It's a reminder of family and happy times, but also the fact that you need to cherish those moments because sometimes they are taken from you."

*

Ken and Stewart tailed the two cars that comprised the Dzhankoy Self Defense Force's mini motorcade through the small Crimean town's evening streets. Ken struggled to hang far enough back that they wouldn't attract the attention of the two cars' occupants. It didn't make it any easier that the militiamen were taking a considerably circuitous route to get to wherever they were going.

"I don't get it," Ken said as he manned the wheel of their Geely.

"What's that?" Stewart replied.

"These guys seem to be trying to drive through every street in this town. Where could they be going?"

"I couldn't tell you."

"Well, neither can I. All I know is I feel like a mouse following two big, mean cats through a maze. ... Please, tell me this is not a stupid idea."

"This is not a stupid idea." Stewart didn't even sound convincing to himself.

Ken rounded a corner and Stewart saw one of the two cars stopped in the middle of the street, blocking the road. A pair of men, silhouetted by streetlights, stood on either side of the vehicle. Ken brought their car to a halt. As he did, bright headlights from another auto that had pulled up behind them illuminated the cabin of the Geely. The second of the militia's two cars had boxed them in.

"This was a stupid idea," Ken said.

"Sorry, mate," Stewart replied in a defeated exhale. "I believe we are well and truly fucked."

Knuckles rapping on the driver's window made both of them jump. They whipped their heads toward the noise in almost perfect unison to see a pair of eyes peering out from behind a balaclava.

"Get out," the man said in Russian.

"He says we have to get out," Stewart translated for Ken.

They got out of their respective sides. Stewart looked across at the masked man standing next to Ken and said in Russian, "My friend speaks neither Ukrainian nor Russian. May I walk around the car to speak to you?"

"Stay where you are," the man said; he was wearing a brown coat with a Ribbon of St. George wrapped around his upper arm. As he spoke, Stewart and Ken noticed that the occupants of both cars had now encircled them.

"What's going on?" Ken asked.

"I'm not sure," Stewart said. "Stay calm and let me find out."

"Do you think we could make a run for it?"

Stewart noticed a couple of the men had rifles.

"Don't," he said.

"Why are you following us?" asked one of the shadowy men. The speaker stepped forward into the Geely's headlights. It was the man in camouflage fatigues with the ripped knee that they had encountered earlier at the polling station. Like all the other men, a balaclava masked his identity. Stewart was pretty sure this one was the leader of the Dzhankoy Self Defense Force.

"You guys looked like you meant business, and we wanted to see if there was a story we could report," Stewart said. "That's our jobs."

"What did I tell you back at the polls?" The man asked as he rubbed his cheek.

"That we should leave the polling station," Stewart replied. "We did that."

Stewart's reply stopped the man. He appeared puzzled about what to say next. This was not Stewart's intention at all. The last thing you want to do when trying to talk your way out of a beating (or worse) from a group of thugs is to make the leader feel stupid. And that was going to be a tricky tightrope to walk because Stewart was quickly getting the impression that this character wasn't all that bright.

"Maybe you don't get the point," the man finally said. "We don't want you Westerners around."

"Why's that?" Stewart asked. He knew he was pushing things, but he had an angle to play.

"What do you mean 'why?'"

"I mean why don't you want us around? We're here with a video camera and filing reports for ETN. We could be a golden opportunity for you to get your message out. Neither my partner nor I have any political agenda one way or the other. All we want is news to report. That's how we make our living. Why not let us follow you and let us report?"

The camouflaged man paused for a moment. The suggestion of leveraging the media was something he had not considered.

"Wait one moment," he said and motioned to two of the five other militiamen. They held a hushed but animated meeting next to the lead car. Eventually, it appeared they had reached a consensus. The large man walked toward Stewart.

"We've decided to let you follow us," he said from behind his mask. "We are on a mission to investigate the possible harboring of Ukrainian agents. Most likely fascists from Svoboda."

"Okay," Stewart said. "Thank you for letting us follow you. We'll stay out of the way."

"I have rules. You may only film us when we are wearing masks. I will instruct you when you can and cannot film. And I want to review your video footage."

Stewart conveyed the instructions to an astonished Ken.

"Is that okay with you?" Stewart asked the Canadian cameraman.

"Yeah, sure," Ken said in surprise. "We'll do what he says. ... Um ... How the fuck did you swing this?"

"Evolution. I think some of these blokes are a few steps back on the scale," Stewart replied, and then spoke to the Dzhankoy Self Defense Force's leader in Russian: "We agree to your terms. Thank you again."

"You're welcome. Follow between our two cars, and do exactly what we tell you."

"Absolutely. Could I get your name?"

"You can call me Dimitry—no last names. You can refer to me as the leader of the Dzhankoy Self Defense Force. Also, don't ask my men for their names."

"Understood."

The militiamen walked to their cars, and Ken and Stewart got in theirs. The three vehicles turned west onto a road that exited the town and crept their way into the moonlit countryside that surrounded Dzhankoy.

"I can't decide whether to feel bad or good about this,"

Ken said. "I'm leaning toward bad."

"My gut says we'll be okay," Stewart replied.

"My gut tells me to punch you in your gut, smartass."

Ken sighed and kept driving. Stewart winced at the headlights in the passenger side mirror and sighed.

"I wonder if there's any good radio out here," he wondered aloud.

*

"Okay, I better go," Danilo said into his phone, and in a moment of younger-brother jackassery added, "I'll be okay."

"Not funny," his big sister advised, getting the bad joke.

"Sorry. Trying to raise the mood. I don't want you to worry."

"That's probably not going to happen until you an Angelina are safe and back in Ukraine, little brother. I'll talk to you later, right?"

"Right. Love you."

"Love you, too."

Danilo hung up his phone. Talking to his big sister made him feel one hundred percent better. He was glad to take Iskandar Nabiyev's advice to make the call. The old man wasn't just a kind host; he was wise counsel.

Danilo had been in the barn to check on his Kawasaki while he called Veronika. He wanted to make sure it was in good shape so that the son of Iskandar's imam could come by and look at it for a possible trade.

The bike was in good shape; started right up and all the electrics functioned as they should. Danilo put it up against the rear wall of the barn; re-covered it with a tarp; and stacked some boxes in front of it. Iskandar's tractor was also parked in front of it, so the motorcycle wouldn't be seen unless someone did a dedicated search.

Danilo exited the barn and headed out into the night. The full moon was out, and he could make out every element of Iskandar's farm: the fields, the small orchard, the farmhouse, the barn, the shed where he and Angelina had initially hidden, and the stone fence. He could almost make out the stand of low, scrubby oaks where he and Angelina had first stashed the motorcycle.

As he stood looking around, Danilo heard the sound of cars. Carefully he crept toward the path that ran from the barn to the shed and alongside the house and out to the front road. When he got to the shed, he saw three cars slowly pull in front of the house. The sight sent him scrambling to the backdoor that entered into Iskandar's kitchen.

"Visitors—at least three cars," he announced to Angelina and Iskandar, who were sitting at the dining table, enjoying Iskandar's paintings and drawings.

The old man got up, walked to the front window and peeked through the curtains.

"I believe it is Dimitry Lebel again, but he has brought some friends," he said calmly. "Please, children, grab your things, quietly go out the back door and run to the trees where you first hid your motorcycle. I will be quickly behind you. Go fast."

Danilo and Angelina moved fast. They had been keeping the motorcycle panniers packed, so they were out the door and into the fields in less than a minute.

*

Despite his worries about Iskandar, Viktor was enjoying the hike to the old Tatar's home. The full moon's light was bright enough to cast shadows, so he didn't even bother with his night vision gear. While he dreaded what would happen when the goons reached old man's house, the walk felt almost therapeutic—like an evening stroll. His steps felt sure and the night air invigorated his chest. Viktor was glad to be doing something, instead of endlessly staring at an intersection where nothing ever happened.

He took a position between two sycamores situated approximately 30 meters across the street from Iskandar's house. Within minutes, Viktor witnessed three compact cars pulling up in front of the house. Their doors swung open, and people began to get out. Viktor spied through the scope on his AK-74M to get a better look.

There were seven men. Five of them had their faces covered in balaclavas, and he was certain that they were the same militiamen that had been patrolling the polling station earlier that day—the so-called Dzhankoy Self Defense Force. Despite the masks, he could make out Dimitry Lebel, whose size and ripped fatigues gave him away. Viktor was angered and frustrated that the militiaman had returned to the old man's home with a bunch of heavies in tow despite Viktor's warning, but he wasn't necessarily surprised.

What did surprise him was the other two men. They were not wearing balaclavas, so it was easy to see that they were the two western reporters he had seen at the polling station earlier that day.

The journalists' involvement in the scene completely changed things. Media being present severely hobbled Viktor's ability to intervene. If he wound up in even a second of video news, the Captain would have him in the stockade in a flash. But, at the same time, he couldn't let the militiamen attack the old man.

Viktor was flummoxed. What were these two guys thinking? Did they not realize the situation? Did they not realize what kind of men they were following? What were they trying to accomplish?

Chapter 22
HOUSEGUESTS

Iskandar joined Danilo and Angelina as they lay together in the fields of the farm. He now wore a fur hat and his fraying wool coat and clasped a shotgun in one hand. A sheathed hunting knife was tucked in his belt, and hanging from his neck were a pair of binoculars. He had slung an old canvas musette bag full of assorted buckshot shells over his shoulder.

"What do we do?" Angelina whispered.

"Nothing," Iskandar replied. "We find a good hiding spot and wait this out. There are several men in the front yard. I heard them speaking in Russian as I ran out."

Angelina, Danilo, and Iskandar relocated to better cover offered by the tangled collection of old oaks situated along the abandoned road. They monitored the old farmer's moonlit fields and modest home. The lights still shined through the windows, and they could see the headlights of the three cars reflected on the trees limbs hanging over the road beyond. Trading Iskandar's binoculars back and forth, the hidden trio could see no movement. They could hear raised voices every so often, but they couldn't make out what was said.

"I can't stand this," Danilo said, handing the binoculars to the gray-haired man. "I feel like we brought this on you."

"Alcohol and stupidity brought this upon me," Iskandar replied. "Neither you, nor I had anything to do with it."

"Remind me to scold you on your choice of neighbors, Mr. Nabiyev," Angelina deadpanned.

"Don't you worry; I make it a regular habit of ruing the day Dimitry Lebel moved in down the way," Iskandar said, and passed the binoculars to her.

"He's the worst," she said.

"Yes," Iskandar muttered. "I believe he is. Danilo, do you know how to use a shotgun?"

Danilo's face must have betrayed his cluelessness in the blue-grey light of the full moon because Iskandar started to provide a brief instruction.

*

Stewart and Ken stood shoulder to shoulder in front of their rental car, Ken dangling the video camera at his side. A semi-circle of five masked representatives of the Dzhankoy Self-Defense Force stood in front of them. Dimitry motioned for Ken to raise his camera. Ken did so and switched on the camera's light. Dimitry blinked for a moment as he got acclimated to the light shining in his face.

"We are here to apprehend two fascist agents from Kyiv and the Muslim terrorist that is harboring them," the big

Russian said, squinting a bit. "Once we have them, we will turn them over to the police."

"We should take them to our brothers at the checkpoint!" one of the militiamen said from behind his balaclava.

"Better still. Okay, I want to start over, Mr. English reporter. Can you do that?"

Stewart nodded.

"We're going to do a second take," he told Ken in English.

"I guess we've got the Russian Martin Scorsese here," Ken wisecracked.

"Looks that way," Stewart said and turned to speak with Dimitry. "We're all set; go ahead," he announced in Russian.

"Okay. We are here to arrest two fascist agents from Kyiv and a Muslim terrorist that is harboring them," Dimitry said. "Once we have them in custody, we will turn them over to a nearby detachment of soldiers."

"Where are the soldiers from?" Stewart asked.

"What? Uh … they are … they are from …"

Stewart was pretty sure he could hear the gears in Dimitry Lebel's brain grinding to a halt as he tried not to admit that the 30,000 men in identical Russian fatigues, carrying Russian arms, and driving Russian vehicles all over Crimea were indeed Russian soldiers.

"On second thought," Dimitry caught himself. "I believe we should hand them over to the police, as they are criminals in my book. I want to start over again."

"Okay," Stewart said, and, switching from Russian to English, he told the cameraman, "One more time."

"Got it," the Canadian said.

"Go ahead," Stewart said in Russian.

"We are here to apprehend two fascist agents from Kyiv

and a Muslim terrorist that is harboring these fugitives," Dimitry said for the third time. "Once we have them in custody, we will turn them over to the police, and the police will determine how to process them."

Dimitry stepped through the front gate and walked toward Iskandar's home. The militiamen followed with Stewart walking behind and Ken bringing up the rear, recording the whole scene. Lit from behind, the group cast shadow-wraiths on the front wall of the modest farmhouse.

Dimitry stepped up to the front door and sternly knocked three times.

"Iskandar Nabiyev!" He bellowed. "This is the Dzhankoy Self Defense Force—open up!"

No sound came from within.

"Iskandar Nabiyev!" Dimitry yelled again. "You are suspected of sheltering foreign agents! You must open up!"

Again, nothing.

"Alright, Nabiyev, we're coming in!"

Dimitry, pulled a semi-automatic pistol from his jacket pocket, took a step back and kicked at the door, near the lock. It appeared to budge but didn't open. The large man kicked again; it didn't open. He kicked a third time, and the door flew open. He turned to the man holding a Kalashnikov.

"Sergei, you go inside with me. The rest of you—including the reporters—you wait until we conduct a search."

*

The two men entered into Iskandar's front room. Dimitry surveyed the room from behind his mask. Sergei stood to Dimitry's left, with his weapon raised, scanning the room. As they surveyed their surroundings, they both stared at a framed passage from the Koran in swooping, stylized Arabic script that hung on the wall behind the couch. The scripture was surrounded by a collage of family photos in an eclectic mix of frames, no two resembling the other.

Dimitry pointed to the closet on the left wall, and the hallway to the left of the couch, which led to the bedrooms and bathroom.

"Search there," he said. "I'll take these rooms and the kitchen."

"Got it," the man with the rifle said.

Dimitry looked around the room. He went to the closet and slowly opened, pointing his pistol inside. There was no one there; just some coats and two pairs of old boots. Hats hung from a row of hooks on the inside of the door. He took one of the hats down, inspected it, and threw it across the room.

He walked to the table, where the old Samovar sat with a kettle keeping warm at the top. Two partially filled cups of tea sat on the table. He pulled up his balaclava and sipped from one of the cups. The drink was still warm. Sketchbooks lay strewn across the table, along with drawings, watercolor paintings and other artistic renditions of rabbits and other small animals; mostly rabbits.

"His fucking rabbits," Dimitry muttered.

Sergei came back in the living room.

"There's no one in any of those rooms," he said.

"They must be somewhere. Let's search the back," Dimitry said.

Dimitry switched on rear porch light as they stepped out the kitchen door that led to Iskandar's yard and fields. The two surveyed their surroundings. Despite the full moon, there wasn't much to see apart from the illuminated grey shapes of the barn and the toolshed.

"Go get a flashlight," he ordered Sergei.

The man with the rifle quickly left to fetch a flashlight. While he did, Dimitry went back inside to get a cup from the kitchen cupboards and filled it with some tea from the kettle. He sipped the tea while standing in the kitchen doorway, looking out over what he could see of Iskandar's fields and small orchard.

"I'm finally drinking your tea, old man!" He bellowed across the fields after a few sips. "That's right. I know you're out there! Hiding like a scared rabbit!"

The large man paused, listening for any sounds. He heard none.

"Your tea tastes like piss, Nabiyev!"

Dimitry punctuated his insult by hurling the cup at the toolshed. He missed.

Sergei returned with a large flashlight and handed it to Dimitry. Dimitry raised the light and his pistol.

"Okay, let's check out these buildings," he said to Sergei and switched on the light.

The pair inspected the toolshed first. After walking around the outside of the small structure, Dimitry opened the door while shining the light in, as Sergei pointed his rifle at the opening. No one was hiding inside.

They repeated the same process with the barn. First, the militiamen checked the outside, but only found a trailer parked at the side of the barn, covered by a large tarp that they lifted to ensure no one was hiding underneath. Then they opened the barn door with the same mix of caution and menace and ventured into the large building. Once inside, Dimitry located a light switch and flipped it; hanging fluorescent light tubes flickered to life. They saw a large tractor parked in front of a large stack of boxes. Tools hung on the wall, and various odds and ends were stacked in two animal stalls that were no longer occupied by livestock. Dimitry looked up.

"I'll search the loft," he said. "You search down here."

Sergei headed toward the stables with his rifle raised. Dimitry holstered his weapon and tucked the flashlight into his belt before ascending the ladder to the loft. He could hear the other man rummaging around below as he climbed.

Once in the loft, Dimitry grabbed the flashlight and scanned the area. There was nothing. With the tractor to help him, the old Tatar did not need to keep working animals, much less the hay to feed them. Despite the extra space, Iskandar apparently hadn't collected anything to store in the barn's upper level. The Russian suspected the aging farmer no longer felt up to climbing the tall ladder. Dimitry did not care. He knew that someday he would own the old man's land and its buildings.

"Hey, Dimitry," Sergei alerted from below. "I think I found something. Come down."

*

Danilo had shuddered when the lights went on in the barn.

"Shit," he fretted. "They're going to find the motorcycle."

"You don't know that," Angelina said.

The trio kept taking turns with binoculars. After several minutes, the two militiamen appeared in the light from the still-open barn doors being cast on the land between the barn and Iskandar's home.

"They're heading back toward your house," Angelina said, peering through the glasses.

"Let me see, please," Iskandar replied. He watched

carefully as Dimitry and Sergei headed back through the kitchen door.

"What are they doing?" Danilo queried.

"I don't know, but I have to go find out," the old man said. "Danilo, I want you to take the shotgun and this bag of shells. Only use the gun if you cannot escape and your lives are threatened. No heroics, okay? These men are better armed, and there are more of them."

"Understood."

"Hold on—What?" Angelina interrupted. "You're going to go out there? You can't. It's far too dangerous. I think that man intends to kill you."

"Of course he does," Iskandar said. "Don't worry. I will stay hidden. That fat fool couldn't find his hat if he were wearing it. Remember, stay quiet and out of sight, and if anyone approaches, head quietly to the west. You will pass through two old fields, and then enter a small wood after that. They will never find you in there, but I will. Stay safe and stay hidden."

"If they find the Kawasaki, our cover is blown," Danilo said.

"Which is all the more reason you need to stay out of sight and make your way to that forest if they head toward you," the old man said.

*

Two of the militiamen chatted quietly, and the third smoked a cigarette with his balaclava partially pulled over his mouth, while Stewart and Ken waited out Dimitry and Sergei's search. They had been gone for a while, and Stewart was beginning to wonder if this was a wild goose chase or the calm before the storm.

As Stewart assessed the possibilities, the pair of

searchers reappeared.

"Did you find anything?" the smoking man asked them.

"Yes," Dimitry said. "Sergei found our fascists' motorcycle."

A cheer went up from the Dzhankoy Self Defense Force.

Stewart cued Ken to start recording. The light from Ken's now-raised camera lit the scene.

Dimitry then turned to Stewart, "Make sure your cameraman gets this," he advised. Then he straightened up, removed his balaclava, smoothed his hair, and tried to adopt a professional-sounding tone for the camera. "I believe our suspects are still in hiding on or near the property, and I plan to flush them out. Come on, Sergei. The rest of you, keep waiting."

*

Iskandar had seen the two Russians go back inside the house as he crept south and then east across his property and was now making his way north through his orchard. The old farmer kept low, moving from tree to tree and trying to stay as much in the shadows as possible. The bright light of the full moon hampered his efforts to remain concealed, but he made his way to the edge of his apple and apricot trees without attracting attention. From there, he had to cross roughly 15 feet of open ground before he'd be able to hide against the southern wall of his home.

He waited patiently, listening to the men rummaging inside his home. He wasn't quite sure what was going on. Had they found the motorcycle? The lights were on in the bedrooms. *Have the Russians been rummaging through my belongings? Are they looting?*

He made a quick, quiet dash to the south wall and crouched below a bedroom window. As he contemplated his next move, he heard the backdoor open. He unsheathed the hunting knife and crouched down, inching his way along the wall so that he could peer around the corner.

Peeking around the edge of the wall, Iskandar Nabiyev saw that Dimitry hugged a large bundle in his beefy arms. As Dimitry and the other man stepped further into the combined light from the porch and the open barn door, Iskandar recognized that the bundle was his tablecloth wrapped around something.

"Come on out, Nabiyev!" The leader of the Dzhankoy Self Defense Force called out. His partner stood to his left, scanning back and forth while holding the rifle across his waist.

Dimitry dumped the bundle on the ground before him. Papers flew in the air. Iskandar now realized the contents of the pile: his drawings and paintings—the ones that he and Angelina had been enjoying less than an hour earlier.

"It's dark out, old man!" Dimitry yet. "Perhaps you and your guests from Kyiv need me to help you see a little better!"

Dimitry walked toward the tool shed, opened the door, pulled out his flashlight, and went inside. Iskandar heard Dimitry rummaging around inside, and soon the big Russian came walking back with the flashlight tucked under his belt and now holding a jerry can of gasoline.

"Let me light your way, you old Turk!" Dimitry yelled as he poured gasoline on Iskandar's art. Once the big man was satisfied, he stepped back, set the can down, and motioned to Sergei to step away. Then Dimitry pulled out a matchbook, lit one, and tossed the lit match at the pile of canvases, sketchbooks, and papers. The spark carved a slow, graceful arc through the night air before reaching its destination.

Iskandar watched decades of work burst into flame. Memories, ideas, emotions, time, patience and small pieces of his soul quickly transformed into fire, smoke and ash that floated heavenward—like prayers. He gripped his knife tightly and thought of the days and weeks his family spent huddled around small cook fires, trapped inside Russian freight cars.

Dimitry and Sergei stared out across Iskandar's fields, obviously frustrated that the bonfire didn't cause any reaction. Iskandar watched as the big Russian went back in the house and returned holding the Samovar up in the air. He heaved it onto the fiery heap.

"Hey old man!" Dimitry boomed. "I thought I might heat up some water for the tea? What do you think?"

Dimitry paused and considered the samovar sitting in the fire.

"You know, I think it's overheating!" he yelled. "I should cool it off a bit!"

The fat man yanked his pistol out of his jacket pocket, leveled it at the old treasure, and shot a round into the boiler. He let out a chuckle. Sergei joined him in laughing.

"There! All better!"

Dimitry then fired a couple more rounds. The two Russians guffawed in mockery.

Iskandar remembered Aysilu unwrapping the samovar on their wedding day. He remembered the woman who gave it to them, how she bestowed her future to them. Such an incredible act of generosity and grace was wrapped into that samovar that every time the aging widower drank from it he was overwhelmed with a combined sense of gratitude and longing for his wife. Every cup he drank was a memorial to her.

And now it was gone.

The old man crouched low and began to work himself around the corner, knife still in hand.

*

"Iskandar's going to do something stupid," Danilo said, surveying the scene from their safe position.

"What do you mean? Let me see," Angelina demanded.

Danilo handed her the binoculars. She could see the old man peering around the corner, the knife in his hand.

"Oh no," she gasped, lowering the binoculars.

Danilo took them from her and took another look.

"What should we do?" he said.

"We have to stop him," Angelina replied.

"I don't think we can get to him in time."

"We have to try."

Angelina slung the musette bag around her neck, grabbed the shotgun, and started rising to her feet.

"Wait! Hold on. Let's think about this," Danilo urged.

"There's no time for that." She started running before Danilo could even stand.

"Damn it!" Danilo cursed, trying to follow after the rapidly fading Angelina.

He chased after her quickly moving silhouette in the moonlight. As they dodged through the old trees on the far side of the property, it became tough for Danilo to tell which dark shape was Angelina and which was a tree trunk. Angelina's running shadow would appear and then disappear. For a moment, he lost track of her, but after staring into the nightscape, he saw her moving again.

"Angelina!" he hissed in a whisper-yell. "Angelina! Wait for me! Please!"

Then, like a phantom, she completely dematerialized.

"Angelina!"

She was gone. Danilo fought to suppress a sense of panic. All he could do now was carefully make his way toward Iskandar and hope the Russians saw neither him nor the woman he loved.

Chapter 23
SHOTS IN THE SHADOWS

Stewart and Ken jumped when they heard the gunfire. First, they had heard Dimitry yelling something from behind the old Tatar's house, and a shot. Then, after a roughly ten-second pause, two more shots cut through the night and made the hair on Stewart's neck stand on end.

"What the hell is going on?" Ken asked him.

Stewart shrugged and turned to the armed militiaman named Andrei, "What was that?" he asked the masked man in Russian.

"It sounded like Dimitry's pistol," Andrei said from behind his balaclava. "I'll go out back and see what's going on."

The man disappeared through the front door.

"I don't feel good about this," Ken said.

"Think of the footage," Stewart said.

"I'm thinking of a stiff drink and a long sleep. Hell, we don't even know where we're sleeping the night."

"The car, I guess."

"I'm starting to feel like we're not going to get any sleep at all."

*

After watching the two western journalists and the Russian militiamen fom afar for some time, Viktor decided the best thing he could do would be to get a closer look. He crept toward the front of the house and flicked on his night-vision sight. He scanned the road but saw nothing. He went back to monitoring the home. Then the road. He kept toggling between the two looking for any change in the situation.

After several minutes, he spotted a small four-door coming down the road. Roughly a quarter mile from Iskandar's house, it switched off its lights and engine and coasted. He kept tracking the small car until it quietly came to a stop at the edge of Iskandar's property. The ghostly night vision shapes of two men got out of the car and crouched behind Iskandar's front fence to survey what was going on out front.

The two men paused and talked, and then crept to the back of their vehicle and popped the trunk to fetch something. *Weapons!* The two men appeared to have automatic rifles stashed in the trunk and were now pulling masks over their heads. *Who are these men and why are they armed?* The last place Viktor wanted to be was Crimea's version of the OK Corral.

The Russian sergeant knew the only thing he could do is keep monitoring. If he got involved, whatever was happening would probably get fifty-thousand times worse. The only thing he could do is sit, watch, and feel useless.

*

Iskandar continued monitoring Dimitry and Sergei, who were now hysterically laughing. He acknowledged he was old and he knew his limitations. He also knew what was the smart, restrained move to make, as well as what was the foolish one. But he had lived through too much misery at the hands of Russians, and rebuilt far too much on his own, to let some drunk bully who had decided to use Russia's invasion of Crimea as an excused to attack him and destroy his things. Tonight, he resolved that he would put Dimitry Lebel in his place.

Iskandar gathered himself and again peered around the house at the two men. The man with the rifle was not paying as much attention to his surroundings as he should, and Lebel was too busy staring to the west and yelling insults. Iskandar could easily creep along the back wall of his home undetected before making a final sprint. If he could rush fast enough, low enough, and quiet enough, he could leverage the element of surprise to spring on the two militiamen and plunge his hunting knife deep in Dimitry's fat neck. Maybe Crimea would experience a tiny portion of justice that night.

The old man crouched even lower and tightened his fist around the knife. He started crawling through the shadows cast along the back wall of his home. If they turned, noticed him, and opened fire, Iskandar decided it would be an honorable way to die.

*

Stewart and Ken leaned against a tree in front of Iskandar's home while waiting for Andrei to return. Ken's camera sat on the ground next to them. The other two members of the Dzhankoy Self Defense Force chatted quietly with each other about ten yards away.

"I'm guessing that Dimitry was firing his pistol in the air or something similarly ridiculous," Stewart mused. "I seriously doubt he was shooting at the man who lives here."

"I have a feeling you're right, but this whole situation is a cluster—and a dangerous one," Ken replied. "These guys want to hurt somebody. If they don't succeed in their 'mission,' who's to say they don't take out their frustration on us?"

"Well, I don't think we had much choice back when they stopped us. We were essentially committed at that point, whether we liked it, or not."

"Well, I don't know if …" Ken trailed off. He was staring at something.

"What?"

"Put up your hands," a voice said in Russian.

Stewart looked at Ken in confusion, who was already in the process of raising his arms. Stewart turned around to see a slender man in an Adidas tracksuit and camouflage-patterned balaclava pointing an automatic pistol at them. Who were these men? They weren't part of the Russian militia.

"I said, put up your hands!" the skinny man said again, this time with more urgency and anger.

Stewart complied. The man motioned with his gun for them to head toward where the three Dzhankoy militiamen had previously been talking, but now they were lying face down on the ground with their hands ziptied behind their backs. A second masked man wearing a jean jacket was covering them with an AK47.

"Lie down next to them," tracksuit said in hushed tones.

"Don't make a sound or we'll open up."

"He's telling us to lie down next to them," Stewart said to Ken.

"What are you saying to him?" tracksuit demanded.

"I'm telling him what to do," Stewart replied. "He doesn't speak Russian."

"Shut up and do it," tracksuit ordered.

They did.

"We're fucked," Ken said as they lay down.

"Shut up," jean jacket hissed.

Stewart was about to translate the command, but it was clear Ken already understood the international language of pissed-off-guy-with-a-weapon.

Once they lay on the ground, the scene went completely quiet. All Stewart could hear was the terrified breathing of the now unmasked militiaman next to him, and Ken's, which was remarkably calm by comparison. He wondered if the next sound he heard would be his last.

*

Angelina jogged through the night taking pains to be as stealthy as possible. *Where is Danilo?* She realized they must have become separated. As she ran, it became clear that the Russians would catch sight of her in the firelight if she maintained her path to Iskandar. A straight line wasn't possible. She considered her options as she ran: Either double back and run around the south perimeter of the property and then cut northeast to Iskandar's current hiding spot, or head to the barn and try to creep behind the Russians.

She opted for the route behind the barn. If she could get there before Iskandar made his move, she could hold the two men at bay with the shotgun.

Danilo's absence was painful. She could only hope that he'd either catch up to her or head toward Iskandar.

In less than a minute, Angelina successfully reached the back wall of the barn and started moving to where she could head along the northern wall of the barn, which butted up against a dense clump of trees. She crept along the far side of the old building with the shotgun raised, ready to blast the first sign of trouble. The gravity of the situation suddenly hit her like an avalanche. She was going up against armed men. Each step became a battle against the urge to turn and run. Her redlined pulse was making her ears ache it was throbbing so hard. *Where is Danilo?*

*

Viktor's mind raced in a thousand different directions at once. *Who are these men? What is going to happen now that they had the journalists and at least three of the militia subdued? What do they intend to do next? Where is the old farmer in all this?*

He knew that intervening would probably end poorly. Then again, not getting involved also seemed like it was inviting bloodshed. No matter how he approached the situation, it seemed to end in a cacophony of rifle reports and bodies. He came to help but was feeling increasingly powerless.

Who are these men?

The man in the tracksuit positioned himself against the wall, on the opposite side of where the front door swung open, but not visible through Iskandar's front window. He had his machine pistol slung by a strap over his shoulder, and he was texting on a smartphone—apparently requesting reinforcements. At the same time, the man in the jean jacket stood so that he covered the Dzhankoy militiamen and the journalists with his AK47. If they made a move, they were done for.

The scene froze like that for uncounted minutes, with Viktor feeling utterly powerless to do anything. His finger nervously rubbed the side of his rifle's receiver. Viktor could feel the sweat from his upper lip permeate the fabric of his mask and inhaled the scent of indecision.

"Shit," he muttered.

The sound of vehicles broke what had felt like an eternity's worth of fear and nervous breathing mixed with dread and anticipation. Two more cars pulled up, cut their lights, and out popped five more armed men in balaclavas. The newest quintet of menacing figures to join the scene headed toward the front gate. Viktor stifled a groan. Apparently, Iskandar's farm was the place to be this referendum night.

Before he could be seen, Viktor ran toward the southern side of Iskandar's farmhouse in the hopes that he could get a better vantage point over the situation.

Chapter 24
CAPTORS AND CAPTIVES

Angelina had successfully made her way along the north wall of the barn, staying hidden from the Russians. Now she had to run the short distance from the barn to the shed, where she could then have the advantage over the two Russians. She took a quick look around the corner and discovered she couldn't see them. *Good. If I can't see them, then they can't see me.*

She ran to the shed and now crept her way along that wall to where she could turn the corner and hopefully have the advantage over the Russians. She could only hope that Danilo was able to reach Iskandar and stop him from doing anything dumb in the meantime.

The shotgun fell out of her grasp and something pressed against her temple.

"You're not as stealthy as you think you are," a husky voice said in her left ear. She could feel a presence emerge from the trees.

Angelina's already racing pulse now exploded in her ears as thousands of alarm clocks and sirens screamed in her mind. Animal terror overwhelmed her self-awareness. She wanted to scream, she wanted to run, she wanted to fight, but all she could do was stand frozen, breathing.

"Stupid bitch. What were you going to do, shoot us?" Dimitry Lebel chided in seething contempt.

Angelina slowly began to turn to view her captor, barely able to control her shaking, adrenaline-soaked muscles in the process, but the pistol the fat man in camouflage held at her head dug even deeper into her temple.

"Don't you fucking think about it," He warned. "Eyes forward, start walking toward the house."

*

Now paused in the shadows, Iskandar sat trying to ascertain why Dimitry had suddenly headed to the trees north of his shed. As he tried to conjure an answer, he watched the other Russian, Sergei, shoulder his rifle, remove his balaclava, and warm his hands over the burning pile of Iskandar's memories.

Moments passed as Iskandar tried to calculate what to do next. Was this a trick? Had Dimitry spotted him and was now circling the house?

Then Iskandar spied a figure coming out from behind the shadows. It was Angelina! What is she doing? Where is Danilo? What he saw next quickly answered that question. Dimitry followed close behind the young woman with a pistol at her back and holding Iskandar's shotgun in his other hand. All-encompassing dread closed around

Iskandar like a collapsing mineshaft. He could barely breathe as he watched the scene unfold.

"Look what I found," Iskandar heard Dimitry gloat to Sergei. "A Ukrainian spy!"

"Not very smart," Sergei goaded Angelina. "You lot aren't very smart at all. Now you're in more trouble than you can imagine."

Dimitry turned toward the back fields. "Hey, old man! Hey, Ukrainian spy! We have your woman!" He bellowed. "If you know what's good for you, you'll come out of the shadows before anything happens to her."

Iskandar peered at Angelina's terrified face as Dimitry called. He didn't make a move. He knew better than to trust Dimitry Lebel, but he was also sure Danilo—wherever he was—wouldn't be able to control the urge to rush in and attempt a rescue of the poor girl. *Where is Danilo?*

Dimitry kept yelling: "You better come out from hiding right now, or I won't be responsible for what happens next! ... Come out; God damn you!"

The two Russians waited for a response. None came.

"Last warning!" Dimitry howled. "Get the fuck out here, right now!"

Iskandar stayed frozen. Danilo was nowhere to be seen.

"Fine!" Dimitry yelled. "You asked for it!"

The big Russian turned to Sergei: "I'm taking her inside. You keep watch."

Dimitry jammed the pistol against Angelina's head until her knees started to buckle, and he grabbed a handful of her hair.

"Now you get to see what happens to fascist spies, bitch," he hissed. "Get inside."

Iskandar watched in irate frustration as Dimitry hustled Angelina up the back steps and the two disappeared through the door into his kitchen. There was no time to waste: the second this Sergei fellow was looking in the opposite direction, Iskandar must ignore the sizable odds against him and attack. Instinctive action was overtaking thought. The old man stayed hidden, felt his muscles coil like springs. He grasped the handle of his knife so hard that it felt like it was now part of his hand.

Sergei surveyed the property, scanning south to west to north. The moment the militiaman had entirely turned his back, Iskandar exploded from the shadows.

*

Viktor quickly made his way to the south side of Iskandar's farmhouse, where he hid behind one of the orchard trees and looked through his rifle's night vision scope to reassess what was happening out front.

The five masked men made their way through the gate and stood before Jean Jacket and Tracksuit, who kept their weapons trained on Stewart, Ken, and the men from the Dzhankoy Self Defense Force, who all now lay face down in the dirt.

One of the five new men said something in a language Viktor didn't understand. *Crimean Tatar?*

Jean Jacket replied in the same tongue, and then all seven laughed.

What are they saying?

Viktor could only watch in hopes their actions would give him an idea of what might unfold next.

*

"So what happened?" asked one of the five, newly arrived men.

"We came here to talk about trading a car for a

motorcycle when we saw these Russian goons' cars parked out front. We switched off the lights, and when we got close, we could see these three in the front yard with these other two, who seem to be Westerners—reporters I guess," Musa, the one wearing the jean jacket, replied. "We knew it must have meant trouble for Mr. Nabiyev. I've already been here once this week because one of these clowns was harassing him. Anyway, we decided to put on our masks, grab our guns, and got the drop on them."

"Yeah, we these guys were definitely up to no good," Azat, who wore the tracksuit chimed in. "We had to step in."

"Impressive!" the leader of the five said. "You lads did wonderfully. God is great."

"Thanks," Musa replied. "God is indeed great."

"So how can we help?" the group of five's leader replied.

"We need some of you guys to help guard these men, while the rest help us flush out any remaining Russians, and find Mr. Nabiyev," Musa said. "I'm hoping he ran to safety."

"You mean you don't know where he is?" the new group's leader asked, suddenly shocked.

"No, but we haven't quite had time to look," Musa said.

"Okay, let's do this quietly," the five's leader said, in a graver tone of voice. He turned to the men laying on the ground and spoke to them in Russian. "Not a word. Not a sound. If any of you makes so much as a peep, we'll make things a whole lot louder."

Stewart and Ken exchanged nervous looks, as did the Russians.

Three Tatars took up guard duty while the remaining four men began fanning out toward the farmhouse.

*

Iskandar rushed toward Sergei with all the speed and strength he could muster. The distance between him and the unaware Russian rapidly diminished as he raised his knife. As he closed the final few feet to the man, he brought it down on a trajectory that would land the blade directly in the back of his neck.

However, at that same moment, Sergei, who was still scanning the property, began to turn his body toward Iskandar. As a result, Iskandar's knife connected with Sergei's shoulder rather than his neck. The Russian groaned as the blade jammed against his scapula. The Kalashnikov fell from his hands, and he and the old Tatar now collided and tumbled to the ground, with Iskandar losing his grasp on the blade, which fell somewhere the darkness.

As they rolled on the ground, Iskandar quickly looked around and spied the Kalashnikov on the grass. He immediately began crawling toward it. A hand suddenly grasped his ankle. Sergei pulled the old man toward him. As Iskandar struggled to get away, his foe crawled on top of him and pinned one of Iskandar's arms with a knee.

"Son of a bitch!" Sergei growled, and raised his fist.

Iskandar tried blocking with his one free arm, but Sergei was swinging so hard and fast that it was impossible to stay completely covered. In the flurry of blows, a fist struck his jaw. Another cracked his nose. A third shot smashed his ear. His head started ringing. Iskandar felt dazed. He tried to cover his face with his free arm and began to close his eyes. He was losing hope. *Is this it? Is this how I die? Beaten to death? What will happen to Angelina and Danilo?* He thought of his children and grandchildren grieving. He thought of seeing Aysilu again.

As these thoughts rushed through Iskandar's mind, he

realized that he wasn't taking any more blows. Sergei had stopped beating him. He felt the weight of the Russian still on top of him but his foe was no longer throwing any punches. Then felt something warm and wet. He opened his eyes.

Sergei was still atop him, but both his arms were at his side. He was staring at Iskandar, but his glowering face began to change expression. The man's brow began to relax. His eyes opened wider. If anything, he was starting to look calm — almost blasé. Then Sergei slumped over to reveal Danilo standing behind him, his blood-soaked fist grasping Iskandar's now-dripping knife.

The two stared at each other for a moment.

"I came as fast as I could," Danilo whispered. "Are you okay? Is he dead? I think I killed him. I didn't know what to do. He looked like he was killing you?"

Iskandar held up a hand as if motioning for Danilo to stop.

"Give me a moment," the old man said in a frail, groggy voice, trying to take stock of himself. The beating was horrible, but he was at least regaining his senses. "I think I'm okay. ... Angelina. We must get Angelina."

"Where is she?"

"Inside."

"Oh good."

"No, you don't understand. Dimitry has her."

Before Iskandar could stop him, Danilo was running toward the kitchen door.

*

"You can struggle all you want," Dimitry sneered as he dragged a struggling Angelina by her hair. He flung her toward the bedroom doorway. She landed halfway across the threshold. Her scalp burned like fire where Dimitry had ripped out some of her hair.

"Get in there," he commanded through clenched teeth as he kicked her in her side. He reached down, grabbed the collar of her jacket, and yanked her to her feet.

"I'm going to show you want happens to Kyiv trash like you."

He smacked her across the face with the back of his free hand. The blow left Angelina momentarily senseless. A trickle of blood came out of her nose. He backhanded her again. The room began spinning.

"You like that? How about another?"

A third backhand sent her ears buzzing in a high-pitched whine. Her vision dimmed.

"I think I might have a little fun with you," the Russian said, the now lascivious tone of his voice sounding even more threatening. One of his hands clasped around her right breast and then began making its way toward her crotch.

Dazed, Angelina instinctively reached out and scratched her assailant's face hard. She felt his blood and skin collect under her nails like mud.

Dimitry bellowed in pain as his beefy arm sent a fist hard into Angelina's stomach. She crumpled to the bedroom floor with the wind completely knocked out of her, helplessly heaving for air. He reached into his jacket pocket and whipped out his pistol and pointed it at her. She held up her bloody hand trying to shield herself. A shot rang out.

Angelina, her eyes clenched shut, felt no pain. *Is this what it feels like to be shot?* The room was quiet. *The gun wasn't as loud as I had expected. Maybe the beating damaged my ears ... am I dying?* She opened her eyes and looked up.

Dimitry towered over her, still holding the pistol. His

face twitched, and he tried to say something. Blood trickled from the four scratch marks that traced deep diagonal wounds across his face. A large, red dot had formed in his forehead, just above his left eyebrow. Blood began to pour down his face from the bullet hole. He made a noise like he was trying to clear his sinuses and gestured with the gun toward the window, which now had a hole in it.

Krack! Another shot came from somewhere. More glass exploded from the window, and a new hole appeared in Dimitry's jacket, near the collar. Blood began to soak his orange-and-black ribbon of St. George. He dropped the gun and tried to step forward, but instead his weight shifted to the side and he collapsed into a dresser, scattering a collection of small, framed family photos that had been sitting on the top. Dimitry desperately clung to the piece of furniture like a life preserver, in hopes it would help him stay on his feet, but his grasp became weak, and he slumped to the floor. He fell on his side, with his head thunking on the wood floor. He stared at Angelina's face, breathed twice more, and then died, his unblinking eyes still locked on hers.

Angelina tried to scream in horror, but all that came out was a raspy, exhausted exhale.

Danilo exploded in the room.

"Angelina! Angelina! Are you okay?"

He stepped over Dimitry's body, crouched down and hugged her tight.

"Come on," he said, helping her rise to her feet. "We have to get out of here."

As Angelina stood up, she turned and looked out the broken window.

"Who shot him?"

*

"Mr. Nabiyev! Mr. Nabiyev, are you out there? Mr. Nabiyev!" voices from the front of the house called to Iskandar as he ran from the back of the house toward the south side of his property — and the Russian soldier who was still looking through his gun's sight in the direction of his bedroom window.

"Sergeant," Iskandar whispered in Russian as he approached. "Sergeant, it's me, Iskandar Nabiyev. You must get out of here before you're discovered."

The Russian soldier whirled in his direction, the rifle still raised.

"Don't shoot!" Iskandar said, his arms spread wide.

Viktor lowered his weapon.

"What in the hell is going on?" the soldier asked. "I just shot Dimitry Lebel. He was about to kill a woman. Is she who I think she is? ... Wait, how did you know it was me?"

"Who else could it have been? You've been my guardian angel for days. We have to get you out of here. Follow me," Iskandar said. "We have to run."

The old man led Viktor into the barn. The Russian soldier paused for a half moment when they passed Sergei's corpse before continuing.

"Hide here. I'll explain everything. They are calling for me," he said. "I need to show myself. You must stay here and keep out of sight. If you're discovered, it'll be trouble for you. You have to trust me."

Viktor nodded his understanding. Iskandar rested his hand on the soldier's shoulder for a moment, and smiled a silent "thank you." Viktor nodded again. He couldn't muster a smile after killing a man — even a man like Lebel. The old farmer then rushed toward the back door of his house, yelling in Tatar "I'm here! I'm all right!"

As he passed through the kitchen and into the main area of his home, he looked down the hall toward Danilo and Angelina, who were emerging from the bedroom.

"Stay here," he said. "Don't leave the house."

He turned and exited through the front door.

"I'm here," he said again in Tatar.

While Iskandar might have had an idea as to what had transpired out front while he had been fighting for his life in back, the scene that greeted him still left the old man surprised: seven Tatar militiamen had complete control of the situation, with the three remaining members of the Dzhankoy Self Defense Force—as well as the two journalists, whom he recognized from before—as their prisoners.

"No names," the leader of the five men said without prompting. Iskandar recognized the voice as Kamil Nasin, a man who went to his mosque. Kamil was in his mid-forties, with a family, and well regarded in the community.

"I understand," Iskandar said, nodding to Kamil in recognition.

"What happened here?" Kamil asked.

"It's hard to know where to begin. First off, you should release those two men," he said gesturing toward Stewart and Ken. "They're western journalists. They're not part of the Russians."

"We'll get to that," Kamil responded. "For now they stay where they are as a matter of caution. Tell me what happened."

"These three men, along with a fourth and Dimitry Lebel as their leader, broke into my home in search of me. Lebel's been harassing me ever since the Russians invaded. He wants to take possession of my farm. Also, he suspected that I was harboring Ukrainian fugitives—which I am."

The seven masked men simultaneously fixed their gaze on the old man, expecting further explanation.

"The fool was obviously going on a drunk hunch, but he was right," Iskandar continued. "I discovered a young man and woman hiding on my property. They had naively traveled here to demonstrate on behalf of those opposed to the referendum, but a scuffle at the Chongar crossing forced them to panic and run through the checkpoint into Crimea. They wound up hiding on my farm, purely out of coincidence."

"And you took them in?" Kamil asked in disbelief.

"'Whosoever alleviates the lot of a needy person, Allah will alleviate his lot in this world and the next,'" Iskandar quoted. "Also, any fugitive from the Russians is an honored guest in my house," he added

"So what happened next?" Kamil asked. "What was the shooting? Where are Lebel and the other Russian militiaman?"

"Dimitry caught the young woman and was beating her. The Ukrainian and I were forced to kill Dimitry's henchman, and then I used that man's gun to shoot Dimitry, who was about to shoot the woman."

Kamil's initial response was a shocked stare. He regained his composure, and said, "We'll take these three," gesturing to the Russian militiamen. "These two," he said, gesturing to Musa, and Azat, "should stay with you, along with the two reporters."

"You two are to stay with us," Iskandar said in Russian to the journalists. "Your hooligan friends are leaving."

"We're not on anyone's side," Stewart replied. "We're just trying to report the news. Can I tell my colleague what's going on? He doesn't speak Russian."

Iskandar nodded, and the journalist explained to his

partner, who sighed in relief.

Iskandar looked at the members of the Dzhankoy Self Defense Force, who now had their masks removed and their hands zip-tied behind their backs. The five masked Tatars had confiscated all their weapons and gear.

"You men made some very poor choices tonight," Kamil said. "Very poor. Two of your friends are dead! Do you know what your biggest mistake was? We know who you are, but you don't know who we are." He turned his attention to his men, "Bag them."

One of the five men put burlap sacks over each militiaman's head.

Kamil racked his Kalashnikov, and the militiamen stiffened. The masked Tatars that had put sacks on their heads now searched the captives for their car keys. Once they found the keys, two of the armed Tatars started marching their captives across the yard toward the cars. The damp musk of fear and uncertainty hung over the three prisoners like a sick sweat.

The journalists started murmuring in English, and Iskandar tried to motion for them to stop.

"Be quiet," Musa said to Stewart in Russian. "Your camera. Where is it?"

The journalist pointed, and the man removed the camera's memory card and stuck it in his pockets.

"Anymore video from today?" Musa asked. "Don't lie, because we'll be searching your vehicle."

"No, that's the lot of it," the journalist replied. "We didn't get much until we met up with the Dzhankoy Self-Defense Force."

"Okay, stay here and be still," he ordered.

They nervously complied.

"We need to get the bodies out of here," Kamil said.

"Let me help with that," Iskandar said, and turned toward Musa and Azat, "You two, come with me."

Iskandar and the men went inside. Iskandar had Danilo take Angelina to the guest room, and then the three of them went out back and collected Sergei's body as well with a wheelbarrow from the shed. Then they wrapped Dimitry's body in an old blanket and wheeled him out. The trio loaded the corpses into the trunks of two of the cars. Iskandar watched as all members of the Dzhankoy Self Defense Force—living and dead—were driven away.

Iskandar shook his head in disbelief and then went around the north of his home to the barn. He crept in and called for Viktor.

"Sergeant? Do you hear me? Come out."

Viktor emerged.

"Yes?"

"The coast is clear. The two Tatar militia who have stayed behind are in my home with the Ukrainians and the Westerners. The rest of the Dzhankoy Self Defense Force is being held by more friends, who also collected the bodies. The only person who would say anything about this night is you, and I don't think you'd say anything considering ... well ... that you killed one of them."

"That's very true."

"So give it a few minutes, and head north around my property before tracing your way back to your compatriots. I'll keep everyone else busy."

"Okay. I'll go then."

Viktor glanced toward the house. The old man spoke:

"You know you saved that girl's life. She'd be dead if it weren't for you."

Viktor didn't say anything. He already knew he'd be thinking about this night for the rest of his life.

Chapter 25

THE MIDNIGHT TEA PARTY

The scorched samovar sat in the center of Iskandar's dining table. Three sets of matching entry and exit holes marred the old treasure. Around the antique boiler sat what was undoubtedly the most unlikely assembly of individuals at any dinner table in Crimea that night: two journalists, two Ukrainian activists-turned-fugitives, two young Tatar men from Dzhankoy, and Iskandar, who had taken a position at the head of the table.

Everyone was obviously shaken up, and Iskandar knew that he, Angelina, and Danilo were going to take some time to get over their scrapes.

Each member of the odd assembly shifted his or her gaze between the unfamiliar faces at the table to the ruined samovar on the table. Danilo had fished it from the smoldering embers of Iskandar's defiled artwork, and now it was essentially useless.

Iskandar stared at the heirloom with moist eyes.

"I'll boil some water in a pot," Angelina said shakily, trying to regain some normality after the evening's nightmare. "It won't be the same, but at least we can have some tea."

"I'll help," Danilo said, rushing to be by her side.

They stepped into the adjoining kitchen and set to the task of heating up some water. At least Iskandar's porcelain teapot was spared from Dimitry's wrath.

Iskandar took a moment to dry his moist eyes with a nearby napkin. This night had been too much. His attention remained fixed on the damaged samovar.

"I'm sure you can have this fixed, Mr. Nabiyev," Musa said.

"Yes, I know a smith who is up to the task, but it will never look the same," Iskandar said, thinking of the day he and his bride received it. "Then again, I don't look much like how I did on my wedding day either."

"A wedding gift?" Stewart asked.

"It was," Iskandar replied, and told a quick version of the story of his mother's friend and how he came to receive the cherished present.

The old farmer finished his story just as Angelina announced "tea" as she and Danilo entered the room carrying a tray holding the teapot and several tea glasses. Soon tea was poured. There was a brief pause as everyone took an initial sip, Iskandar realizing that he didn't quite know how to initiate the conversation.

"Sir," Stewart said to Iskandar in Russian, "I'd first like to thank you for helping free us, but I have to ask why. Why have you assembled us at this table?"

"Because you are all tied in a knot—a series of intertwined problems that need solutions," Iskandar said, grateful for the nudge. "Now that knot must untangle itself. The first problem, Dimitry Lebel and his men, has been solved. Now we must work on more difficult problems."

"Wait," Stewart interrupted. "Exactly how will the surviving members of that militia be 'solved?' Does that mean they are going to wind up in a ditch? You know I don't like what they stand for, but I have to know what's going to happen to them."

"Dead in a ditch? We're not terrorists," Musa said. "Unlike these pro-Russian thugs, we do not operate that way. We are going to apply firm pressure to them so that they know that they have grown too brazen and too aggressive. The only thing they understand is force—and they won't soon forget that two of them were killed."

"We know their names, where they work, where they live," Azat picked up. "We know whether or not they have families, where their kids go to school. And right now, our friends are explaining all of that to them on an individual basis in a very dark place, where they will stay until tomorrow evening. Then after sunset, we'll dump them in front of their homes."

"To give you an idea of what the pro-Russian thugs are up to, already two Tatar activists have already gone missing near Simferopol," Musa said. "They are likely dead. We know what we are up against. These men are murderers who have now been given authority to do whatever they want. We know that the Russians will make it impossible for us to find justice or protection through any official channels. We must focus on self-defense."

"Are things really that out of control?" Stewart asked. "Is modern Russia focused on oppressing the Tatars? The deportation happened 70 years ago under Stalin."

"Mustafa Dzhemilev," Musa said plainly, and let his reply hang there.

"Who's that?" Stewart asked.

"He's the chair of the Mejlis, our representative body," Musa said. "That used to mean something until today's referendum, which we all know is a foregone conclusion."

Musa sipped his tea and continued.

"Mustafa Dzhemilev is currently in Turkey, where he had been in meetings. Because he has a five-year ban from entering Russian territory, then this so-called referendum is destined to keep him from being able to return here. Thus, we won't have our leadership here in Crimea, where it is needed. That will confuse the Mejlis' efforts and give the ethnic Russians here in Crimea the opening to treat us how they please, which is fine by the Russian government because they want to quash any possible source of dissent. So, we have no political voice and no one advocating for us. We must focus on self-defense — and that means keeping people like the Dzhankoy Self Defense Force in check. The Russian forces certainly won't intervene on our behalf. We have to take care of ourselves."

"I wouldn't be too sure," Iskandar said, thinking of the Russian sergeant. "Anyway, this is a discussion for another time. My point is that Dimitry Lebel and the Dzhankoy militiamen were a problem — primarily my problem — which has been solved. However, I look around the table, and I see a few more problems that need solving: Two of you need to escape Crimea. Two of you are part of a Tatar organization that must remain private. And, two of you are reporters that need a story, but must not report on what happened here tonight"

*

Viktor's walk back to the checkpoint was uneventful and gave him plenty of time to reflect on what had surely been the strangest night of his life. Cold, dry leaves cracked under his boots as he strode along a line of sycamores. Already, new buds and tendrils were starting to sprout from the branches above.

Eventually, Viktor reached the fields to the west of Checkpoint Anna. He considered what Musa and Stewart had said about the referendum. If his Squad was indeed mobilized to Eastern Ukraine, the mission would likely see more activity, and not the good kind.

Soon, Viktor could make out the shape of the Pav Tigr sitting behind the sandbag wall. Two of his men — one of them was easily identifiable as Boris due to his glowing cigarette — were manning the barrier.

"I can see your smoke a mile away," Viktor said as he approached.

"I thought I'd light a candle for you," Boris replied, his face becoming illuminated as he took a drag.

"No one likes a smart ass," Viktor advised.

"Is everything all right?" Albert asked.

"Everything is fine, boys," Viktor replied. "Where's Sasha and Pavel?"

"They're both in the truck," Albert said. "I think Pavel is sleeping."

"Got it," Viktor said, heading toward the Tigr. Sasha was in the passenger seat. Viktor opened the driver's door and swung himself into the cab.

"So how'd it go?" Sasha inquired quietly.

"Don't ask," Viktor sighed.

"Anything I need to worry about?"

"Nope."

"Anybody see you there?"

"Nope."

"Things get violent?"

"I don't want to talk about it."

"I saved some tea. Want some?"

"Yep."

The two sergeants sipped at the tea and stared out the front window. Their eyes, now adjusted to the moonlight, took in a scene that hadn't changed since the day they established Checkpoint Anna. For more than two weeks Squad B had been in a semi-autonomous region of Ukraine. Tomorrow they'd be in Russian territory. Viktor wondered if he'd notice anything different.

"Glad you're back," Sasha said.

"So am I."

Chapter 26
GOODBYE

Dawn light invaded Iskandar's home as everyone slept. A chorus of birds chirping in Iskandar's small orchard eventually interrupted their slumber. Everyone began to collect around Iskandar's table once again.

"Already morning," Stewart said, yawning. "That came fast. ... So we're all agreed then?"

Everyone nodded. Iskandar had solved the remaining problems—Danilo and Angelina, Musa and Azat, and Stewart and Ken—with a simple, straightforward plan:

Danilo would trade his beloved motorcycle in exchange for Musa's Toyota. This would ensure that Angelina and Danilo would be free of the highly identifiable Kawasaki. They signed their titles over to one another with backdated signatures to make it appear they had acquired the vehicles some time ago. It wasn't a perfect ruse, but it should suffice given that none of the authorities in Crimea had any idea who Danilo or Musa was, let alone why they would know one another.

Then, Angelina, Danilo, Stewart, and Ken would split off into two pairs and travel in the freshly traded Toyota and Ken and Stewart's Geely. They would cross back into Ukraine at Armyansk. Angelina would pretend to be Ken's guide and translator, and Danilo would pose as Stewart's guide and Ukrainian translator. Stewart and Danilo could speak to one another in Russian, and Angelina knew some English from school so that she could speak with Ken.

They would play the parts of journalists following the story, from Crimea into Ukraine, where unrest was starting to brew in parts of the East and South. It was an easy ruse since it was the reality for Stewart and Ken. The big story now was that Russia was fomenting unrest in Ukraine, and it looked as though that story could become far worse than what happened in Crimea. Like the vehicle exchange, this cover story was not exactly a flawless deception, but believable enough to get them across the border.

"You two will escape your pursuers," Iskandar said to Danilo and Angelina. "And you," he said to Stewart and Ken, "will get your story."

Musa and Azat arranged for a friend with a van to pick them up with the motorcycle later in the day. That way they could get it off Iskandar's property without riding it in broad daylight—something Musa wouldn't be able to do until he could paint over the bike's highly recognizable bright, metallic emerald livery.

"That'll be better anyway," Danilo had said. "Then it will become your motorcycle."

"I'll give it a good home," Musa said, grinning and

shaking Danilo's hand to seal the deal.

Iskandar watched the transaction and remembered saying goodbye to Wind. He knew precisely how Danilo was feeling at this moment, but he decided to keep his story to himself. Instead, he clasped his hand on Danilo's shoulder and said, "You are doing the right thing. You're doing the thing a man should do."

With the arrangements finalized, they had only to pack and eat a little breakfast in the morning before parting company. Angelina had regained much of her composure, and offered to reheat some leftover borscht Iskandar had in his refrigerator and prepare a salad. A fresh pot of tea helped them break their fast. The group shared a chatty meal together as though they had known each other for years.

As Danilo finished his meal, he pushed back his plate and stood up.

"I think I should call my sister and let her know what we plan to do," he announced.

Danilo freshened up his cup and exited the kitchen door to the backyard so that he could place his call in private. The warm tea helped fight the chill of the early March morning. The excitement of going home eclipsed whatever lingering trepidation he still felt over using his phone. He dialed the numbers, and his sister's line rang.

"Danilo," his sister said. "I'm so glad you're calling. What's going on? When are you coming home?"

"I think we have that figured out. It's a very long story, but we now have two cars and have met up with two reporters—an Englishman and a Canadian—and we are crossing the border with them at Armyansk."

"How is crossing with them going to help?"

"We're pretending to be their translators. The

Englishman speaks Russian, but the Canadian doesn't speak Russian and neither speaks Ukrainian, so I guess, in that case, we're not pretending."

"Aren't you worried about getting separated?"

"Well, I think we ought to be okay. I figure we'll follow each other most of the way and then meet up once we cross the border."

"Aren't you worried about getting caught?"

"I don't think it should be too hard to cross. The authorities don't have much to go on regarding any descriptions of us. We were together, on a motorcycle, and wearing helmets at the time this whole mess started. Besides, it seems like the Russians, Berkut, and Cossacks at the crossing were more worried about letting people into Crimea than out. That's what caused this whole mess in the first place."

Veronika paused and then spoke: "Well they might be paranoid about both directions, now."

"What do you mean?" Danilo asked.

"Haven't you watched the news this morning?"

"No."

"You know there was a referendum yesterday."

"Oh shit. They voted to join with Russia."

"If you want to call it voting, sure. But either way, I'm sure you're not the only people trying to flee the peninsula today."

"Shit. I better let the others know. I ought to hang up."

"Call me when you decide what to do."

"I will."

"I love you, little brother."

"Love you, too."

Danilo raced back in the house through the kitchen.

"Turn on the TV," he said.

"Why's that?" Iskandar asked.

"The election," Danilo answered.

"Damn. That's right," Stewart said. "They probably concocted the results before the vote was even over so that they could report about the outcome first thing in the morning."

Iskandar switched on his television. Since Russia had invaded, it had removed Ukrainian television from the airwaves and cable, and the only news being broadcast was from Russia. Given that all but one Russian news outlet was state-controlled, Crimea had been receiving propaganda dressed up in the guise of cable news as its main source of information for more than two weeks. Regardless, everyone in the room found a spot to sit in from of the set.

"The citizens of Crimea voted overwhelming to support merging with the Russian Federation, with ninety-eight percent in favor of the move, and only two percent against," a generic Russian anchorwoman read from a teleprompter.

"Ninety-eight percent!" Angelina gasped.

"It's a lie," Iskandar said calmly.

"What shite," Stewart said.

"What's going on?" Ken asked Stewart, not understanding the Russian news anchors.

"The results of the referendum are in," Stewart replied. "Ninety-eight percent of the votes approved merging with Russia."

"Hah!" Ken laughed. "You're kidding me."

"Wish I could say I was."

"What a fucking joke. I guess Putin is betting no one remembers their history classes."

"What do you mean?"

"Ninety-eight percent is the same percentage of yes votes that the population of the Sudetenland supposedly voted in

Hitler's phony referendum in 1938. He staged it after his troops invaded to 'protect' ethnic Germans living there," Ken said to Stewart. "Sound familiar? Cripes, at what point does the entire world finally call this guy on his bullshit?"

The other five members of the tea party shifted their attention from the television to the two journalists.

"It's a fuckin' joke," Ken added, breaking the awkward silence.

"What's he saying?" Musa asked.

Stewart related Ken's history refresher to the rest of the group.

"He's right," Iskandar said.

The six Russian speakers continued to watch the news, with Stewart updating Ken every so often. After about an hour, it became increasingly clear that expecting any actual news beyond the televised equivalent of the Russian government high-fiving itself was a futile endeavor, so Angelina switched off the set in an act of collective mercy.

"Unbelievable," Danilo spoke up. "Putin stole Crimea. He actually stole the entire Black Sea peninsula. How do you even do that?"

"Thirty-thousand triggermen helps," Azat suggested, which got everyone chuckling enough to shake themselves back into action.

"Does this situation change our strategy for crossing the border?" Danilo asked. "My sister worries it might."

"I don't think so," Angelina replied. "Our cover story is a good one, and it makes sense that we'd be heading to Ukraine, as it looks like things are heating up there; particularly in the east. Don't forget, we dodged a riot the night before we left."

"It's a safe bet that Russia is going to try and back similar unrest in Ukraine," Stewart added.

"Of course Putin will expand from Russia into the East of Ukraine," Iskandar said. "Putin needs a land bridge to Crimea. He'll pick the Chongar crossing, I imagine."

"He already has," Danilo said. "A lot of those pro-Russian guys in the riot were bussed in. It was pretty clear they were 'tourists' from across the border."

"So we're agreed that the plan still makes sense?" Stewart asked.

Everyone in the room nodded.

"Then I suppose we ought to get packing," he said.

*

With the teapot emptied and their bags crammed into the cars, there wasn't anything left to do but say goodbye. Iskandar insisted on jotting down everyone's mobile phone number, and he also traded mailing addresses with Angelina and Danilo.

"I want to keep in touch," he said to the young couple, who returned the sentiment.

Soon Iskandar, Musa, and Azat accompanied the four to the two cars parked on the road. As they began saying their goodbyes, Iskandar said he forgot something and ran back into the house. After a brief moment, he came back out the front door and across the yard carrying something substantial wrapped in a towel.

He approached Angelina and handed the object out to her. The young woman pulled a corner of the towel back to reveal Iskandar's samovar.

"For you and Danilo," the old man offered. "Once you get settled, I shall ask my friend who's a smith for a good recommendation for someone in your area who can do the repairs. He knows everyone in his trade."

"I … I can't accept this," she said. "It has too many

memories for you."

"And it will have just as many memories for you," Iskandar replied. "Every time you make tea, you shall make new memories and recall old ones. Just as I did with my Aysilu."

"Oh ... Mr. Nabiyev," Angelina said, breaking down in tears. She hugged the old man as though she was holding fast against a hurricane. "You've been so kind," she said in between sobs. "Your risked everything. They invaded your home. They even destroyed your art. I don't know what to say ... thank you."

When Angelina regained her composure a bit and pulled back, it was clear Iskandar's eyes were welling up, too. He again handed Angelina the samovar.

"Please," he said, holding it out once again.

Angelina accepted, adding a second, choked-up "thank you" from the back her throat.

"We'll toast every pot to your name," Danilo said. He paused and changed his tone. "What you have done for us ... I can't describe how brave, how generous, and how kind you have been to us. Whoever drinks from this will know the name Iskandar Nabiyev."

"Please," Iskandar implored, "you would have done the same. The key for all of us is to stay safe and keep our homes."

"I will," Danilo said. "We will," he added, taking Angelina's hand in his.

Iskandar smiled.

"Thank you, to all of you," Stewart said to Iskandar, Musa and Azat. "You, Mr. Nabiyev, you saved us, and you two spared us. My partner and I are truly grateful. And you saved this young couple, as well. You should be proud of what you have done. Just assure me that you'll stay safe from those militiamen."

"Spasiba," Ken said mustering his best Russian accent, sticking out his hand.

"You're welcome," Iskandar smilingly replied in his best English, shaking Ken's hand. "Have no fear," the old man continued in Russian, now addressing the group. "If what Musa here says is correct, the local thugs should be cowed."

Danilo and Angelina hugged and reassured one another. Then Ken and Angelina got into the Geely, stowing the blanket-covered samovar in the backseat. Danilo and Stewart hopped in Musa's Toyota. They started up the cars, rolled down the windows and started waving and trading final goodbyes with the Tatars to whom they owed their lives.

Iskandar kept waving until the cars had traveled out of sight and into the uncertainty of Crimea. The old man then lowered his hand, reached into his pocket and pulled out a handkerchief. He began to wipe his eyes.

"What you did—saving those people's lives, protecting them—was the bravest thing I've ever seen anyone do," Musa said, putting his hand on the old farmer's shoulder. "Mr. Nabiyev. I feel proud to say I know you."

Iskandar nodded his thanks to the young man. He was too overwhelmed by recent events and the sad parting to speak.

Chapter 27
FOREIGN ROADS

The two-car convoy motored along the M17 through the fields of Crimea. Farm after farm scrolled past the windows of both vehicles as their passengers sat mostly quiet, each person nervously anticipating the border checkpoint located roughly thirty minutes ahead.

Would the crossing go without event, a mere review of identity papers and passports? Or would the Berkut, Russians, or Cossacks detain them at the border? Would they be dragged from their cars and arrested? Beaten? Summarily executed? Every possibility had an almost equal chance of morphing into reality in the unknowable realm that was post-annexation Crimea.

The only certainty was that, at this very moment, they were no longer traveling through the Crimea of yesterday.

They now drove on a Russian road, past Russian farms, along a Russian agricultural canal.

"What a difference a day makes," Ken mused to Angelina as he piloted the Geely.

"What's that?" Angelina asked.

"It's an old song. It says how much things can change in just a day. It's originally a love song, but I think it makes sense about Crimea today," he said.

"Because Crimea is different now," Angelina confirmed. Her English was rusty.

"Indeed."

"Well, the more things change, the more they stay the same."

Ken looked at the young woman for a heartbeat and let out a laugh at Angelina's joke. A massive language barrier stood between them, but he could tell she was a pistol. If only he spoke Russian or Ukrainian. For now, basic English with some of his crappy high school French to help fill in the gaps would have to make do.

*

Behind, Stewart and Danilo were having the same conversation. Was this Russia? Was this Ukraine? Was this Crimea? Russia's blunt-force foreign policy had forced reality to somersault into strange territory.

"Geopolitics," Danilo said, drawing on his unused degree.

"Eh?" Stewart replied.

"This is about geopolitics," Danilo repeated. "Russia was afraid of losing the Black Sea ports if Ukraine became part of the EU.

"That, and gas," the young man continued. "Russia gained most of Ukraine's natural gas reserves by annexing

Crimea." Danilo paused for a moment, and said, "What we need are EU association and an IMF loan. That'll bring us genuine independence."

"So, you said you were an electrician," Stewart replied. "No slight on electricians, but you have a pretty broad perspective on all this."

"I have a Political Science degree—undergraduate."

"Ah ... so how did you become an electrician?"

"Well, I like electrical work, and it pays better than being a staffer in the government. Plus, have you seen the Rada? Ukrainian politics are a mess even without Russian meddling. Why would I ever want to get involved in that? I really should have picked a different degree."

Stewart laughed. "I think you made the right choice."

The morning's drive had been uneventful and traffic light thanks to their dawn departure. Farms quickly gave way to houses as they reached the outskirts of the city of Krasnoperekopsk which sat on the isthmus that connected Crimea with Ukraine. After passing through the warehouses, apartment complexes, and factories of the city, the buildings ended at the lake. Soon, the scenery transitioned back to farmland.

Eventually, the two cars arrived at the outskirts of Armyansk. Soon, they would reach the border. A massive concrete and tile sign emblazoned with the city's name and coat of arms signaled the city line. Towering apartment blocks dominated the Armyansk skyline. Reflections of Crimean apartments scrolled past their windows; row after row of addresses that now called Russia home.

The M17 cut north through the city until it reached a large traffic circle around which the two cars sling-shotted to the northwest. In the middle of the roundabout sat a stone monument topped with a Second World War-era T34 tank sporting a Soviet star, a reminder of Russia's modern influence over a region with a much older history.

The two cars then passed a soccer stadium and more homes. Now, the border checkpoint lay right ahead. Soon they would encounter the modern Russian military. Would one of those soldiers' cast-off vehicles someday become a monument in Crimea, like the old tank?

Traffic began to back-up as commercial vehicles and private cars now waited their turn at inspection. Eventually, the motorway came to a crawl. In the course of their driving, Stewart and Danilo's Geely had pulled ahead of Ken and Angelina's Toyota. Danilo turned around and looked out the rear window at Angelina in the Toyota behind him. He dialed Ken's mobile phone and held up his phone and waved it to signal to Ken and Angelina that it was he who was calling. Ken pulled his ringing phone from his jacket pocket and handed it to Angelina who answered.

"Nervous?" Danilo asked in Ukrainian.

"Yes, but not as bad as at Chongar—or last night," Angelia replied. "I don't know why ... I guess I'm eager to get home."

"I'm nervous," he said. "I hope this plan works."

"It will. Have some faith," she replied.

"Are they feeling clear on what they need to say?" Stewart interrupted in Russian.

"Did you hear that?" Danilo asked Angelina.

"Yes," she said. "I do." Angelina turned to Ken and asked in English, "Do you understand the plan?"

Danilo heard a muffled "yep—got it" in English in the background.

"He understands," Angelina told Danilo.

"They sound like they're ready to go," Danilo told Stewart.

"Excellent," the Englishman replied.

"Danilo?" Angelina asked.

"Yes?"

"Call your sister again," she advised in Ukrainian. "You know she's worried sick. I'll be okay. Call your sister, okay?"

"Okay, I will," he confirmed.

"Good. Also, promise me something."

"What's that?"

"Keep calm at this checkpoint," she warned, reminding him of Chongar. "We need to be very calm and matter-of-fact this time around—even if something unexpected happens."

"I will. Okay. I'm going to call Veronika now."

"Good. Do that. I love you."

"I love you, too. We'll be safe. "

Traffic inched forward as Danilo dialed his big sister.

"Hello?" Veronika answered.

"Hi big sister," Danilo announced. "Guess what?"

"Danilo! What? What should I guess?"

"We're waiting in line at the border."

"Really? Where? Did you make it to Armyansk?"

"Yep. Armyansk."

"Oh, that's terrific! I'm going to drive over to just before the Ukrainian checkpoint. I can't wait to see you. Call me when you're across."

"I will."

"Okay, I better go and get ready. Be safe and get across!"

"I will."

As the traffic thickened, soldiers—ostensibly Russian—hidden by balaclavas began directing the cars into two lanes and trucks off to a third lane. As this happened, Ken and Angelina in the Toyota came alongside the Geely. The occupants of both cars looked over at one another. Angelina smiled and waved to Danilo. He waved back. Ken held his crossed fingers up to the window. Then the Toyota's lane slowed a bit, and the Geely pulled ahead.

A soldier with an AK74M hanging across his chest motioned for Stewart to stop. He did so. The soldier motioned for Stewart to roll down the window and the reporter complied.

"Pull ahead to the second barrier," he instructed in Russian.

"Alright," Stewart said, nodding at the solider. He put the car in drive and drove to a spot in between two concrete barriers where two more soldiers stood, waiting.

"Documents," one of the Russian soldiers demanded, his voice partially muffled by his balaclava. Stewart handed them his passport, along with Danilo's driver's license and passport.

"Purpose for exiting the Russian Territory of Crimea?" the soldier asked as he reviewed the papers.

"I am a journalist for ETN, and heading to report from Ukraine," Stewart replied. "This man is my guide and Ukrainian translator."

"Mmm-hmm," the Russian said as he reviewed the papers. As he did so, Danilo could see that Ken and Angelina's Toyota was pulling into a similar set of concrete barriers set up for the second lane of traffic.

*

"Please hand over your documents," a Berkut officer wearing his agency's distinct blue-and-grey camouflage instructed as Ken rolled down his window.

"He wants us to hand over our papers," Angelina said.

She turned to the Berkut officer: "He does not speak

Russian. I am his translator."

"Okay, I'll come over to you."

The special police officer walked to the other side of the car as Angelina rolled down her window. She handed him Ken's passport and her driver's license and passport. He began reviewing the documents.

"Purpose for exiting Crimea?" the Berkut asked.

"He is a journalist — a photographer — and he is traveling to Ukraine on assignment. I am his Russian and Ukrainian translator, as well as his guide," she said.

"Do you mind if we inspect the vehicle?" The Berkut asked Angelina.

"No," she said.

"Okay, you'll need to step out," the officer said.

Angelina instructed Ken to get out, and the two stood near the front of the car as two additional special police officers came to search the vehicle. They first opened the trunk and began to unzip Ken's camera bags while the officer still holding their documents supervised.

*

Back at the Geely, the Russian soldier lifted his gaze from the passports and looked at Stewart.

"These papers appear fine except for one thing," the soldier said, leaning down and looking through the window over to Danilo. "Your passport doesn't show entry to Crimea."

"I didn't need to have it marked when we came to Crimea," Danilo said.

"And why is that?" the Russian asked incredulously.

"Er ... That was before these checkpoints were established," Danilo replied as calmly as he could. Up until the Russian invasion, traveling to Crimea was no different than driving to any other part of Ukraine.

"Ah." The soldier said. "That makes sense."

The soldier flipped through the documents one last time. Danilo glanced over at the Toyota. To his horror, he could see Angelina and Ken standing outside while Berkut officers searched through the car. Danilo's mind began racing with recollections of the catastrophe at Chongar and the news reports of the beaten and abused Euromaidan activists who were detained earlier in the month.

"You can move on," the soldier said, handing Stewart their documents.

Danilo continued looking at Ken and Angelina.

"Thank you," Stewart said. He tapped Danilo's shoulder with the Ukrainian's passport and driver's license, saying "Here you go."

"Uh ... thanks," Danilo said.

The soldier in front of the Geely, motioned for them to drive between two concrete barriers that formed a "chute" that exited the checkpoint. Stewart did so, and they slowly merged onto the open road, passing several Russian trucks and armored personnel carriers that were lined up in front of some recently erected temporary buildings. Danilo craned his neck to look out the back window at the diminishing figures of Ken, Angelina, and the Toyota.

*

The lead Berkut officer approached Ken and Angelina.

"We've completed our search," he said. "The camera equipment appears legitimate, as does the luggage, but we have one question about the samovar we found in the back seat."

"Yes?" Angelina asked.

"Why are there bullet holes in it?"

Chapter 28
LEFT BEHIND

Worry infected Danilo's nervous system like a super virus. A thousand horrible thoughts simultaneously fired through his synapses and his skin prickled as though a swarm of crazed hornets were stinging him from the inside.

"They're searching their car," Danilo said, horrified. "We have to pull over."

"Wait—what?" Stewart asked. "How do you know?"

"Angelina and Ken were getting out of the car while the Russian soldier was handing you our papers. I looked over as we were pulling away, and some Berkut were opening the trunk."

"Shit."

"We have to pull over."

"We can't pull over."

"What do you mean we can't pull over? We can't leave them behind!"

"They'd be on us in a second. Look at where we are. Why would we be pulling over right after a border check? We have to wait until we're at least at the Ukrainian checkpoint."

The M17 made a straight shot from the Russian border checkpoint established on the northeastern edge of Armyansk all the way to a similar cluster of buildings, trucks, armored personnel carriers and barriers that the Ukrainian army had installed on their side of the Crimean border. Nothing but open road sat between the two sides of the border crossing. Pulling over would attract attention.

"Couldn't we pretend to have car trouble?" Danilo argued.

"Sure, and what do we tell the Russian soldiers who come to check in on us?" Stewart said. "What if one knows a thing or two about cars? Anyway, how would that help Ken and Angelina? Danilo, I know you're worried about her. I'm worried about Ken. He and I have freelanced together for nearly fifteen years. This is incredibly nerve-wracking—but we have to get to the Ukrainian side of the border before we can pull over."

Stewart kept driving. Danilo kept looking back. The Russian border crossing now seemed a million miles away and grew exponentially distant with every second.

Within five minutes, they were slowing once again for the Ukrainian checkpoint. Several cars and trucks inched along ahead of them. The line wasn't long, and the process seemed to be going quicker than it did at the Russian border.

"Okay, have your papers ready," Stewart advised. "It won't be long before they'll ask for them."

"Mm-hm," Danilo confirmed, feeling hollow.

"Don't worry. They'll be okay. It's normal for journalists to get searched, especially a cameraman. They carry too much gear for guards not to be suspicious. Plus, a lot of these guys try and steal camera equipment for extra cash, so the big worry is actually making sure Ken doesn't get ripped off. It's more likely something like that will happen than the Russians holding them for questioning."

Soon Stewart and Danilo were pulling into the thick of the crossing. A Ukrainian soldier standing in front of concrete barriers painted in the yellow and blue of the Ukrainian flag motioned for them to pull up to him. Stewart did so and rolled down the window.

"Are you returning to Ukraine or visiting from Crimea?" The Ukrainian asked in Russian.

Before Stewart could answer, Danilo chimed in across the car from the passenger seat.

"We're coming back to Ukraine," he said in Ukrainian. "He's an English reporter, and I'm his guide and Ukrainian translator. He speaks Russian."

"Welcome back," the soldier said, again in Russian. "Can I see your documents please?"

"Certainly," Stewart said, handing him their passports and Danilo's driver's license.

"Purpose of returning?" The soldier asked.

"I'm on assignment," Stewart said. "Heading back into Ukraine for a story."

"Donetsk, I take it?"

"Yes."

"Well, let's hope we can put a lid on that situation before we have more of Putin's tourists visiting our country."

"You can say that again," Danilo said from across the car.

The soldier crouched down and addressed the pair with

a matter-of-fact disclaimer:

"Okay, we're going to let you cross back into Ukraine. Understand that this Russian occupation of Crimea is temporary and we don't recognize Crimea as a federal district of Russia. That means we won't be stamping your passport with an entry. Also, be advised that most travel from Ukraine into Crimea is restricted, so if you want to return to Crimea, you will need a special travel permit from the Ministry of Foreign Affairs."

"Understood," Stewart said.

"I understand," Danilo echoed.

"Okay, you can move along," the soldier said, as he pointed to a group of three soldiers standing next to a gap between two more sets of concrete barriers. "Please head over there and pull into traffic when you are signaled to do so."

One of the three Ukrainian border soldiers looked down the road and gestured for Stewart to pull back onto the M17. The Geely turned back on the road. They were now in Ukraine. That was it, no going back, not even if Ken and Angelina were still stuck.

"Okay, now I'll pull over," Stewart said. "We'll wait for them."

The Englishman brought the car to a halt on the shoulder about 150 meters past the exit from the Ukrainian checkpoint.

"This makes no sense," Danilo said while they sat. "The whole thing is crazy. I understand the politics of it, I grasp it from an academic perspective, but I don't think anyone would have expected this to happen so fast and to have played out the way it did."

"Things have certainly taken a turn for the surreal," Stewart replied. "But this is standard operating procedure for Putin. Look at Georgia and Chechnya."

"That's true. Maybe what no one wants to admit—I know I don't—is that he has become a full-fledged dictator."

"That, and the fact that he's working on behalf of his fellow oligarchs. I'm not sure what worries me the most, Putin, or the men aligned with Putin—wait ... what's that?"

The two could very clearly make out the unmistakable report of a Kalashnikov: *Krak! Krak-krak! Krak!*

"Oh no!" Danilo practically moaned.

"Relax, we don't—" Stewart couldn't finish his words before Danilo had opened the passenger and practically flung himself out of the car. He was halfway at the border checkpoint by the time Stewart was able to get out and follow.

"What happened? What happened?" Danilo yelped as he ran up to three soldiers at the checkpoint. One was intently peering through binoculars at the Russian border station.

"We're not sure," one of them said matter-of-factly. "We're trying to figure it out. Who are you? You really shouldn't be here. You need to get back to your vehicle."

"I'm ... sorry," Danilo said, speaking between heaving gasps for air, the full effect of his sprint now taking hold. He was bent over with his hands on his knees. His oxygen-starved body convulsed with each breath. "I ... have ... friends ... stuck ... there."

*

Angelina and Ken crouched behind the Toyota, terrified. Angelina was shivering with fear, and Ken patted her shoulder, trying to calm her down.

"It's okay ... it's okay," he shakily repeated.

A Berkut officer stood above them, his finger resting on

the trigger guard of his half-raised Kalashnikov. He stared down at them, a stern look on his face.

"You can get up," the border guard said.

The Berkut officer who had been leading the search of their car walked back over to them.

"A truck tried to go through the crossing without stopping, and we suspected he might be a criminal. We had to fire warning shots," the border official said nonchalantly. "Now about the samovar — why are there bullet holes in it?"

Angelina inhaled and did her best to maintain her cool. The lingering terror from her run in with Dimitry Lebel was welling up and she struggled like Hercules to force it back down.

"I bought it from an old woman in Simferopol during our travels," she lied. "The woman said her ex-husband had shot it in a drunken rage. She wanted to sell it because it was a reminder of bad times. I thought I might be able to have a smith fix it."

"I see," the Berkut said.

"It's very beautiful," she added with a flustered smile.

"It is," the officer agreed. "Can your journalist friend corroborate this?"

"Well he was in his hotel room, working, so he's only going on my word. Plus, since I'm translating for both of you, you'd be going on my word as to what he's saying …"

"Well, I can't see a reason why you'd be shooting a samovar. We couldn't find any firearms or anything besides the camera equipment …" the Berkut officer trailed off.

Angelina waited for him to continue.

"You're free to cross," he said. "Here are your papers."

The Berkut officer handed Angelina their documents, and she passed Ken's passport to him.

"Is he telling us we can go?" Ken asked.

"Yes," Angelina said with obvious relief.

"Good Lord that is great news. Let's get the hell outta here."

"Thank you," Angelina said to the Berkut.

Ken echoed her gratitude with a "spasiba" in just about the only Russian he knew.

The officer nodded to both of them, and the pair got in the Toyota and started following the various Berkut and Russian soldier's directions through the maze of concrete barriers and back onto the highway.

"Goodbye, Crimea," Ken said as Angelina turned the car onto the M17. "It hasn't been fun."

Angelina laughed. "Soon we will be in Ukraine," she said in her best English. She knew she had said the words correctly, but they sounded strange. A day ago, Crimea would have been Ukraine.

After a short bit of driving and another bit of traffic, Ukrainian soldiers herded Angelina and Ken's Toyota through the Ukrainian border crossing. This time there was no inspection and no gunfire. After a perfunctory set of questions, a Ukrainian soldier granted them passage back into Ukraine with the same warnings Danilo and Stewart had received.

Angelina pulled through various yellow-and-blue painted barriers and got back on the M17. Two men were walking on the side of the road, one with his hand clasped on the other's shoulder in reassurance.

"Wait a second," Ken said. "Is that them?"

"It is!" Angelina beamed. She pulled the Toyota off on the shoulder and flew out of the door and ran up to Danilo, repeatedly yelling his name.

"Angelina!" the young man exclaimed as she flung her arms around him. The young couple clasped each other in a long embrace.

"I take it you guys got through before the gunplay," Ken asked Stewart as he walked up.

"You two had all the fun," the Englishman replied.

"Yeah, those Russians know how to party. You have no idea how glad I am to see you guys. I don't know what prompted the search—I figured I was going to get a shakedown for my camera gear—but this time they seemed genuinely suspicious of something. I was sure we were going to spend the night getting the third degree."

"I'm glad you two made it safely through. We heard the guns, and Danilo insisted on running back to the crossing. The soldiers shooed us off once they determined that they were warning shots."

"Yeah, some hotheaded truck driver or something," Ken said. "Who cares? Let him spend the night getting questioned at the Berkut Inn. ... Hey, let's get the hell out of here."

"Yes, let's go," Stewart said. "Let's go," he repeated in Russian.

Danilo and Angelina broke their embrace.

"I love you," he said.

"I love you, too," she replied.

"Do you mind if we take the Toyota?" Angelina said to Stewart.

"Not at all!" Stewart replied, and then switched to English: "Ken, let's leave the lovebirds to the Toyota. You and I should probably figure out how we can generate a good story from all this. We're you getting any footage or snaps?"

"I got some stills and low-res video with my point-and-shoot," the Canadian replied.

"I got a little from my cell phone," Stewart said.

"We should be able to cobble something together. Especially if we get an interview with the young couple over there."

"Great idea. Let's hit the road."

*

The four of them met up with Veronika outside of Kherson. Danilo had called his big sister the moment he and Angelina got in the Toyota to let her know they were safe and on their way. Veronika got impatient and drove out to meet them along the M17.

When they pulled up to Veronika's parked car, she ran to the Toyota and wrapped her little brother in a bear hug the moment he stepped out of the passenger door. Tears were streaming down her face, and their embrace lasted nearly as long as Danilo and Angelina's roadside hug.

"Oh Danilo," she sobbed in Ukrainian. "I'm so happy to have my stupid, brave, little brother back."

"I'm sorry," he said. "I'm sorry."

Then Veronika broke off her hug and put her arms around Angelina, as well.

"I'm so sorry my ass of a brother got you mixed up in this," she apologized. "He should have never done it."

"It's my fault as much as it is his," Angelina replied. "He didn't strap me to the back of the motorcycle. But I'm so glad to be out of there."

The two hugged again, and then Veronika turned to Danilo. "Little brother, are you going to introduce me to your friends?"

After a brief exchange of introductions, expressions of thanks, and pleasantries, everyone got in their respective vehicles, and they were now a three-car convoy. Veronika lead them back to Diligence Inn, where rooms remained available. After some clean-up and repacking, the five enjoyed a long dinner where talk of Crimea only made brief appearances in the conversation. Tomorrow, Stewart and Ken would interview Angelina and Danilo about their ordeal, but for now, they wanted to savor the moment as much as the meal. They were home.

Chapter 29
SEVENTY-NINE DAYS LATER

Wedding preparations are always maddening—particularly when those preparations include moving out of a town occupied by armed militants and insurgents.

Within a day of crossing the border back into Ukraine, the couple instinctively acknowledged that they would marry. "Destiny is undeniable," Angelina had told Danilo. However, the logistics of such an undertaking were atypical at the least.

Both had wanted a traditional wedding, but the situation in the East had already spiraled out of control. It was clear that, starting from the riot in Donetsk—which in retrospect seemed to be timed in almost perfect synchronicity with the invasion and referendum in Crimea—that events were being stage-managed by Moscow. The "unrest" that sprouted up seemingly out of nowhere in the oblasts of Donetsk and Luhansk after the Crimea invasion bore a closer resemblance to theater than they did popular political sentiment.

Russia's official position on Eastern Ukraine was much like its official position in Crimea: denial. To hear it from President Putin or Foreign Minister Lavrov, Russia wished for no unrest in eastern Ukraine, but would "protect" Russian speakers in the region from Ukrainians that Russia was labeling fascists.

The irony was rich. The self-appointed "people's governor" of the newly formed "Donetsk People's Republic," Pavel Gubarev, was a former member of the ultra-nationalist, anti-Semitic group Russian National Unity, which went so far as to use a stylized swastika for its logo. Russia was trotting out any story possible, including calling any and all Ukrainians fascists, to obfuscate the fact it was sparking a civil war within Eastern Ukraine in order to advance its territorial objectives.

Now, seventy-nine days after Russia invaded Crimea, Danilo and Angelina were less than a month from their wedding day. They were both in Kyiv, but, out of respect to tradition and Angelina's parents, Angelina was living with Veronika until the wedding. Despite having to forgo some pre-marital formalities, Danilo and Angelina were able to travel to Poltava so that Danilo could ask Angelina's parents for her hand. In lieu of the traditional ransom, he did one better and offered her little brother, Adam, a job as an apprentice. Angelina's mother and father gave them their blessing, and they slated a date in June.

The real trick was moving Angelina out of her apartment in Donetsk. The situation in the city had blossomed into a fully formed crisis within days of Danilo and Angelina's return to Ukraine. Danilo and Adam rented a nondescript van and Angelina joined them on their trip to the city to move out.

The trip was more stressful than the actual move. Danilo, Angelina, and Adam had to pass through armed checkpoints manned by militia members. The men were not keen on anyone leaving the city, suspecting they were supporters of the Euromaidan, but the three made it through under false pretext that they were moving Angelina for a new job.

For nearly three years, Donetsk had been home to Angelina. She had found good work there and had grown to love the industrial town. It was different from her hometown, Poltava, which was an ancient city, more than one thousand years old. Donetsk was relatively new, a coal and steel town founded by an enterprising Welshman roughly one-hundred-fifty years ago. Until she had met Danilo, she believed she could have lived there for many years. She had even toyed with the notion of trying to convince Danilo to move there.

"The mood's changed," she said as they carried her mattress down the stairs. "This city always felt pleasant—full of people living their lives. Now I'm not sure what it is."

"I'm sure those people are still here," Danilo said.

"They're either hiding or they've left," she said flatly.

Angelina cried for nearly an hour on the drive to Kyiv.

*

That was six weeks ago. Now, Danilo, Angelina, and Veronika were preparing to host company in Veronika's apartment overlooking Independence Square—the Maidan, the crucible that had forged Ukraine's autonomy on more than one occasion.

"This spread looks amazing—the table is practically sagging there's so much food!" Danilo exclaimed as he surveyed the various dishes Veronika had set out.

"This is nothing," his big sister replied. "Wait until you see the wedding."

"I don't know if that will be possible, big sister," Danilo said as he reached down to try some eggplant mezhivo.

"Hands off, or there will be trouble," she warned in a mock threat. "That's for our guests."

The three continued to prepare, under the direction of Veronika. A knock came from the door just as they were wrapping up.

"They're here!" Angelina said.

"I'll get it," Veronika said, hurrying to open the door.

"Hello," Stewart said in Ukrainian. Ken was standing next to him in the hall. "Thanks for having us as guests. … I'm sure my accent is terrible," he apologized in Russian.

"It is—but hey, you're trying," Danilo replied from behind his sister's shoulder, laughing.

"Come in," Veronika said, switching to Russian.

"Thank you!" Stewart said enthusiastically.

Ken uttered his now familiar "spasiba" as he entered behind, shaking everyone's hand.

They hadn't seen the two journalists since parting company two days after they had crossed the border.

Prior to their parting, Stewart interviewed Angelina and Danilo on camera about their experience—the terror at the Chonghar border checkpoint; being on the lam; crossing back with the journalists. The interview, edited together with the border crossing footage, made for a compelling, in-depth report that garnered both reporters substantial attention, but they all agreed they would stay mum about the events at the farm belonging to Iskandar Nabiyev, who had truly saved them all. Iskandar would remain in safe, peaceful obscurity as far their report was concerned.

"How about we start with some tea?" Angelina asked.

"That would be lovely," Stewart replied.

"Angelina turned toward the table, to fetch the kettle, which was keeping warm in a familiar spot: atop the samovar that the old farmer had given her.

"Hey, you fixed it!" Ken exclaimed. "Fantastic."

"Yes," Angelina replied in event better English than before. She too had been practicing. "We still keep in touch with Iskandar by phone and letter. A tinsmith he knew recommended another man here in town."

"That's great," Stewart said in Russian.

"It wasn't cheap, and you can still make out the spots where that drunk ... psychopath shot it, but as far as I'm concerned, they represent one more tale to tell for a very storied heirloom," Danilo said.

There was a long lull in the conversation where Angelina, Danilo, Stewart, and Ken each privately recalled Dimitry Lebel and the horrifying night at Iskandar's farmhouse.

"I'm sure it makes the tea taste even better," Stewart observed.

"I love it," Angelina said. "Iskandar says it's our wedding present."

As soon as all the glasses were poured they all toasted the aging farmer.

"To the humble, beautiful man who saved our lives," Stewart said, which was followed by a group cheer of "Na zdorovie!"

"So what's next for you?" Danilo asked.

"Maybe Donetsk," Stewart said. "Ken and I are still deciding. It's turning into a war zone, which means maybe we should skip it."

"Why's that?" Angelina asked. "Isn't that where the headlines will be?"

"We're both middle-aged at this point," the Englishman said. "I can't run and duck like I used to. Neither can Ken. Political unrest or an overnight occupation is one thing, but active warfare with bullets whizzing all over the place is another."

"Well, what do you call what happened at Iskandar's farm?" Danilo asked.

Stewart sipped his tea and let the question hang there. He didn't have an answer. At least not right away. No one did. They allowed the conversation to shift to the wedding, with each savoring the visit as much as Veronika's meal.

*

Despite the nightmare in March, calm had quickly returned to Iskandar's farmhouse. The day after his guests had departed for Ukraine, the body of a Tatar human rights activist had been discovered. His name was Reshat Ametov, and he had been abducted in broad daylight in Simferopol by men that looked like pro-Russian militants, according to eyewitness accounts related in the foreign press. Ametov's naked, bound body was later found and showed signs of torture. He wasn't the only Crimean to disappear, either.

But while the Russian invasion had emboldened thugs and militants in various parts of Ukraine, the deadly events at Iskandar's farm and the swift action and threat of retribution by Musa and company had cowed the louts that once called themselves the Dzhankoy Self Defense Force.

Iskandar's thoughts drifted to Dimitry Lebel often, and his overwhelming feeling was one of disappointment. Lebel was a man who wasted what could have been a good life if he had not succumbed to abusing alcohol and bitterness in equal portions. Both vices ate at the man's soul, and Iskandar hated to watch it unfold. What would their relationship have been if Lebel had decided to make the most of the lot life had given him? The answer was unclear, but Iskandar knew for sure that at least two men wouldn't have died that night at his farm.

Now it was April 18, and he was in Simferopol. He had traveled here with Imam Mustaffa and Musa. They had come to recognize the seventieth anniversary of the Sürgünlik, the Soviet Union's 1944 deportation of each and every Tatar man, woman, and child to Uzbekistan and other unfamiliar and inhospitable places. In three days, the Soviets had ethnically cleansed Crimea of its entire Tatar population. On the drive down to Simferopol Iskandar couldn't help recalling the endless journey inside Stalin's rail cars that had claimed so many lives.

Once in Simferopol, Iskandar, Mustaffa, and Musa joined twenty thousand other Tatars to commemorate the 1944 deportation. While Crimeans had been holding such rallies in Simferopol's Lenin Square since their return to Crimea in the 1990s, Russia's recently installed authorities decreed they were banning the assembly and all others until June 6, citing fears of "unrest."

"Already, the Russians are off to a good start," Mustaffa remarked as they drove. "They paint their 'X's and anti-Tatar slogans in our neighborhoods, and murder our activists, but turn around and call us the terrorists."

"We've hosted this rally for twenty-three years," Musa said. "Now all of a sudden we're Al Qaeda or something."

"The truth is that Russians don't want this rally at all," Iskandar said. "They don't want to admit the Holomodor. They don't want to admit the Sürgünlik. They are afraid of the past—so much so that they don't realize their present policies will force them to acknowledge it."

Only four days after becoming part of Russia, Crimea's recently installed government ministers had asked select Tatars to vacate some of the lands where they had resettled in the 1990s. Russia told them it was to accommodate "social needs." Once again, Russia was making Tatars leave their land and homes. Moreover, once one factored in the political violence and threatening atmosphere that had followed Russia's annexation of Crimea, it was no surprise that, by this time, five thousand Tatars had opted to flee Crimea for Western Ukraine. The writing was literally on their walls in the form of "X"s.

But Crimea was the Tatar homeland. Russia's ban didn't stop twenty thousand Tatars—Iskandar, Musa and Mustaff among them—from showing up in Simferopol for the annual rally. When they got into town, word had gotten out that the event was moving to a different location and would be held after a march. Iskandar was getting too old for marching through town, so he waited with many others in a sea of blue Tatar flags at the new rally location on the outskirts of town.

When the marchers finally arrived, Iskandar almost cringed at Russia's official response. The marchers, many bearing flags and all of them chanting "Crimea! People! Motherland!" stuck mainly on the sidewalk, but a procession of riot police from Russia's Special Purpose Mobile Unit marched alongside them in the street—riot police at a memorial. Cars and trucks flying Crimean Tatar flags honked their horns as they drove past the parade.

Mustaffa and Musa met back up with Iskandar shortly after the marchers arrived.

"Do you like our escort?" Musa joked to the old farmer.

"I'm amazed by it," Iskandar replied.

"These Russians certainly aren't shy about reminding us exactly who did the deporting seventy years ago, eh?" Mustaffa added.

Despite the blue-and-grey camouflage ring of riot police surrounding the crowd, the event carried on. Soon, various speakers launched in to deliver addresses and recite prayers. As they did, a rush of memories flooded Iskandar's mind: Recollections of his childhood in Crimea; his father repainting the door; his mother cooking in the kitchen; the Soviet rail nightmare that killed Zilya; re-learning how to live in the strange, inhospitable land of Uzbekistan; riding Wind; meeting Aysilu; starting a family — all these small movies played at once in his mind's eye. The speakers told not only the story of Crimea's Tatars, they told his story. They told the story of every person in the throng massed around the stage.

Suddenly, a strange thudding sound interrupted the stream of Iskandar's recollections. He looked up. Two large Russian helicopters were now orbiting above the rally. The machines reminded Iskandar of a pair of chubby beetles lazily buzzing around his plot of strawberries. They slowly rotated at low enough altitude to distract the audience. The gray helicopters hung in the gray sky, while the crowd below waved bright blue Tatar flags.

"Dear compatriots, dear people, you know why these helicopters have arrived here, who sent them, and what can be expected of them?" Refat Chubarov interrupted his original speech to tell the crowd. Chubarov was the chairman of the Mejlis, the Crimean Tatar representative body. "They want to scare us. They want us to leave.

"The way forward for us is building mosques and holding Friday prayers," Chubarov continued. "The right way is not to leave the homeland. This is Crimea. So it was, so it is, and so it will be."

Iskandar watched the helicopters, slowly turning in their lazy, low rotation. As he did, his eyes fell lower. He thought of Chubarov's words. "The homeland." He was now looking at the faces in the crowd, which were either looking toward the stage or up at the helicopters. This is Crimea, he thought. Faces of everyday people — the faces of Crimea.

*

Sixty-five miles to the north, Checkpoint Anna remained dull. Viktor and Sasha sat in the cab of the Pav Tigr sharing a thermos of tea as Albert, Boris and Pavel kept watch at the sandbag post. Mercifully, Captain Lukyanov had varied the weekly assignments between the various squads, so the members of Squad B had received different patrols and duties since their initial deployment to Crimea. However, this week they manned the now-too-familiar Checkpoint Anna.

Seventy-nine days had passed since their IL76 had touched down on Crimean tarmac. Thirty-one days had passed since the referendum. Crimea was now Russian, and Squad B was still here.

"Do you think they'll move us north?" Albert asked his fellow privates leaning up against the sandbag barrier.

"Naw," Boris said, pulling a pack of cigarettes from his pocket. He put one in his mouth, touched his Zippo's fire to it, snapped the lighter shut, and returned the shiny device to his pocket in one, fluid motion. "As much as that place is going to shit, there's no way they'll want us up there."

"Why's that?" Pavel argued. "They wanted us to come down here. Why not send us up there now that things are secure down here?"

"We hardly fired a shot down here," Boris replied. "Eastern Ukraine is headed toward a Civil War. Who wants to take sides in that kind of mess?"

"Maybe we should help them out," Pavel replied.

"It would sure be more interesting than this place," Albert added.

"If you want to go up to some shitty town in some shitty Oblast far away from home to die for some guy with a Russian last name, be my guest," Boris said exhaling a blue cloud that momentarily hung in front of him before dissipating in the breeze. "I'd rather die of boredom right here."

Viktor and Sasha had eavesdropped on the three privates' conversation.

"So what do you think?" Sasha asked. "Think we'll go north?"

"I do not know," Viktor replied, lingering on each word as he said it. "I hope not."

"I'm with Boris," the bigger sergeant declared. "I don't think we will. From what I can tell, the West is going nuts over what's happening. There have already been two rounds of sanctions, and some of them have been targeted specifically against Putin. I guess the Yanks and the EU want to make things personal."

"Yeah," Viktor replied. "I guess they'd go crazy if we rolled into Donetsk or Luhansk in force. Better to send in aid and 'tourists' to prop up the locals."

The two sat silent for a long moment, gazing blankly out the Tigr's windshield at the same trees, pavement, and field that had dominated their view for more than two months.

"This place does not change," Sasha said. "Ever."

"Nope," Viktor replied.

The two stared at the road and the fields for a bit.

"Do you think we've accomplished anything here?" Sasha asked.

"For who?" Viktor replied.

The question hung in the air like cold breath.

Viktor sipped from his cup and thought about that night at the old Tatar's farm. The so-called Dzhankoy Self Defense Force had gone silent ever since those events. He recognized some of the men while on patrols in town. All but Dimitry Lebel, the man he had killed. Meanwhile, the rest of his militia appeared to have returned to living quiet, regular lives, as though Dzhankoy Self Defense Force and Dimitry Lebel had never existed.

The Russian sergeant had checked in on Iskandar Nabiyev from time to time. The aging farmer continued to work his field and tend his orchard. One day, Iskandar invited Viktor to his farmhouse for tea and showed the Russian sergeant a small painting he had been working on — a rabbit sitting in the field. It was beautiful and full of delicate detail.

"I'm painting it for you," Iskandar had said.

"Me?" Viktor said. "Why?"

"You deserve some art," the man had said. "Also … the painting somehow fits you. I can't quite explain it."

Viktor bought a suitable frame for the little painting in town and stashed the treasure in his pack until he had a good opportunity to mail it back home. He wondered what his wife Klara was doing right now. She was probably enjoying lunch with a friend or maybe watching television, perhaps the news. Would it be reporting on Crimea?

"I wish I was back home," Viktor said.

"Me too," Sasha agreed. "More tea?"

Viktor's cup had gone cold.

"Yes," Viktor affirmed. "Please."

Outside the Tigr, the three privates continued chatting. A breeze brushed across the treetops, dislodging a resting crow from its swaying perch and sending the big, black bird cawing through the grey sky. Viktor and Sasha watched the road and sipped their tea.

Thank you for reading *Tea in Crimea*

I'm genuinely grateful that you took the time to read *Tea in Crimea* and I hope that you enjoyed and valued it.

Please consider writing a review on this novel on Amazon or Goodreads. Good or bad, short or long, your feedback helps me in terms of encouragement and focusing my creative direction. Moreover, when you write a review, you help other readers find my work by making it more visible in the rankings and search results. Reviews are the highest compliment you can pay me and the most effective way you can help me.

Also, if you want to receive alerts about new releases, read short stories, and get other updates, follow me on Twitter, Facebook, and Instagram via @davidkfiction and subscribe to my enewsletter at davidkfiction.com.

Made in the USA
San Bernardino, CA
29 November 2018